House of Vampires 6: The Fate of Magic

Samantha Snow

ABOUT THIS BOOK

The 6th book of the epic series!

Lorena has the weight of two worlds on her shoulder. While a war rages in the fae world, the fate of magic in the human world grows in her belly.

Thankfully, she's got an all-star lineup of vampire boyfriends to help her with the coming baby and the war.

Then comes **the curveball.**

Now she's being haunted by a ghost, and solving the riddle of the dead only gets more complicated when a handsome new neighbor moves into town.

What's a girl to do when everyone wants her dead or alive?

There are only two options for Lorena Quinn: fight clean or fight dirty.

CHAPTER ONE

The Matrix is all about free will.

Sometimes, choices can make you feel really, really good.

The choice can lead to the sort of good that makes you want to frolic around hillsides in Austria. Feel the warm wind as it whips through your hair with the fragrance of alpine roses tickling your senses while Julia Andrews leads you in a euphoric tune dedicated to your favorite things.

Sometimes, a choice is less like a Disney song and more like the first fizzling note of a fresh bottle of Dr. Pepper. It's the building of the bottle's chilling condensation on your fingertips as you respite underneath the heat of a blazing summer sun.

It's the feeling of that cold liquid sliding down my throat and tracking the sensation as it slips through my body and settles somewhere low.

Have I had fantasies about Dr. Pepper? You bet.

I mean, if it's a choice between the reenactment of *The Sound of Music* or a bottle of Dr. Pepper, what choice do you think I'd make?

But not all choices are good for everyone. Often enough, someone makes a choice that ruins the lives of everyone around them, devastating dreams and crushing hope into a powder so fine that a simple breath could carry it away and render it forever forgotten.

Choices can have a domino effect, tripping up one person after another, rippling like the drop of a stone in a lake and building into a mighty wave that eventually crashes and takes everything with it.

But the happiness and the pain all have the origin of choice, and without it, neither could exist. Not in any organic form of the word. Choice is the catalyst for human beings. Otherwise, you're just a mindless bot constructed of artificial intelligence.

And no one wants to be that.

Well, no one outside the warlock cult that my mother and sister were once a member of before they died, but that's a story for another time.

And that time is never.

The end of my theory was met with a silence that was only disrupted by the sounds of chittering sparrows whose biological alarm had yet to register the presence of winter that told them to pack up and head south.

Alan narrowed his potent blue eyes and stared at me like I'd grown another head and that the other head was another me that was just as confusing as the first.

Even mystified, Alan had one of those faces people paid millions for.

Unlike me.

This, I knew for a fact.

During my half of a semester stint in college, I went out on a date with a guy I liked and who I thought liked me. When he asked for a selfie, I thought nothing of sending him one. The photo wasn't dirty by any means. It was just me stretched out on the bed and fully clothed, yet somehow the photo ended up on a prostitute site.

To say I was pissed would have been the understatement of the year.

I'd been shocked.

Appalled.

Outraged.

And not because my photo was on the site but because of my photo rating.

Three out of five stars.

Three out of five?

Really?

I left it up for another week to see if the rating changed. When it dropped to two point five, I finally reported the photo and buried the memory under a heavy quilt of adolescent lessons and shame.

But now when I thought about it, had that photo been of Alan, the internet would have shut down across the world.

His beauty had probably inspired paintings of angels in old Catholic churches. He was old, but his vampiric lineage rendered him forever young.

His features were romantically soft. His skin was almost pale enough to blend in with the sheets that covered his lower half. Alan didn't have the body of a fighter. Only a few inches taller than my five-foot-nothing height, his slim form camouflaged the relentless strength that lurked just underneath the surface.

His hair, which had once been long golden locks that simmered like sunlight, was now cut in a modern, short style thanks to an event that I refused to think about.

I pushed back the flicker of annoyance that tried to take hold of my otherwise mellow disposition and turned my focus back to his eyes. Bewilderment pinched his brows. "Darling, I have no clue what you're talking about." The French accent added a tantalizing purr to his words.

I was resting on my front in the middle of the bed. My arms were crossed and pillowing my head, but at his words, I popped up my head. "Seriously? You got nothing from all of that?" I knew the *Matrix* wasn't something everyone understood, but I was sure I did a pretty good job at explaining the first half of the theory behind the film.

Heck, I could give a Ted Talk on it.

Did they have Ted Talks for that?

I needed to get a hold of Ted and fast.

Or maybe I could do those deep theory videos for YouTube. How much did those creators get paid anyway? Was it based on views? Could I get sponsors? I should probably look into that since I wasn't allowed to work at the mini-market anymore. Actually, I'd been banned from the establishment altogether, which wouldn't have bothered me so much if I were in a bigger city, but out here in the mountains of Virginia, going to the mini-mart was a trip to Disneyland.

Alan's lips twitched in a way that told me he was holding back a laugh. "While the movie's premise eludes me, I understand that you are desperately in want of Dr. Pepper."

I smiled. I couldn't help it. There was a chance that Alan would live for a thousand years and never understand *The Matrix*, but he one hundred percent got me. I didn't elude him at all.

Looking into his eyes, I found it hard to believe that it had only been a year since we'd met. I wish I could say every moment of our acquaintance had been bliss, but between the attempted murders, near-death accidents, and fights that were absolved to full-blown wars, I'd manage to find sanctuary along the way.

That sanctuary came in the form of the men who held my heart.

Yes, I said *men*.

It was something I never thought I'd possess. While most people collected cars and engraved teaspoons from around the world, I'd collected love. More specifically, lov*ers*.

Even more specifically vampires. Four dark, sensual creatures who took just as much as they gave.

Alan rubbed my lower back in leisurely strokes and then slipped his fingers to my hips. "You're obsessed with the stuff. I see why Marquessa and Jenny have warded you from returning to the mini-mart."

And there was the reason I was out of a job.

Two weeks ago, my friend Jenny and her grandmother Marquessa found me in the back of the shop. There I was, crouching in the corner of the storage room. A bottle of bleach and mop on one side. A six-pack of Dr. Pepper on the other. It wasn't my finest moment, and at the young age of twenty, I was almost sure I hadn't had my finest moment yet, but that moment had been pretty bad. They'd called in reinforcements.

I was dragged out, kicking and screaming, which everyone found amusing except for me.

And Alan hadn't used the word "ward" lightly. The witches were magically blocking me from going back.

Some friends.

At least I wasn't a cheapskate. I paid for the sodas! What more did they want from me?

But I already knew what they wanted from me. It was what the whole world wanted from me. It was the reason my boyfriends' mansion was currently filled to the brim with werewolves, fairies, and witches.

The baby.

"You know we're doing this because we care."

I huffed, but deep down inside, he was right. The baby was the answer to a zillion prayers. My child would return magic to the world, and everyone wanted to make sure the baby was healthy.

But what everyone seemed to pleasantly forget was the fact that this was inside my body.

"Dr. Shaw said Dr. Pepper isn't good for the baby."

"Dr. Shaw said," I mocked, hissing to replace the many, many vulgar words that came to mind. So many words came to mind that selecting just one became an impossible feat. Every time someone said, "Dr. Shaw said," it was like a switch went off in my mind, striking up a spark and turning my rage into a live wire.

My skin tightened.

Alan frowned. "Lorena, calm down. You know what Dr. Shaw said. Anger is poison to the blood."

My left eye twitched.

Dr. Shaw, who was a witch and OBGYN, had blown into my world like Mary Poppins, bringing the medicine but without leaving the spoonful of sugar behind.

Refined sugars were on the witch's "no-no" list. In fact, in the last month, Dr. Shaw's no-no list had grown so long that she all but put my name on it.

No being Lorena Quinn.

All the delicious, delectable delights that I craved were being replaced with whole grains, lean meats, and organic fruits and vegetables.

I'd eaten so many carrots that my skin was starting to look orange.

Seriously, it was, but no one believed me, and whenever I told one of my boyfriends—yes, plural—that I was starting to look like a mandarin, they all made some lude comment about how sensational they found the fruit.

And then they proved their hunger in ways that had nothing to do with fruit and everything to do with me, which happened to be the upside of pregnancy.

I'd become a live wire craving every touch.

But the pleasure only distracted me for a time, and then I was on the hunt for my next shot of high fructose corn syrup all over again.

This need went beyond addiction. Foods that came wrapped in bright wax paper were embedded into my DNA, but it didn't matter how much I told Dr. Shaw that I was a girl whose dad dragged her across the country and that I'd grown up on nothing but fast food and sandwiches; my doctor wasn't listening.

"One bottle won't hurt," I whispered. My body jittered at just the thought of eating something on the no-no list.

I actually had two bottles stashed away in the kitchen. Peter was hiding them for me. Though my boyfriends had forbidden him from buying me any more, Peter was the only one I could trust them with.

As I thought about how good those bottles would be, I was sure I looked like a junky. I was fiending and trying to convince Alan to become my dealer. "Come on, Alan. No one has to know."

He cracked a smile and chuckled. "It's for your own good."

When did my men become so bossy? It was like, suddenly, I was pregnant, and they all forgot who the necromancer in the room was.

By the way, if you didn't know it, I'm the necromancer, and my vampires were all tied to me.

I could feel their emotions, dip in and out of their thoughts. I knew their pleasures, and I knew they wanted to make me happy.

I knew that each and every one of them loved me.

Now, I just needed them to prove it. "One six-pack a month."

"Lorena …" I could tell he was weakening. If anyone was going to get me the good stuff, it would be Alan.

"You let me sip, and I'll let you sip." My blood was another thing the men were forbidden to, thanks to Shaw Law. Everyone feared the blood loss would hurt the baby.

But a sip wouldn't hurt. In fact, a sip would feel really, really good. Having sex without fangs was good, but there was nothing like the feel of my men piercing me in every possible way all at once.

I lay my head back down and purposefully arched my neck in offering. I also tried to make my expression as seductive as possible. If it didn't work and I ended up looking as awkward as I felt, I'd pretend that I was stretching.

Fortunately, it *did* work.

I knew it worked when Alan's eyes darkened, and the deft fingers that had been playing on my hip tightened.

Alan had really deft fingers, and when I say deft, I mean those puppies possessed some serious skills.

I'd introduced him to my PlayStation, and within weeks, he was kicking my butt, but remembering all the other things he could do to me with those hands spread tingling up my spine and down my shoulder blades.

My hair was pulled away from my throat by someone else's hand; the strands whispered across my shoulder, away from my back, and onto my other side. I felt Dimitri's breath fan my neck right before he kissed me over my pulse. My blood sped wildly as I felt him press closer.

His woken manhood was impossible to ignore. He rubbed himself against my side just a few inches lower than where Alan's hand rested.

His voice was thick with desire. "You almost fell for her trick, didn't you?" He spoke to Alan between the tender kisses over my throbbing artery. His gentleness was a strong contrast to everything else about him.

Alan blushed as his eyes followed Dimitri's lips with covetousness that made me wonder what he wanted more, my throat or Dimitri's mouth. "You're right. I did almost fall for her trap. I do enjoy planting myself inside her in every possible way. She knows this and is very clever."

"Hey! *She* is laying right here." I tried to put some heat behind my words, but my stupid lungs weren't working correctly, so the words were kind of breathy. There might have also been a whimper I was ashamed to admit.

"We know exactly where you are." Dimitri turned me around.

Dark hair covered his brow and cradled his resilient masculine visage. Onyx eyes stared down at me with the heat of a thousand suns from a thousand galaxies.

He was Romani and carried the blood of great wanderers, yet somehow, he'd claimed me as his home.

His gaze was possessive in a way that was threatening. The lethalness seemed to ripple in his muscles as he crouched over me, balancing on his elbows and pressing the rest of his bulk on top of me. That dangerous part of him rested heavily on my stomach and made me quiver.

Out of all of my men, Dimitri was the most violent. He was broody by nature, and thanks to his father, Vlad the Impaler, he had another form that came out when he was ready to rage.

He'd frightened me once. Dimitri was massive. Tall with broad shoulders and built with the intention to contain the beast that rested inside of him.

I remembered the dreaded night when his beast cornered me in the library. His body had twisted and contorted until he was unrecognizable. I thought I'd die, but if my record for getting in and out of trouble proved anything, I wouldn't. Not before I fulfilled the prophecy. I touched his solid cheek. I was no longer afraid of him and not because of my destiny but because he'd proven his devotion to me over and over again since that terrible night.

"How are you feeling?" he asked.

If he was asking if I was ready for some action, the answer was yes. In answer, I wrapped my leg around his hip. The move triggered both men into action.

The sheet was ripped into the air and fluttered to the ground like a cloud as my men presented me with their blatant beauty. Their blunt erections made my mouth water and gathered moisture in another place as well.

A tongue went to my mouth while another went to my nipple and flicked it until it was taut.

I sighed and grabbed Dimitri's hair as I shamelessly rubbed myself against him. My other hand tracked down Alan's body and wrapped around his jutted member.

He was warm in my grip, like hot iron that had been covered in velvet.

And so sensitive.

I squeezed.

He gasped against my mouth and then gave me more of his tongue.

I was so long in the sensation that I barely noticed when their mouths switched.

And suddenly, I tasted both of them on my tongue. I sucked them in deep, one after another as a hand crept down my stomach and fingers I knew well attached themselves to my clitoris, teasing me with strong circles before slipping through my wet folds.

Dimitri's chest rumbled against mine right before we gasped.

I broke from the mouth I was latched onto and looked south.

Down the line of my body, I watched Alan's fist work Dimitri into a frenzy while he did the same to me. Those beautiful fingers twisted and worked deep inside until I was dancing on the fine line of pain and white-hot bliss.

Dimitri's canines extend to the point that they could be called nothing but what they were. *Fangs.* The sharp white points forced a shiver through me and not in fear.

Alan leaned over and took the larger man's open mouth in a hot kiss of fangs and tongues, and I was done. I could see it a million times, and my reaction would always be the same. I often went into this prepared, knowing what to expect, and yet my feelings never changed. The pressure of Alan's hand and the sight of two men kissing was too beautiful.

I rode Alan's strong fingers and crashed just as Dimitri jerked and coated my stomach.

A rough knock came on the door as I pulled Dimitri down and kissed him again.

We ignored it.

My Romani flipped us until I was resting on his warm bulk.

Alan closed us in a second later. Their heat and strength befuddled me to the point that I forgot there'd been a knock at the door.

I turned back and caught Alan's mouth with mine while Dimitri entertained himself with my breast.

The knock sounded again and tried to shatter the bubble of desire we were in, but it barely made a ripple.

Peter's voice was barely muffled by the solid wood. "Dr. Shaw is here."

The bubble didn't just pop. It detonated. One minute it was there, and the next it was gone.

Alan pulled away first.

Dimitri blinked like he was coming out of a trance.

I wanted to shout. I wanted to tell him to come back into the trance, but I knew it wouldn't work.

The moment was gone, and now I had yet another reason to hate Dr. Shaw.

CHAPTER TWO

I'd like to say I didn't complain as they led me into the shower or while I got dressed at the speed of molasses. I'd also like to say that I didn't have debt collectors chasing me down for all those credit cards that I still hadn't gotten around to paying off.

But I did complain, and the creditors were starting to sound like a remake of *I Know What You Did Last Summer.*

The former was because of Dr. Shaw. The latter was because of a clause in my grandmother's estate.

I'd inherited everything Loretta Quinn had left in the world after she'd died but could only get the money and the house after living in the house for a year.

Somehow, her lawyer had found out that I'd gone missing last year, so I was being forced to start the timer over again.

Eventually, I got Alan and Dimitri to leave so I could get ready alone.

As I combed out my hair, slipped on my underwear, and poured myself into a pair of jeans, I felt like I was preparing for war.

In my drawer, I rummaged through my T-shirt collection and pulled out a Wonder Woman shirt before I decided the occasion called for the entire Justice League.

After that, I put on some socks, forwent boots, and trudged from the room.

The sound of music and laughter reminded me of the hundred-plus guests in the house. The walls were soundproof, so I often forgot about them.

A few of the merry fae had managed to break the werewolves from their reserved nature. They'd been here for two months. The two groups had come for different reasons.

While most of the dryads were here to avoid the war that was taking over the fae world, the werewolves were here to protect me.

With a house full of vampires and myself having my own witchy abilities, it would be easy to assume that I didn't need the added protection, and a year ago, I would have agreed.

But times had changed, and after a year of being the prisoner of the queen of the Unseelie, I had no intention of going back anytime soon. Not only did the hateful woman take me away from my home and my family, but she erased my memories and killed my first boyfriend.

So, for now, the wolves were welcome to stay.

But as I maneuvered through the crush of bodies and tried to find air around the stale scent of liquor, I admitted that their presence was something I was still getting used to.

I remembered the first time I'd come to the mansion. It had been a very quiet place. Now, in order to find solitude, I had to sneak into the library or a bedroom.

The hallway was long, and I walked slowly and talked to a few people to buy myself some more time. I admired the fine rug that ran the length of the great hall or the dynamic portrait that hung on the aesthetically pleasing wallpaper.

It was stuff I'd seen a hundred times, but I took extra care and noticed the gilded frames and the sconces.

The mansion of the sons of Vlad was a big, beautiful masterpiece, but neither the art nor the crowd was the reason I was taking half steps to the sitting room downstairs.

The truth was I dreaded my meeting with Dr. Shaw and not just Dr. Shaw but any doctor. It was irrational and stupid, but there was nothing I could do about it. Growing up on the road, I didn't get to grow up with one pediatrician. I had a different one for every shot, every cut, every accident. I'd grown up with a montage of faces, and while most of them had been kind, a few had given me the sort of nightmares that only death could eradicate.

A memory from my past rushed up and attacked me so hard that I almost tripped as my feet came to a halt. I was six. My father and another nurse were holding me down while a doctor drove a needle through my arm. He'd missed my vein the first time, so he'd had to do it again.

As the needle pricked through the first layer of skin and sunk through the next, I remember the pain, but more than anything else, I remember the doctor's mute disposition.

He hadn't cared about my tears or my pain. They were as much a routine to him as the doctor's visits were a routine to my father. He'd looked just as annoyed as the doctor, but no one seemed to care about my fears, and knowing the shot had been for my own good didn't make it any easier to accept.

I'd lived years without anyone ever listening to anything I said.

My dad had stolen me from my mother and treated me like little more than a burden his entire life, and though we were not on better terms now, the past still hurt.

A heavy hand on the shoulder shook me from my dark reverie.

I turned, looked up, and was met with a pair of eyes so viciously verdant that it seemed unfair to just call them green. A whole universe of greens had come together to compose the majesty of Ewan's irises.

He carried the essence of his home in his eyes. The Emerald Dream was sometimes what the fae world was called.

Ewan, Prince of the Night Court, the Unseelie, and Master of Shadows, stared down at me with all the unspoken compassion this world and his world had to offer.

Ewan understood me in a way that the others couldn't because, for most of our lives, we'd been journeying down the same road just in parallel worlds.

We'd walked a very silent and lonely path.

Being half-fae and half-vampire had made his existence unbearable to many of his people. They'd rejected him while I'd never had people to begin with. All I'd ever had was my father, and all he'd ever had was his other.

And both of them were more or less dictators.

13

Our words, actions, and thoughts had been muted by them.

Ewan's mother had ruled her son like she had ruled the Unseelie. Differences in opinions weren't tolerated.

Though Ewan and I didn't talk about it, two months ago, we'd been engaged, but I didn't count the proposal as sincere since he hadn't asked me of his own volition. He'd been doing his mother's bidding at the time.

Would he ask me again?

None of the vampires had brought up marriage, and I wasn't sure if they ever would or if they should. It was just another thing that I planned on bringing up, but not now. That would come later. Currently, I was still wrapping my head around the pregnancy.

He took my hand, and I knew where it was going. He brought my fingers to his lips. The kiss invoked a flutter low in my belly.

The old-fashioned gesture was our thing.

It had taken me time to accept that I had people who were dedicated to me. Now, I had to get over the fact that I had a *thing* with each of them, something that was traditional and would remain that way until I turned to dust and ash.

The only tradition I'd had before these men was watching my most anticipated films on opening night.

Now, I got soft kisses on my hand and eyes that had the power to make me blush in places covered by clothes.

A growl from down the hall caught their attention. A she-wolf had been cornered by two male dryads. They pressed their bodies into the woman while their hands investigated her muscled form. The she-wolf's expression was of pure bliss.

"Do you remember when you asked me out on a date?"

I lifted my chin and studied him, wondering where this was going. I remembered. I remembered how skeptical he'd been about the entire occasion. I'd been granted a gift from the Old One, the tree that begets all magic.

When the tree couldn't give me my first request, I asked for a date with my fiancé.

That night had been Ewan's first date, which I still found ridiculous, considering he was one of the most handsome men I'd ever seen.

When he'd followed me out of the fae world, he hadn't come prepared, so he'd had to work with the designers my world had to offer. And I had to admit that the tailored jeans, turtleneck, and boots looked good on him. All of it was black, which seemed in sync with his nature. In a trice, he could vanish into a cloud of smoke.

His skin was that beautiful translucent shade that the vampires were known for. His hair was as dark as midnight and hung in loose waves around his shoulders.

The fact that women in the fae world hadn't been crawling all over themselves to get close to him was mind-boggling. They'd rejected him because of his father's blood, but I couldn't get enough of him. In fact, I'd proved it that night when I all but begged him to touch me ... amongst other things.

Finally, I responded to his question. "I remember our date."

He jerked his adorable head in the direction of the wolf and the dryad explorers who were trying to conqueror and map her body. "Who do those dryads remind you of?" His eyes gleamed with humor, and I knew what he was playing.

I punch Ewan in the arm. "Hey! I was nothing like those dryads."

He roared with laughter, which only made me hit him again. "Look at you. You still can't keep your hands off me, can you?"

I laughed, and the muscles in my neck relaxed. "Keep it up. My next hit will connect somewhere else."

He moaned. "I'd love to connect with you as well." He wrapped his arms around me and gave me a kiss that was more chaste than his words.

I shook my head. "I've never met a virgin with such a dirty mind."

Ewan was still a virgin and unashamed. He grinned and pulled me close enough to feel his hardness. "Sorry. You make it difficult to think of anything else when I'm around you."

I was flattered to know I inspired filth in this man's mind. No, seriously, I really was. "You better clean up your act."

He waggled his brow. "I'd rather clean something else." Then he bent down and kissed me again, but this time, he used his tongue to remind me of all the wicked things he could do with it.

He pulled away too soon. "Let's go downstairs."

The fog of his seduction lifted as I remembered why I was dressed and standing in the hall at all. "I'd rather stay up here."

He smiled and backed away. "Come on. Doctors in this world can't be all bad." He held his hand out in the direction of the staircase.

I begrudgingly led the way. "Tell that to every comic in existence. Many of the villains are doctors."

"Why is that?"

It was a fine question and one I latched onto as he guided me to my doom. "While part of me thinks it's used as a means to come up with some really cool tech and add more possibilities to the comic universe, humans are also given the benefit of the doubt once they have a medical degree notched to their name. Their villainy is then hidden under the guise of science."

"So, science in itself isn't evil?"

I smiled. "Nah. Science is awesome, especially when they attach the word fiction at the end."

He laughed, but my humor died when our feet stopped moving, and I quickly realized that we'd made it to our destination. And there in the middle of the room was my greatest enemy yet.

Dr. Kimberly Shaw's smile was dainty and friendly. "Hello, Lorena. How are you feeling?" She had the voice of a swan.

Or at least her voice made me think of swans. I wasn't actually sure what swans sounded like, but her voice was buoyant and floated in the air like a swan could float on a pond. It was peaceful and graceful.

It should have calmed me, but instead, my hackles rose.

I compared the woman to Mary Poppins because that's who she looked like, and not the Emily Blunt version but the 1964 film version with Julia Andrews.

She was the reason *The Sound of Music* was currently stuck in my head. I'd had a friend once who'd invited me for a sleepover in grade school. My dad didn't allow me to sleep over. He picked me up around ten that night, but I was there when one of the girls popped the film in and never forgot a second of it.

I'd loved it, but not for any of the reasons most people adored it like the music and the escape from Nazis, but because Maria had swept into the lives of the Von Trapp kids and given them the mother they no longer had.

And I'd been envious and enchanted by her.

I'd felt every moment of the movie. I'd felt the loneliness and lost state of the children and the harsh father who didn't seem to care.

The idea of a stepmother had been a completely foreign thought to me until that moment, and it only got better when Maria managed to make Captain Von Trapp's heart of ice melt and beat renewed.

For weeks after seeing that film, I looked at every woman differently. My father wasn't a bad looking guy. Maybe he could love again. Maybe my teacher or the store clerk or some woman on the road would catch his eye and change our lives forever.

That idea died when we moved again. How was dad going to fall in love if he didn't stay long enough to take a woman out on a proper date? The answer was simple.

He wouldn't.

As I stared at my own Julia Andrews, I felt a million conflicting emotions about her.

I wanted to hate her because she was a doctor. I wanted to love her because she smiled at me with a familiar tenderness that my mother, the mother who'd tried to kill me, never gave me. I wanted to scream so she'd leave, but I kept my mouth shut because I wanted her to stay.

The very idea that she could make me act differently than who I truly was made me lash out. "I don't remember scheduling this appointment."

Her tone never changed as she approached me. She walked with an elegance I'd never possess but always admire. "You didn't. I just came by to see how you were doing."

Damn. There went my heart, leaping with all the skills of a ballerina.

Dr. Shaw stopped right in front of me and held my stare with her tranquil, glittering blue eyes. "Your aura is burning very bright this evening. I'm seeing a dark-red when I'd hoped for blue."

She'd asked me to keep a food journal so that I could keep track of my protein and iron levels. There was also a stone with a rune hanging around my neck that matched the one around her neck. It allowed her to keep track of my aerial changes. That we were rocking matching jewelry felt odd in both a good way and an awkward way.

I hated that the first piece of personal jewelry anyone had ever given me came from this woman. Ewan's ring didn't count since the object had actually been a weapon to suppress my memory. Unlike my fake engagement ring, this rune had been made just for me. Dr. Shaw had broken a stone in half and crafted them herself.

The idea would have been sweet if it didn't also have the stalker effects.

"It was probably red because I was having sex," I snarled, hoping my tone would put her off.

It didn't. Instead, she laughed, and even that was like a merry tune. "All colors have a positive and a negative side, and I can see the difference. Red holds passion, but it also holds anger. Last night, there was passion, and then there was dander."

Dander? Who used words like dander? People like Dr. Shaw was the answer.

I threw my arms out. "What? I can't get angry now? Should we put that on the no-no list?"

"It's already on the no-no list."

"Well, angry is who I am," I cut her off when she tried to speak. "I'm not finished."

She pressed her lips together and tucked her chin. I was aware of the eyes that watched us. There was Dr. Shaw's assistant, her pretty daughter, Blair. She stood in the corner of the room with one of those old-fashioned doctor bags in her hand. She wore a style similar to her mother. The dark-green dress with its quarter length sleeves, sweetheart neckline, and hoop skirt looked like something that belonged on the set of *Grease*, but it worked for her charming personality.

She had soft, round features with a permanent Mona Lisa smile, and I never stopped wondering what thoughts lived behind those clear blue eyes. She said nothing unless someone asked her a question. She was two years younger than me and my opposite in every way.

For one, I was sure she was doing great in school, and when high school was over, Blair would go to college and excel there as well.

Like Dr. Shaw, Blair was some sort of auramancer. Their spells were emotionally based.

I wondered if the women would ever try to use their abilities on me to try to control me, dragging me from the edge of my rage. So far, they hadn't.

Aside from the Shaw family, only my men were present in the room.

Zane was the only boyfriend I hadn't seen that morning, but I felt his golden gaze track me just as soon as I walked through the door. His dark skin gleamed in the light of the fireplace, where he stood, leaning against the mantle with his arms crossed.

He'd had me all to himself last night. He, unlike Alan and Dimitri, wasn't into sharing, which was fine with me.

Out of all the men, Zane was the one I spoke to the most about my fears. He was just so easy to talk to. Once I opened my mouth around Zane, words poured out faster than I could think. Since the day we'd met, he'd felt as familiar to me as my own skin.

With Zane, I was blunt, and he was blunt with me.

I was surprised he was here. Zane liked to leave on the nights we weren't together. I didn't know where he went, but I knew he was feeding. When I'd finally gotten him back from Titania, he'd been skin and bones. Now he was more muscled but still leaner than Dimitri.

And tonight was all about Dimitri, but since Alan and Dimitri were a pair in themselves, I often got both of them unless Dimitri said otherwise.

I visited my guys on a scheduled rotation. The arrangement worked not just because we loved each other but because each and every one of them had become as vital to me as an organ. We fit together.

And one of the reasons we fit so well was because the men not only adored who I was but loved every part of me.

My fury included.

"You have no idea what my life has been like, Dr. Shaw. A year ago, I finally found my mother, and do you know what she tried to do? Kill me! Also, I found out I had a sister, and what do you know? She tried to kill me as well. As quickly as I knew them, I knew they hated me."

She opened her mouth, but I kept going. I was on a roll.

"And then, two months ago, I found out my mother, who'd I'd assumed was dead, wasn't. Instead, she'd infused our souls together with the intention of taking over my body, but then she sacrificed herself and now her soul sits in a rock, and I need to decide what the hell I'm going to do with it."

That was the reason my aura had probably mirrored an inferno last night. While talking to Zane, I'd gotten worked up. My mother was sucked into a Soul Stone and not only her but Wei.

Wei.

I considered him boyfriend number one. He was the first vampire I had fallen in love with.

It had been over a year since I'd seen him, but I still remembered the feel of his weighty, angsty gaze. His eyes had been as dark as onyx and his need for me as great as his hatred for past and failures.

It had taken hard work for us to get to the place where I could say he was mine and he wouldn't flinch away.

And just when it was starting to get good, Titania took it all away from me.

So now, he too was locked in a Soul Stone, and I didn't have the first clue as to how to break him out. According to legend, there was no way to reverse the process, but I was going to find one even if it killed me.

"I've been shot with arrows, clawed open by werewolves, attacked by a hag, choked out by a psychotic vampire, kidnapped, imprisoned, and betrayed by some of the very men in this room on more than one occasion."

I felt the energy in the room shift. As a necromancer, the emotions of the dead were hard to ignore. I felt pain and shame, mostly from Zane, Ewan, and Dimitri. Even Alan flared a little, though I didn't know why. Out of all of them, he'd been the most loyal, though his feelings for Dimitri had made dating him impossible at first. It was only after I learned that I could love more than one person that I discovered so could he.

I loved them all, but I missed Wei, and my past had left some scars that weren't evident on my body.

"I am who I am," I finished, feeling a little exhausted as I did.

"What have you eaten?" Dr. Shaw asked.

The sudden change in the direction of the conversation put me off.

I crossed my arms and shifted on my feet, feeling unnerved. "I just got up."

Dr. Shaw nodded and turned to Peter, who stood by the door. "Would you please make Lorena a smoothie?"

"I don't want a smoothie," I fired the words with hate that was dwindling. I liked that Dr. Shaw said please and thank you to Peter. When Vlad had come with his army of women, they hadn't been so polite, especially Anja.

I could still recall the sound of the smack she'd given Peter in the kitchen. That was while I'd been caged in a room under Vlad's command.

Dr. Shaw folded her hands in front of her and pressed them against the front of her blue skirts. "What do you want?"

The question was a loaded one. What the hell did I want? I wanted a lot of things. I wanted to bring Wei back and figure out what to do with my mother. I also wanted to stop the war that was happening in the fae but fighting in my condition was also on the woman's no-no list.

"I don't know." I didn't actually *not* want a smoothie. In fact, a smoothie sounded good. What I wouldn't allow was for this woman to come in here and dictate my life.

She turned back to me and waited.

I groaned and looked at Peter. "Fine. Make the smoothie. Thanks." I grumbled the last because I didn't want to take my acrimony out on Peter. As a brownie, he'd been through enough. Also, I'd learned to never piss off the hand that fed me, and Peter had the remainder of my stash.

Turning back to Dr. Shaw, I asked, "Are you happy? You can go."

Dr. Shaw nodded and turned to her perfect daughter Blair. "Let's go."

I ignored the churning in my stomach and stormed out of the room. I rushed toward the back of the house and out the back door.

The December wind backhanded me so hard it all but called me its bitch. I was knocked back and stunned for a second, but the shouts from the people who'd followed me forced me out the door. "No one come near me!" I shouted to everyone in the room.

My power flicked on like a switch in my blood. Since the beginning of the pregnancy, I no longer had to look for it. It found me every time. My magic added force to my words, and I felt my men stumble back as if they'd run into a brick wall.

For once, I didn't see anyone on the back porch or in the weather-beaten garden, and I planned on taking full advantage of the peace.

I shivered in the cold and grabbed my arms as I moved forward. The bitter air slipped through my thin clothing and froze the hair on my arms. I could feel my lips tingling as my every breath turned into a cloud.

The cold pressed against my fingers. I was probably minutes from hyperthermia.

If Dr. Shaw wanted me to be blue, she was about to get it.

I thought about going back inside for my coat and boots, but something demanded I didn't. Call me crazy, but I'd been feeling a pull to the outdoors for the last month. I blamed it on the dryads. They were fascinated with nature while I was more into video games and a plethora of other activities that could take place inside and preferably in pajamas.

I measured my steps against the wooden porch and then quickened them once I reached the field.

The grass crunched underneath my feet.

I stopped to look over the garden. Before the dryads had arrived, the place had been pretty barren. A short hedge wall had surrounded a large square that had two dead beds and a water fountain that had been covered in leaves and algae and hadn't looked like it had been used in years.

Now the flowerbeds had been cleared of their weeds and debris with the dryads planning to plant some herbs and other vegetation in the spring, but only if the war went on for that long.

To the right in the distance were the stables and to the left another barn used for storage. Their lights made the night bearable.

I could feel eyes pressing in on me and imagined the faces pressed against the glass, watching me.

CHAPTER THREE

"I'll be Watching You" by The Police popped into my head, and the tune wouldn't leave as the eyes from the house continued to stalk me.

Seeking the solace of the dark, I started for the fountain, but something grabbed my foot.

I looked down, and my heart tried to punch a hole through my chest.

The wind blew, and I blinked to make sure what I was seeing was actually happening.

The frosted grass shook off the winter and erupted from underneath my feet. Vines had latched themselves around my socks. They shot up and twisted out of the soil. In the dark, the vines looked like the mangled fingers of the dead.

They crawled away from me as they grew.

I stood there in wonder as the first calendula bloomed.

The flower was native to Virginia, and I only knew that from my time working at the mini-mart. There was a small shelf of seeds for people who didn't feel like walking the one block over to the actual store.

So, thanks to the laziness of the townsfolk, I knew this flower well.

The vibrant-orange petals were soft moonlight, and I was struck dumb when more little buds popped up. They burst into an array of purples, yellows, and more sunny oranges. Pansies and winter jasmines sprouted up, and between those blooms known to earth were once known that could only exist with magic.

I lowered myself to the ground and stared at the petals that looked more like gems.

They glowed brilliantly in shades of blue and green and mocked the heavens as they formed their own celestial sky. They sparkled like stars.

A deep groaning in the distance made me look up.

I expected to see a giant, but instead, the tall, red oak trees in the distance that surrounded the property swayed. They bent until they canopied and twisted together. Their whining was the same sound people made after waking from a long slumber. They stretched their branches like arms and grabbed one another as they formed some sort of structure in the trees.

The magic blooms spread past the garden and were now twining around the trees. They looked like lanterns hanging from treehouses.

I hadn't done a thing to cause this wonderful phenomenon.

My hand went to my flat stomach before I fell to my knees.

I couldn't move, mostly because I was frozen solid but also because of what was happening.

This magic wasn't coming from me yet at the same time it was.

I became aware that I was no longer alone when a pair of hands grabbed me and helped me up.

Dimitri cradled me in his arms. I snuggled against his hard chest, seeking his warmth while Zane tossed a warm blanket over me.

The cold began to melt away, and I realized I was shivering. My skin thawed, but I barely registered a thing besides what was happening in the yard.

Murmurs filled the silence. Voices were carried on the wind as more and more people poured out of the house. I heard the questions, but it took some time before anyone directed one at me.

It was Alan who asked, "How did you do this?"

I said the only thing I could say. "I didn't."

A gasp had me stretching my neck to see where it had come from.

Dimitri turned his bulk around just in time for me to witness Willow coming down the porch steps. Her long, red hair was billowing around her like a cloud.

She, like the rest of the dryads, was dressed in a manner that was more fitting for summer than winter. The dryads didn't feel cold in the way humans or even other fae did. Being related to the earth, they could withstand everything the weather could throw at them.

Willow was all long limbs, much like the trees she adored. Her eyes were large as she took in the magic that had spilled and overtaken the front yard. I had never seen anything but an abundance of happiness displayed on her face.

She didn't disappoint me then either. "Who did this? Marula?"

Marula was another dryad who'd come with the pack. I loved her just as much as I loved Willow. She was powerful with dark skin and copper eyes, and I'd only had to tell her to stop kissing me once before she stopped.

The dryads were very sensual beings and thus became fixated on new sensations. My humanism fascinated them.

"I didn't do this," Marula said in response to Willow's question.

"Then who?"

"I did it," I answered. "Or, I mean … the baby did it."

Willow rushed over and slipped her hand underneath the blanket. She didn't ask permission before she slipped her hand over my belly. The dryads weren't really good at that. I tried to explain sexual assault to them. Let's just say the conversation hadn't gone over well, so in the end, I told them not to leave the mansion, and they agreed.

I stiffened as it dawned on me how important this moment was. The baby and the prophecy were no longer an abstract of reality, but a real-life, breathing thing, and the freak-out only grew when I realized something else.

I was a mother.

This singular thought stayed on the back of my mind only to jump out and attack me every time I remembered that I was pregnant. I was a mother, and I was expected to raise the bundle of cells in my stomach.

The information was enough to make me dizzy, but now that I knew my child was powerful … I was speechless.

And my speechlessness wasn't a standard occurrence.

Willow's hand was warm. The dryads were always so warm. Her smile was radiant. Pale, golden tresses danced across her face. Her voice was soft with wonder. "Fae."

My stomach did a somersault off the diving board and missed the water. "What?"

"Fae." The thrill from her eyes spilled into her words. "This is fae magic."

I glanced out to the garden and took in the gleaming flowers and watched as the dryads gathered them, which was probably a good idea since flowers like that didn't belong on earth.

My child was fae?

Did that make Ewan the father? "But Ewan and I never …"

"All magic is rooted in the fae," Willow said. "The magic that rests in his world also came from the Old One. It is all connected. We are all connected." She emphasized her words by rubbing my belly again.

I hadn't known that, but now, when I thought about my visit to the Earth kingdom, it made sense. The Old One had given me a gift because I'd been kind to the trees in my world. If our trees were connected, why wouldn't our magic be?

So, Ewan wasn't the father, but then who was?

That was another discussion I hadn't had with my boyfriends. No one had asked about DNA, but I was sure they all wondered who the father was.

I looked over at Ewan, who stood on the other side of the driveway. Under the fall of the light that emptied from the open door, I could make out his features, but it was hard to see his face. Still, I could feel his gaze on me like a vice grip of a firm hand.

I opened myself to the magic that was now suffocating the air and was sidetracked by the cords of magic that were visible. The silver threads not only covered the sky and ground but looked like veins against everyone present. There didn't seem to be any pattern in the framework of the magic, but it was beautiful in its wild state. The colors all varied where they touched.

Ewan's was red.

A second after I thought his name, his emotions drenched our connection with anxiety and a longing saturated with distress. He needed me.

His heart thumped like a furious drum down the line, knocking my own heart off rhythm until it was in tune with his.

His pain bloomed into thoughts, and I read his mind with the ease of a book.

Out of all the men, he was the only one who couldn't be the father, and that was because of a vow he'd made to his mother. Until Ewan and I were married, we'd never get past third base, and that pained him. It hurt him that he couldn't connect to me the way the others did, and he thought that made him less than the others.

He felt like an outsider, and I hadn't even known it until this moment. He'd hid the feeling so well. I'd wondered if he'd missed the fae world or even his diabolical mother, which wouldn't have upset me. Who was I to tell someone they couldn't love their parents?

I should have known he was feeling this way, but I'd been so caught up in myself that I hadn't noticed.

Tonight wasn't Ewan's night, but he needed me.

I tried to get down, but the arms that held me tightened. I turned my head to Dimitri. "Put me down." I felt him tense.

"Your socks are wet, and your feet are frozen. Let me at least take you inside before they fall off."

Deciding I wanted to keep my feet, I relented. "Fine, but I need to speak to Ewan alone." I didn't bother calling over to Ewan since I knew he could hear me.

Dimitri sat me down in one of those fancy wingback chairs by the fireplace. The upholstery was deep-green velvet and came with a matching footrest that Alan put in front of me.

Peter brought tea and a bowl of a thick soup that smelled wonderful. "Dr. Shaw changed the meal plan when you ventured outdoors. She thought you would want something more."

"Of course she did." But I couldn't stop the warmth that penetrated my heart.

I blamed the fireplace.

Then an idea came to mind, and I smirked up at the brownie. "I'll be by the kitchens to discuss the menu for tomorrow."

He knew what that was code for—I needed another hit.

Peter cleared his throat. His uncharacterized graveness put a trickle of fear into my blood. "Dr. Shaw suggested the soup while I was in the kitchen."

"What does that mean?"

"She came into the kitchen to look over your menu."

My shoulders dropped. "What does that mean?"

"She took it."

My skin prickled, and I took a deep breath.

Anger wasn't good for the baby. Anger wasn't good for the baby.

The chanting didn't work.

In the last month, every emotion I felt was heightened, especially my wrath.

"She had no right! Dr. Shaw is banned from this house, you hear me? Banned! Barred! I don't want to hear her name spoken again. Tell Marquessa I don't need a doctor."

It had been Marquessa who'd said I needed a doctor. Marquessa had been my grandmother's friend, and since Grandmother Loretta was no longer around to see over me, Marquessa tried to step in where she could.

I knew the woman had good intentions. Everyone had good intentions, but I refused to be a hostage in my own home.

"I will make sure your message is delivered," Peter said.

I didn't actually mean to give him that order, but I let it go and told him he could leave when he asked.

Ewan closed the door behind himself when they were finally alone. "You wanted to talk to me?" He stayed as far away from me as he could get, and it wasn't because of what had occurred. I could still feel the loss and sadness that came from him.

Immediately, my troubles were set aside so I could focus on him.

Ewan and I had gone through problems in the beginning. I'd be the first person to admit that I was not the easiest person to get along with, but I thought he knew how I felt about him. That he doubted my feelings for him hurt.

I held out my hand, and Ewan flew across the room and took it.

He knelt by my chair and brought my fingers to his lips again, but this time, I saw everything he was holding back. How could I have missed the melancholy?

I knew my fingers were cold, but I needed to touch him, so I grabbed his face in my other hand. "Hey, how are you feeling?"

He cringed before he smiled. "That's not important. The only people who matter to me right now are you and the baby."

The phrase "heartache" had never been truer than every second that I could feel the honesty seeping from his words. I didn't know who the father was, and I didn't want to know, but Ewan knew the baby wasn't his and was still willing to stick around.

The heaviness in my chest was too much to bear. I wasn't built for this emotional stuff. "I love you just as much as I love the others. Just because we haven't had sex yet doesn't make you any less my boyfriend than they are."

The tightness in his features told me my words had missed their mark. "I don't want to be …"

I didn't know what else he'd planned on saying at the moment because a second later, the door opened, and I was tackled to the ground a second before I heard the ping and thump of metal.

My back slapped the coarse rug, knocking the breath right out of my lungs.

Ewan was over me and had cradled my head for the landing. "Stay down."

I covered my belly. "What's going on?"

We were behind a couch. Then I was behind the couch by myself because Ewan flew away.

And when I say flew, I mean he moved like a dark cloud. His body became incorporeal. I watched his face empty right before he went out of sight.

I heard the ringing of metal and continued thumping and breaking of wood. I heard furniture move as it slid across the floor.

Something gleaning flitted over the couch and hit the wall.

They were stars. The sort I recognized from anime movies with ninjas.

I thought, 'What the heck?' and then whispered, "What the heck?"

Turning on my side, I looked under the couch and tracked a single pair of boots. The style looked handmade, and the material wrinkled like hide. In the firelight, I could also see Ewan gliding in the air. His shadow abilities came from his father.

"Still trying to kill my bride, I see."

A male spoke. "I'm not here to kill her. Had that been my intention I would have used a sword to sever the head from her shoulders."

Ewan's reply was cold. "Then be prepared to lose yours."

"She comes with me alive or dead!" More furniture moved, and more stars were tossed.

I stiffened. I didn't like being threatened, and I knew that voice well.

I'd waited for him to come after me.

Lord Corridan.

He'd been part of the Unseelie court until I exposed him as the traitor he was. I'd told Ewan's sister, Princess Aisling, how he'd been using her to try to get the throne and remembered the brokenness she'd tried to hide.

I hated it when people said they were going to kill me, but I really hated it when people used others.

I stood. "Hey!"

Corridan turned, but before he could toss a star, I tossed my magic.

It flung from me just as sharp as a two-edged blade, nearly cutting me as it leaped from my fingertips.

Corridan sprinted, missing the blast and came right for me. "Lorena!"

I know what he wanted me to do. He wanted me to hide, but instead, I braced and took a breath. As my lungs filled, my body vibrated with energy.

I could feel Corridan's hatred for me as he picked up speed. His rage empowered him.

But if it were a contest between whose rage was the biggest and stiffest in the room, then I was going to win hands-down.

Everything happened at once. The world slowed around me.

Ewan poofed into wisps of smoke.

Corridan flicked his wrist.

I threw up my hands and shoved my enraged magic out with all my might.

The trajectory of Corridan's star turned just enough that it missed its mark for the center of my head and scraped my cheek with all the impact of a fingernail's whisper.

He was thrown back against the wall, his other star knocked from his hand.

Ewan appeared and elbowed him in the face.

Corridan's head snapped back against the furnace. His eyes rolled back, and he slumped to the floor.

Ewan had the bloodied fae tied up before the room was flooded with people.

Everyone was asking questions at once. Hands touched me, ran up my arms and down my legs. Someone suggested Dr. Shaw be sent for, and that's when I snapped.

"Back up!"

I marched over to Corridan just as he was coming around and grabbed him by the collar of his dark-green tunic. When I'd left the fae world, the color was all the rage. I suppose the war had slowed down fashion's evolution.

"Where's Aisling?" That was the first thing I wanted to know. Yeah, yeah, I know the guy wanted to kill me or take me in or whatever, but I was worried about Ewan, and though the siblings didn't get along, I wanted them to.

Ewan stiffened as if just remembering the story I'd told him about how I escaped the palace. His sister had helped me, and in return, I'd pointed out the enemy she'd been keeping far too close.

Corridan spat in my face.

The shit hit my eye and stung.

My mouth dropped.

No one had ever done that to me before.

It was worse than a slap. It was debasing me and reminded me of how inferior I was in his eyes. To the fae, I was just a stupid human, unworthy of Ewan and the throne he was destined to take one day.

I was paralyzed by his degrading action.

But Ewan wasn't.

Corridan cringed and screamed. His face was red in agony. He lifted his arm. Where there had once been a hand was now nothing more than a bloody stump. The bone was visible. My stomach rolled, but I managed to hold it back so I could look tough.

Ewan dangled the severed appendage in front of Corridan and let the blood drop on the man's face. The prince of shadow's green eyes glittered with hate and retribution. "I'll be taking a finger for every offense you took against my fiancée, and you have committed many offenses this night."

I glanced around the room at all the stars that now decorated the furniture and walls. There were way more than ten.

I didn't bother correcting Ewan's assumption that I was his fiancée because I knew he was speaking in the heat of the moment. Or at least, I hoped it was. However, now wasn't the time to correct him.

Ewan stood, and someone else lifted me. My back hit a wall made of hard muscle. I looked up and over and saw Dimitri holding me. His features were more vehement than the others in the room. I could feel him trying to hold back the beast that clawed at him to get out and do damage.

Ewan shouted an order. "Let's slow the bleeding so he doesn't bleed out and take him to the basement. My mother's charms still have hold of the space."

Titania had used her magic to bind anyone who walked into the basement. Victims were immediately hit by drowsiness that was almost too heavy to shake off. The queen of the Unseelie had held my men down there for a time. I doubted that I'd have been able to make it in and out of there myself if it weren't for the connection I shared with the vampires.

Zane picked up Corridan by his uninjured arm and jerked him to his feet. When I found Zane two months ago, he'd been almost skin and bones, but he'd filled out since his return. He was still built like a swimmer with lean muscles. They rippled as he marched a wailing Corridan from the room.

Some of the dryads followed. There were a few healers in the bunch.

I hadn't realized so many people were in the room until that moment. It had been so quiet, but now everyone was talking in hushed tones. I heard one of the dryads suggest they leave. It seemed the war had finally made its way to my doorstep.

Dimitri brought a warm, moist cloth to my face and wiped where Corridan had gotten me. "Are you hurt?"

"For once? Only my pride is scattered." It was a miracle that I wasn't bleeding or broken somewhere. I expected injuries after a fight like people expected sunrise after nightfall.

Whenever someone tried to kill me, I usually wore the evidence of the battle in my skin. My arms were covered in silver lines from the attacks I'd survived. To the Court of Fire, the scars were as good as memorabilia. I was kind of glad I didn't have any keepsakes from this one.

I slipped my hand in Dimitri's and locked our fingers together.

He squeezed. Before I could speak, the mountainous werewolf who went by the name William stepped forward. He was the first commander of the wolves and had been sent by Evelynn, their queen.

His voice had a certainty that only came with years of challenges. Surprisingly, he was only eighteen, but he was wiser than many of the adults I knew. He could also be easy going when there wasn't a pending battle. He was the perfect leader. Dependable and kind.

"The wolves and I will rotate shifts so that you are always protected. Two at the door and two at your side at all times. If you need anything else from us, please let me know. You are one of our queen's top priorities."

"Well, ain't that sweet," I muttered. "Look, the last thing I need is a bunch of people following me around all day, so thanks, but no thanks. What we need to know is how he found us and how he got in."

There were murmurs of agreement.

"We'll get answers," Ewan vowed. The coolness in his tone was just as troubling as was the fact that he was still holding Corridan's detached hand. Black swirled around him like a dust cloud.

"Ewan?"

He looked at me, and my magic picked up on an emotion he was hiding. *Fear.* "I need to find my sister."

CHAPTER FOUR

I felt like I had spent the last year waiting for the final fight. When would the day come when I could finally use the phrase, *"Let's finish this!"* Instead, I'd encountered one trick boss after another.

It was like I was stuck in *Super Mario Brothers* or *Final Fantasy IV, VIII, and XIII*.

The question of art mimicking life or life mimicking art made me realize that my life was a video game.

And as I stared into Corridan's angry eyes, I wondered, would Corridan be the final battle?

If so, then I was going to find the manager of his reality and ask for a full refund.

The vampires and I had formed a plan before dragging Corridan out of the basement. By then, daylight had begun to threaten the sky, so Zane, Dimitri, and Alan had been forced to retire for bed. Ewan was half fae and had the ability to walk through the day and the night.

So, for the time being, a group of the werewolves, led by William, stood around me like a bloodthirsty wall.

If Corridan so much as flinched, he'd lose a lot more than his hand.

I'd had to stop Ewan from taking the other one. I know, I know. Corridan deserved to walk the world without hands and a lot more, but the thought of it unsettled me. So, for the moment, he'd keep the hand and his life.

"Where did you learn to throw stars?" I asked.

Corridan narrowed his eyes, but a wary glance in Ewan's direction had him giving me the right answer.

We may have agreed not to kill Corridan, but he didn't know that. "It was a talent I picked up. I've always been good with my hands."

The last statement was like nails to the chalkboard of my senses. My head exploded at the memory of him almost forcing himself on me. He'd shoved an elixir down my throat that had prevented me from moving or using my magic. Then he'd crawled on top of me and groped me.

Suddenly, I wanted to be the one to cut them off. "Where's Lady Aisling?"

"Who knows? I ran once I knew she wanted me dead." He shrugged. "I haven't seen her since."

The fae's strict rule of truth ensured that everything that left Corridan's mouth was factual content.

But that didn't mean he was being honest. The fae worked in riddles, and riddles were a game I was working at. "You haven't seen her, but has she seen you?"

Corridan's sudden hesitation said yes. "I'm aware that someone is following me and trying to hunt me down. It is likely her."

Ewan released a breath, and his posture became less rigid. "Tell us what happened to her after we left." I'd told Ewan how I escaped and how Aisling had been the one to help me do it. "What happened when my sister confronted you?"

Corridan swallowed. Bitterness marred his mouth. "Your sister didn't confront me. At first, after you left, everything seemed fine. They sent out a search party for you and your bride, but I was treated the same. Aisling didn't act differently toward me, and I assumed it was because she didn't know about my affair with Mustardseed, or she had decided she didn't care. I thought she'd chosen to look past my betrayal because of her love for me."

I took some time to consider the fae before me. Corridan was tall and handsome with deep-blue eyes, but it was hard for me to get the image of him trying to kill me out of my head. His currently calm nature was in direct odds with the crazed individual who continued to try to kill me and would have raped me had his girlfriend, Mustardseed, not shown up when she had.

He looked at me, and before I realized it, I was shuffling back. I stopped when my back hit something. The pair of hands on my shoulders told me I'd bumped into William.

His presence gave me the boost of strength I needed. I wasn't the victim here. Corridan was.

"What happened next?" I asked.

Corridan, still holding my eyes, said, "Her pleasantness was all a ruse. At dinner the next evening, Titania honored me with a gift for all my hard work. A box was brought out for me, and I realized that Mustardseed wasn't there. I wanted her to see me step into my glory."

I tried not to roll my eyes, but they rolled. His glory? The man was really delusional.

"My mother does have a flare of dramatics," Ewan said. "Let me guess. Mustardseed was in the box."

"Only her head," he spat, and I wondered if he was using anger to hide his pain. He'd seemed in loved with Mustardseed, but then again, he'd been willing to rape me so who knew his real feelings.

"The guards came after me, so I jumped through the window and ran," Corridan went on. He struggled in the ropes that bound him to the chair, but the binds were unbreakable, not because of magic but because Ewan was just really good at tying knots.

I knew from experience.

And if you're wondering just how deep my kink went, let's just say we hadn't hit bottom yet. Though my own bottom was getting hit. Repeatedly.

"While I'd wanted to believe the best, I'd been prepared for their betrayal. My horse had been waiting on the other side of the window."

The fae horses flew. My own horse, Airgead, was in the stables.

"Where did you go after?" Ewan asked.

Corridan sighed with feigned annoyance. "I went to the only place I had left to go if I still wanted the throne."

"Your father," Ewan finished.

Corridan nodded. "I told him who I was and told him what had happened to me. I also told him of my failed plan, so we made another." He'd been looking at Ewan but found my eyes before he spoke again. "I was to find you and take you back to him. Once I accomplish my task, my father will give me the Unseelie Kingdom once he's won the war." His chin lifted slightly.

Even bound to a chair, he was confident that he still had a chance at victory.

Either the man was smoking something, or he was the most confident person I'd ever met.

"How did you find me?" Only one person in the house was in contact with anyone in the fae world, and that was Willow, but she communicated through the trees, and I doubted the trees had given me up.

"I shouldn't have to answer to you, human!" Corridan shouted. The sudden eruption had me tense. The man was unhinged. "Prophesy or not, you and this filthy-blooded prince have no authority over me. You're both despicable. I can barely stand the sight of you."

Ewan's sword made a sharp whining sound as he unsheathed it. "Then perhaps I should take your eyes next."

My stomach dropped, and Corridan's eyes turned to white balls of terror.

"Answer the question," I said as I grabbed Ewan's hand to still his movement.

"I have my ways," Corridan cried.

"And I have your hand," Ewan leaned into me. "Shall we keep going?"

Corridan closed his eyes in defeat.

Ewan's comebacks were solid gold. I'd almost forgotten how witty he could be.

Ewan put his sword back and crossed his arms. "We can continue this little game of tit for tat if you wish, but know that I will win in the end." He sounded more princely by the second.

I could tell he was in his element dealing with Corridan. I wondered what sort of man he'd have become if his mother had loosened the short leash she'd always had on him.

This was a take-charge, no-nonsense Ewan that I'd glimpsed very few times in the fae world and even less here until this moment.

"How did you find my bride?" Ewan asked. "Who helped you?"

And again, I said nothing to correct him. Besides, this wasn't *Keeping up with the Kardashians*. We didn't really owe Corridan explanations about our relationship anyway.

"Oberon," Corridan hissed.

"How?" Ewan asked.

That made Corridan clam up.

Ewan stepped forward. His hand was on his hip again, close to his weapon. He'd picked up his blade somewhere in the last hour. His fingers danced on the helm.

But I didn't want the blood ruining the room. Also, I needed answers and wasn't sure Corridan would be able to give them to me once Ewan was done with him.

So, I blocked him, planting myself firmly in front of Ewan as I narrowed my eyes at Corridan. "How?"

His lips twitched mockingly. He doubted I could hurt him. Still, he gave an answer. "I've had someone scrying for you for weeks but couldn't find you."

Scrying was a talent that fae of the Court of Airs possessed. Ewan had explained that to me when he'd come looking for me months ago. I'd explained to him that the mansion and my grandmother's house were protected from any divination by means of mirrors and crystals.

My adoration for indoor activities was the reason Corridan had failed to find me. Before tonight, I'd only gone outside to see Airgead or to go to my grandmother's house—my house—to read more about her life.

Ewan said, "Only the Court of Airs has the ability to scry."

"Oberon has forced the Court of Airs to bend the knee."

That was a surprise.

I rotated my eyes to Ewan. I wanted to know what this meant for his mother's kingdom. I wanted to know how that made him feel.

But he gave me nothing and kept his attention on Corridan. He'd drawn his features into that blank look he dawned for polite company. "That's ... interesting."

I wanted more than that, but I wasn't going to get it with Corridan in the room, so it was time to bring this conversation to an end.

Now that I knew who wanted me and why Corridan had finally come, I still had one question. "Why does Oberon want me alive?"

His reply was the last one I'd expected. I'd assumed Oberon wanted to kill me or use me in some way. Maybe he thought Titania would surrender in exchange for my baby and me. Maybe he'd heard about the prophecy and wanted the baby himself.

But Corridan said the one thing I wouldn't have seen coming. Not for a million years. "He says he has the answers you seek. He can reverse the soul stone."

CHAPTER FIVE

I woke to the soft knocking of the ceiling fan as it made its rotation at a moderate speed. Ewan had carpenter skills and had offered to fix the fan so it would run silently, but I'd turned him down. I liked the noise. The rhythm was soothing and perfectly timed.

Outside the window was an overcast bright, gray sky that made it impossible to see the position of the sun. I didn't know how long I'd slept, but it felt like mid-afternoon.

I felt rested, but I didn't want to get up. I kept my face planted in my pillow and squeezed the stone in my hand.

I'd fallen asleep with Wei in my palm.

It was his day.

Technically, it was my day, but I'd told myself that it would be Wei's day once I got him back.

Closing my eyes, I saw the eyes that had been a gift of his Chinese ancestry. I saw his rare smile and remembered the press of his lips against mine.

When I pictured him, he was always in the ancient battle stance he'd taken when we had first met.

He'd been so determined. Determined never to like me, to protect me but never love me.

He'd ended up doing all three.

And I would not stop until I got him back.

My decision to go to the fae world and confront Oberon had been an easy one to make, but how we'd go about doing it and securing my safety at the same time would take a great deal of planning.

42

Ewan had continued to question Corridan after I had left and would share his findings with the others once the sun had set. I feared the men would try to make me wait until after the baby was born. I feared the divide that would be created when I told them I wouldn't. I had to get Wei now or as soon as possible. Waiting eight more months wasn't an option. Who knew what life was like inside the stone? Getting pulled inside was a painful experience that I'd only survived because of my mother.

Was he in pain? Was he awake in the stone?

It was possible that he wasn't awake, and that Oberon was lying, but what if he wasn't? Should I do nothing?

There wasn't even a question of whether or not I was going to do nothing. All I needed to know was who would go with me because I wasn't foolish enough to go by myself. That would be suicide.

I tightened my hands around Wei's stone until the edges bit into my skin.

Flipping over onto my back, I brought the stone to my face. The soul stone absorbed light. I'd have been able to see straight through it were it not for the shadowy area in the center. Was that Wei's soul? My mother's stone, which sat in one of my grandmother's old jewelry boxes at the house I'd inherited, looked the same.

"Wei, if you can hear me, I want you to know that I'm coming for you. I may have found a way to do it, but I'm not sure." I didn't try to analyze whether or not Wei could actually hear me. Talking to him made me feel better, so I did it.

My stomach growled, and I remembered I hadn't eaten much last night. I'd wolfed down the soup Peter had given me, but the meal hadn't been filling. I rolled out of bed and placed the stone onto the table before hopping into the shower.

I dressed in a long-sleeve, black shirt and matching ripped jeans. Then I put on my boots, placed Wei in my pocket, and started downstairs.

The first thing that hit me in the hallway was the silence. I looked up and down the hall and saw no one. Where were the dryads and the wolves?

The quiet reminded me of the months before the queen of the Unseelie took me away. This was how the house had been when I'd lived with the vampires. I could hear my every step as I walked toward the landing in the grand foyer.

Even my thoughts were louder.

The air was cooler.

In the kitchen, I found Peter. He was standing at the sink, staring out the window. A tiny pink demifae sat on the windowsill also looking out. Peter's gaze switched from whatever was going on outside to the small creature who had enthralled him.

When Titania had come and taken over the mansion and stolen my men, she'd left behind a wrecked house and a crowd of fae who'd held the residents in the house spellbound.

Neither of them turned around when I entered, so I went about getting my own food, a luxury I missed.

I'd already had the bread, roasted turkey, and bacon out before Peter spoke. "Lorena, I didn't know you were here. Can I get you anything?"

My sandwich assembled, I took a bite. I even tried to speak. My teeth tore through the soft bread and smoked meat. When it hit my tongue, my stomach caved in, begging to take part in the party in my mouth.

I admit, even I thought a sandwich tasted better when someone else made it, but this was heaven. My groaning turned to moans of pleasure and pain. I'd finished half the meal, sounding like the soundtrack to a porno, before a coherent word left my lips. "I've never known you to be capable of dividing your attention when Azalea is in the room. What's going on outside the window?"

Peter was looking like a tomato, and I wondered if it was my words or my moaning that put the color in his cheeks. "It cannot be described. You must look."

I took the last of my sandwich to the window over the sink and looked out.

I gasped, and food was lodged in my throat. Thankfully, it came up when I coughed.

Once the tears cleared from my eyes, I quickly finished the sandwich, cleaned my hands, and rushed out the door in the kitchen that led to the yard.

The gardens were beautiful. The flowers that my child's magic had planted last night had taken over everything. The purples, yellows, and oranges made the yard look like spring. I was warmed by the sight even as the cold seeped into my clothes and gripped my fingers.

"Miss."

I turned around and shrugged into the coat Peter held out for me. "Thanks." I turned back to the unbelievable sight as I buttoned up the coat. Peter put on my gloves, but I was too excited to pay attention or even assist him properly.

Past the gardens was some sort of massive house that had been created out of twisted trees. The dryads had picked all the blue flowers, but what remained was still magical. I could feel the currents of power in the air. The outdoors pulled me in just as it had last night.

What kind of witch was my kid?

I started toward the fountain and met the eyes of the dryads and wolves I passed.

Only the wolves would look at me. The dryads actually dropped to various bows and curtsies.

I stood and looked around. A number of them had paused their activity to point the top of their heads in my direction. It made my skin crawl. "Cut that out."

One of the wolves, a big guy who was all muscles, said, "They are not bowing to you."

My stomach took that moment to flip. "The baby can't even see this happening."

The wolf shrugged a meaty shoulder. "They don't care. They simply want to show their respect."

"That doesn't make sense. The baby doesn't even know what respect is."

It got me another shrug.

One of the dryads popped onto her toes. "Oh, I know. We could sing to the child." Then she threw back her blond head and made some cawing sound. It rattled the atmosphere and crescendoed through the trees. The other dryads joined in. The rhythm was wild and loud.

As the noise grew with the voices, I yelled, "I take it all back!" I cried. "Bowing wasn't so bad."

But they didn't stop.

What had I done?

Then Jenny jumped in front of me. "Boo!"

I screamed, although not in fear but joy. Having her arms around me gave me the same feeling I got when I found old photos of me. It's a gentle reminiscence of easier times.

Jenny had gone to see her girlfriend, Reikah, two weeks ago. Reikah was in her second year of college. The distance was killing them, so Jenny often went to visit. I always missed her when she was gone, but I knew I had no room to complain, not when I had four boyfriends of my own.

Five, I corrected myself. I had *five* boyfriends. One of them was just stuck in a stone, but he still counted.

I pulled back and looked up into Jenny's eyes. Her deep skin tone had the extra glow that always came after she'd seen the love of her life. Her copper eyes glittered. She was dressed in a thick, red jacket with a yellow beanie on her head.

She spoke when the weird song died. "I heard your baby decided not to wait until he was outside the womb before he started performing miracles."

"Yup. The kid's a showoff." I looked down to see if anything had grown from my feet, but not this time. Maybe the baby needed the moon to pull magic from, or maybe I had to remove my shoes for something to happen.

Since I wasn't going to remove my shoes, the answer would have to wait.

Jenny looped her arm through mine as we continued down the center path of the garden, walking around the stone lady in the fountain that someone had cleaned out, even though the water wasn't going. "Lorena, this is a big deal. Witches are never this powerful at birth. Some of them never possess this much power even after living for a hundred years. Your kid is incredible. Amazing!"

I covered my stomach. "Look, would you cut that out? I'm trying to keep the kid humble."

"Sorry." She laughed. Jenny thought the baby would be a boy while Reikah thought the baby would be a girl. Depending on who I spoke to, I would say, "he" with Jenny and "she" with Reikah. The gender didn't really matter to me either way.

"But let's be real. Other babies don't stand a chance. My ovaries are intimidated."

I laughed. "Are you thinking about having a baby?"

"I'm thinking about a lot of things." She got quiet for a moment and then stopped and dug in her pocket. Out came a small box that could only contain one thing.

I fanned myself and fluttered my eyes. "Oh, Jenny. I didn't know you felt this way about me."

Jenny barked a laugh. "You're such an idiot. It's not for you. Look at it. Do you think Reikah will like it?"

I took the box and popped the lid. The ring was plain, and the diamond was cut into a square with perfect lines. "It's perfect and very Reikah."

Reikah had been trained to believe magic should be performed on a grid. Her magic looked like it had been drawn by Picasso, while mine usually looked like it had been drawn with the hand of a toddler.

And then that toddler threw up.

But hey, it worked.

I talked to Reikah a few times a week. We video-chatted so she could keep up with the baby and me. She and Jenny were the godmothers. I had asked them weeks ago, and they said yes.

"I think she'll love it. I'm happy for you."

Jenny tucked away the ring. "Well, she hasn't said yes yet."

"But she will."

"You think so?" Jenny became hesitant. "You don't think it's too soon?"

"Well, it doesn't really matter what I think. Have you discussed it with Reikah?"

She sighed and shrugged. "We've talked about it, but we didn't make any plans."

"Hey, I'm probably not the best person to ask about this. Remember, I was going to marry Ewan, and I didn't even know half the stuff about him that you know about Reikah. Also, I'd only known him for a day or so when he'd popped the question."

"Yeah, but you only agreed because you thought marrying the prince of the Unseelie would keep you safe."

"He's also not that bad to look at."

Her smile seemed to shake off her melancholy. "No. That's true."

"Reikah loves you, and I don't think anything else matters. You can't time love." After all, I'd fallen for my men within weeks of knowing them, and I loved them deeply. Even if I never married any of them, I was committed to them for as long as they were committed to me.

"Thanks, Lorena."

To lighten the mood, I said, "How's Marquessa? She knows I'm not mad at her for kicking me out of the shop, right?"

Jenny chuckled. "You mean dragging you out? Yeah, she knows, but if you think we're going to take down the wards, you're wasting your breath."

What a silly thing to say. Wasting breath was one of my finer traits. "Please?"

"No."

"Just a bottle a month. The guys even check my Amazon orders. I'm dying out here."

"I've never met anyone addicted to processed food as much as you." She giggled. "I missed you."

I placed my head on her shoulder. "I missed you too." Then I leaned back and looked at her. "But I want to get a new doctor. I don't like Dr. Shaw."

Jenny narrowed her eyes. "What did she do now?"

I tried to come up with something really good, but my reasons were flimsy, even to my own ears. "She came unannounced to the house and tried to make me drink a smoothie last night. All but bullied me into it."

Jenny laughed again. "You're so averse to doctors. I'm starting to think this whole sugar obsession has more to do with your not liking Dr. Shaw and less to do with an actual craving."

I thought about her words as she got closer to the trees.

Was the reason I wanted sugar and white bread linked to some need to provoke Dr. Shaw?

I smiled at Jenny. "If you're right, then we should definitely get rid of Dr. Shaw. I couldn't provoke her if she's not around. Then everything would go back to normal. Problem solved."

"I wonder if your baby will be as strong-willed as you."

"I hope so."

Jenny grinned. "Me too."

As we neared the trees, I was starting to wonder about my child's personality when a kiss landed on my cheek.

I turned toward Ewan. He had his foot on the end of a thick vine that curved up into the trees like a rope. He held it in one hand and circled my waist with the other. Before I could say a word, he gave the vine a yank, and my stomach hit my toes as we flew up into the trees.

I gave a shout and wrapped my arms around his shoulders. I buried my face in his chest until we came to a jarring stop.

He carried me from the vine.

I didn't look until he said, "There's a floor underneath your feet." I looked down, and sure enough, the thick oak trees had formed a footpath with their twining branches.

I glanced around and found an entire network with floors and walls with green vines lacing everything together and adding color to the wintery surroundings. The walls also blocked some of the cold.

The beauty of the design was almost enough to make me forget how afraid I was of heights.

Almost.

I snapped at Ewan. "I hate heights. You know that!"

Ewan lifted my chin and, with a slow and deep kiss, turned my fire into desire. When he pulled away, I had to admit I was enchanted and in heat. There were people around us, but I was tempted to drag him into a dark corner and have my way with him.

His smile was arrogant. He was completely aware of just how good he looked.

I'd been telling Jenny the truth when I said I'd agreed to marry Ewan for more than one reason. I hadn't loved him, not then, but I'd wanted to love him, and I'd wanted him to love me.

He grabbed my fingers and locked his around mine. Light shined through his emerald eyes and made them gleam in otherworldliness. "Keep looking at me like that, and I'll bury my tongue between your legs, never mind who sees."

I clenched my thighs together even as I said, "Is that supposed to be a threat?"

He growled and pressed his lips to mine again. The kiss got so hot that his fangs scraped my lip. He licked the blood away, and my toes curled.

A zipping sound behind me made me break the spell.

One of the male dryads carried up Jenny and dropped her off on the same floor as me.

I moved away from Ewan and watched him adjust the object that had grown between his legs before he turned to Jenny just before she saw us. "Hello, Jenny."

"Ewan," Jenny replied in greeting. She glanced around the treehouse and then turned to me. "This is beyond impressive."

I had to agree.

It was beyond impressive.

I was nervous about how I would teach my kid magic. I was still trying to learn the craft myself. I'd had a necromancing teacher for a few weeks, but Marco vanished some time ago, and no one had seen him since.

Marquessa and some of the other witches were looking for him, but for now, I had Jenny, and she was an excellent teacher if I did say so myself. Maybe she could teach my baby. Maybe the kid wouldn't need a teacher at all.

The last thought was comforting.

Ewan showed us around the treehouse that almost stretched the expanse of the mansion. The dryads were moving in and planned to sleep in the tree. Some of them were speaking to the trunks as we passed by.

Ewan had been up hours before me, and I was surprised by the amount of energy he had considering he'd gone to bed after me, but then again, he wasn't growing another being inside him.

At the back of the forest was a view like no other. In the distance were more mountains. To the left and right were the few blocks that made up Colt Valley. There was a field that Ewan had taken the horses out to ride through.

Not far beyond that, I saw a beautiful stone and glass house that looked out of place in the valley. The design was modern. "What's that?"

Jenny was next to me. "New neighbors. I met them at the shop a few weeks ago. Their names are Sirius and Lilac. They seem like good people."

I wasn't surprised Jenny knew the new neighbors. There were only so many people in the valley. "Do you think they noticed the trees?"

Jenny laughed. "Yeah, I think they'd notice that the trees decided they wanted to be a house." The structure was massive. It couldn't be missed.

"Are they kinfolk?" Ewan asked, and I assumed he was asking if they had magic.

Jenny shrugged. "I didn't think to check. They looked regular."

"Well, sooner or later, they're likely to wander over and ask questions. How are we supposed to hide this structure from human eyes?"

"It's going to require magic." Jenny looked around and grimaced. "Probably more magic than you and I possess."

That was comforting.

I decided I didn't want to wait until the guys were awake to ask Ewan questions about last night. "What did Corridan tell you?" The topic couldn't be avoided any longer.

Ewan leaned back on a branch. "Oberon knows where my mother keeps the answer to reversing the soul stone. She told him one night. He's kept the information to himself until it was useful."

"So, your mother can reverse them?"

"Apparently. I'm going to have to go to the fae world. I leave in an hour. Time is of the essence."

I stiffened. "Wait. Run that by me again?"

He gave me a grave look. "I have to find my sister. So much has happened that I've been unaware of. Many have died. While Oberon has taken hold of the Court of Air, the Court of Fire has joined alliances with my mother. Now both kingdoms fight for the Court of Water, but so far, the water fae in combination with the Earth and demifae courts have managed to hold them back." He shook his head. "I can't stay here while my people are dying and while my sister may be in danger."

He made a good case. I couldn't even fight him on his convictions because I believed the same and would do the same under the circumstances. Staring into his eyes, I knew it didn't matter that the fae had mistreated him, rejected him, and wouldn't have cared if he lived or died. Ewan wanted to do the right thing, and the right thing involved saving lives.

"What are you going to do?" I asked.

His expression relaxed. "You're going to let me go?"

"Of course." I grabbed his hand. "But I'll admit, I'm scared. I don't want you to go, but I understand you are needed there." The prince of shadows was capable of things other fae weren't. He'd be unusual in battle, but the thought of losing one of my men to that world …

No, I couldn't think that way. I wouldn't lose Ewan. He'd come back to me.

My heart felt like something was poking it with knives. I didn't want him to go.

He cupped my cheeks and placed his forehead against mine. "Who are you going to give my nights to?"

"I don't know. Maybe I'll take them for myself."

He lifted a brow. "You mean you'll give them to Wei. You spend too much time with that stone."

"That's not true."

"It's in your pocket right now, isn't it?"

I pressed my lips together. "I loved him."

"Don't spend too much time in your head. Promise me you'll have fun." The way he talked, you would think he knew me. Which he did. He did know me. I did spend a glorious amount of time thinking, thinking about how I was going to stop a war in another world and what kind of mother I'd be and how we'd get Wei back.

"I'm used to being alone. I like thinking. Thinking is my happy place." I was lying. Thinking was not my happy place, but I didn't want him to worry.

He stroked my cheek. "I'd rather you get used to being loved."

He kissed me quickly. The sparing press of his soft lips was hardly enough before he pulled them away. Still against my forehead, he said, "When I come back, we finish this."

"Finish what?"

"I want to be complete with you."

My heart flipped. "What does that mean?" But I knew what he meant. I just wasn't sure I was ready to hear it.

He stroked my hips. "Plan to take me inside of you."

"Oh boy," I whispered.

There were only two ways that was going to happen. Either his mother broke the curse, or we were getting married.

CHAPTER SIX

We left the house right after Ewan walked into the portal.

Watching him leave, I felt a part of my spirit go with him. I was broken and numb.

I closed my eyes and leaned against the car door, remembering how he'd looked right before the portal closed.

He'd dressed in the same royal costume he'd come to earth wearing. While he'd been here, he'd worn jeans and a shirt, and it had been easy to forget his royal bloodline. When he'd left, he'd looked every bit the prince that he was, a man destined to become king.

I fiddled with the stone that hung around my neck and hoped today wasn't the last time I saw Ewan.

Jenny—in an attempt to distract me—decided we should drive over and welcome the new neighbors.

We were also on an investigation. I wanted to know if the newcomers were magical or not. Could they see the treehouse from their position in the valley?

Maybe it didn't look any different than it had been before. Maybe they wouldn't notice that the trees had turned into a house with the ease of a transformer. Maybe they were blind.

Maybe I was delusional.

Since I couldn't bake to save my life, we weren't taking a pie to Lilac and Sirius. Instead, Jenny grabbed a few treats from the mini-mart that she thought they'd like based on the things they'd purchased when they'd come. There was mostly trail mix and fruits.

I placed the snacks in a basket I'd found in the house, and Willow had made a bow out of dried twine. I had to admit it looked great.

As we drove, Jenny filled me in on the details of her trip and how much Reikah was enjoying college, even though she tried to hide it from Jenny.

Jenny seemed a little worried about losing her girlfriend, and I understood. The lesbian pickings were nonexistent in Colt Valley, but that didn't matter. She wouldn't have wanted another woman besides Reikah. She loved her.

"You're not proposing so she won't leave you, right?" I asked as we turned into the long gravel driveway that led up to Sirius and Lilac's home. It was a legitimate question considering the fact that Jenny had lost her last and only other girlfriend when the chick had gone away to college.

The car rumbled over the stones. Jenny kept her eyes forward. Her mouth was a line of determination. "Of course not. I love her." She glanced at me. "Do you think she'll think I'm proposing so she won't run off with someone else?"

"I can't pretend to say that I know what's going on in her head, but I hope it works out for you both."

"Me too."

The house came into full view as Jenny turned the car into the circular driveway.

The foundation of the glass fixture was a gorgeous sandstone. The beige had hints of burned orange and deep red. The house had been built with a slanted design. The stones were stacked in one direction while the glass shot out in the other. The windows in the stone had been framed with oak shutters that matched the stunning wooden box that made up the car garage.

"It's a masterpiece," Jenny said. "I wonder if one of them designed it."

So did I. The house was amazing. It seemed like something straight out of a magazine.

Jenny said the couple who lived in the house was young, and by the looks of it, they were obscenely wealthy. I could see through the glass and into a lovely living room with white couches and a large TV over a double-sided fireplace.

Since the fire was going, I assumed someone was home.

"Why would people like this want to live in Colt Valley?" I asked out loud.

"Maybe the view?" Jenny offered. "They could be really private people. I haven't seen them in the store since the first time they came."

"When was that?"

"About two months ago."

I grabbed the basket and got out. The cold swept around me, so I buried my face in my collar. "Two months? So, they'd moved in around the time I came back from the fae world."

Jenny started for the front door. "Pretty much."

She knocked, and I waited and marveled at the wooden door. Everything about the house was meant to wow the senses.

The door opened, and a woman with long, raven hair opened the door. Her eyes reminded me of cinnamon. They were a pale brown with a hint of red. Very pretty and wildly unique. Pretty did not describe her. The word was too soft for the strong features of the woman I was assuming was Lilac.

Her skin had a soft Mediterranean tan. She was thin but hippy, wearing a long, black, sleeveless turtleneck dress that emphasized her femininity.

She looked at my basket and then at Jenny. "I don't remember Sirius ordering anything."

I looked at the basket and could see how the woman could assume we were delivery folk.

Her comment confused Jenny for a moment and then shook her head. "No, we came to say hello and welcome you to the town. This is my friend Lorena. She lives on the other side of the forest."

Lilac's posture changed, and she turned toward me. "Oh, I'm Lilac. Come in." She moved back, and I followed Jenny inside.

Lilac closed the door and then crossed her arms. She stared at me for a moment that bordered too close to impolite before she charged ahead. "Follow me. I'll give you a tour of the place. I'm sure that's one of the reasons you came over, right?" Lilac looked over her shoulder at Jenny and me with a smirk. "You're not the first person to come by to see it."

She motioned a graceful hand to the stainless steel and white kitchen. "You can put the basket with the others." Sure enough, there was a group of baskets on the counter. I counted five as I put ours with the others.

I looked over at Jenny, who looked just as embarrassed as me. The jig was up. We were being nosey, and Lilac knew it.

I turned to the homeowner. "You caught us. We are curious about you. I'm sorry. As you've probably found out, there isn't much to do in this town. You're new. That makes you as fascinating as a trip to France. Your house is gorgeous. Thank you for offering us a tour, but if you'd rather we leave, then that's what we'll do. No hard feelings." I knew what it was like to be gawked at. No one liked to feel like they were being put on a petri dish and studied underneath a microscope.

Lilac blinked, and then her eyes widened. "Wow. That's pretty direct."

I shrugged. "That's me. Ms. Direct."

Jenny stepped forward. "Lorena never beats around the bush."

"That's right. I never beat bushes. No bush brutality from me."

Lilac laughed and shook her head. Her shoulders fell as she uncrossed her arms. "All right. Come on. I'll show you around."

She had a distinctly indistinct American accent like me, so I had to ask, "Where are you from? If you don't mind my asking. If you do mind me asking, then let's pretend I asked about the weather."

Lilac laughed again. "I'm more or less from everywhere. My family moved around a lot."

"Me too."

Her eyes flashed. "Really? Military?"

"Nah. My dad just had to move a lot for his job."

She nodded as if she understood. "My father too. I jumped from base to base, but we're trying to make Colt Valley home."

"We" must have included her boyfriend, Sirius.

"Come on."

We toured the entire first floor, and every room was just as beautiful as the next.

From the first-floor office, I could see the trees by the house of the sons of Vlad.

The great tree was stark against the landscape. The setting sun acted more like a spotlight, telling everyone, "Look here! Look here!" A neon sign wouldn't have made the trees anymore obvious.

There was no way Lilac could miss it. The trees looked as big as a mountain, a rock of trunks being held together by vines.

In a way, it mirrored the Old One from the fae world. Was that how the baby would bring magic back to our world?

Either way, there was no way anyone with eyes could miss it, and Lilac, unfortunately, wasn't blind.

She stood by me and looked out at the tree. "I didn't know the people who lived over there were doing any construction. That treehouse looks so real. I'm surprised I missed it." She laughed. "I didn't even see you clear out the land, but then again, Sirius and I do get rather busy here."

She thought the tree was fake.

This was good. This we could work with.

Should I tell her that I lived across the field? Technically, it was my boyfriend's house, so I left the subject alone.

I glanced around the office. It blended well with the rest of the house. Absolutely nothing about the entire first floor gave me a witchy vibe. There were no crystals or spell books. The couple seemed normal.

Jenny asked, "Did you design the house?"

Lilac's face softened. "I like that you asked me if I designed it as opposed to asking me if Sirius designed it."

I frowned. "What? A woman can't design houses?"

Lilac grunted as we made it back to the kitchen. "That's the assumption everyone else made when they came. Coffee? Water?"

Were we being invited to stay?

I didn't know Lilac well, but I liked her. Though, I liked anyone who wasn't actively trying to kill me. "Water, thanks."

"She's pregnant," Jenny said.

"Congratulations. Have a seat." Something sad passed in Lilac's eyes before she turned to the fridge and pulled out water for Jenny and me. "I didn't design the house. My sister did. She's an architect and a professor at Piuther University." It was pronounced like peu-ward. The term was Scottish Gaelic for sister.

I only knew this because it was the same school Reikah was attending.

Jenny smiled as she took a seat at the counter. "That's where my girlfriend goes."

Lilac smiled and leaned against the counter. "Really? What's her name? I'll make sure my sister looks out for her."

That was really nice.

Jenny was in the middle of telling Lilac everything about Reikah's studies when a man walked into the kitchen.

My heart stopped as my eyes caught sight of the softest bedroom eyes I'd ever seen. The man had blue puppy eyes. They were tilted down at the corners, reminding me of Chris Hemsworth. He had deep-red hair that was kind of longish at the top but cut short on the sides.

He was tall and dressed in black jeans and a gray shirt that cupped his wide shoulders and sculpted chest magnificently. His mouth was surrounded by a tamed beard, and I wondered how it would feel against my skin.

I felt my mouth hanging open and closed it before I swallowed and looked away.

I turned to Lilac and noticed her eyes were on me, and I knew from her cool expression that whatever friendship I'd started to gain with the woman I'd lost with my lecherous glance.

Shame slammed into me. I wanted to apologize, but I didn't want to draw the male's attention.

I glanced over at Jenny and noted that if I'd been undressing him with my eyes, Jenny had already jumped his bones in her mind.

I knew my friend preferred women and loved Reikah, but that didn't mean she couldn't admire the sight of the opposite sex. Even I had my own share of lady crushes, but Jenny was doing a better job at hiding it. She didn't let her gaze settle on him. Instead, she just kept glancing up and down at the counter over and over again.

The male smiled at us. "I see we have guests."

Lilac straightened. "Yes. Sirius, this is Jenny and her friend Lorena. They're our neighbors. Lorena lives by the forest east of here."

Sirius looked directly at me. His eyes were a springtime blue and glittered like tranquil pools. "I remember Jenny. Lorena." He bowed his head. There was a black earring in his left ear.

"Nice to meet you. Thanks for the tour." I hopped down from the bar. "We should get going."

58

"I'll see you to the door." Lilac wanted us out just as much as I wanted to be gone.

"Wait," Sirius called.

I only stopped because it would be impolite to run from our host.

"Lorena is pregnant," Lilac nearly shouted. She fisted her hands at her side.

Sirius looked at her, and I could tell something private was being communicated between them. There was a story behind their locked gazes that made me uncomfortable. I didn't know why my pregnancy would be a big deal to him, but Lilac thought he should know.

I was used to awkward situations mostly because I recreated them, but this was straight-up weird.

I was inching backward when Sirius looked at me again.

Did I say he had puppy eyes? Now when I looked at him, the eyes were bedroom eyes. They didn't possess the magical charm of Ewan's eyes, but the man had a charm of his own. How could I be thinking about this man when I had so many of my own?

"I'm having a party tomorrow night," Sirius said. "You should come."

I frowned. "Thanks, but no thanks."

"Are you sure?" He lifted a brow. "Half the town is coming."

"Only half?" I glanced around the large interior. "I'm sure you can fit more than five people in here."

He chuckled. "There were a few more than five in town. In fact, I found a hundred at the house across the meadow." Was he referring to the werewolves and the fairies? Had he been to the vampire house? Why wasn't I told about this?

I'll admit, I expected Sirius to have an Irish accent, but he shocked me with a strong Boston accent. What was a city guy like him doing in a backward place like this? I wanted his story but not enough to come to the party.

There was a part of me that felt drawn to him, which was wrong, considering he had a girlfriend who was standing right there in the room.

This was not like me. Maybe it was the hormones from the baby.

"You both should come." Sirius glanced at Jenny and then me again. "We could get to know each other."

Was he seriously flirting with me in front of his girlfriend? There was no mistaking the heat in his voice. He was looking at me like he intended to make me his entertainment for the evening.

"Sirius," Lilac called to get his attention. There was a plea in her voice.

I didn't know what was going on, but now I didn't care. Sirius was the worst sort of man to flirt with me in front of his girlfriend, who was clearly in distress. I didn't judge couples who swung, but if emotions were telling me anything, then the only thing Lilac wanted to swing was an ax to my head.

"I don't want to get to know you," I said matter-of-factly.

"Are you sure?" Sirius asked. "Isn't that why you came?"

I turned away. I was walking out, and there was nothing he could say to stop me. "I decided ignorance is bliss."

"You didn't strike me as the blue pill sort."

Wow. I know I said I wouldn't stop for anything, but I stopped like I'd run into a wall. Was that a *Matrix* reference?

I could have laughed to myself. Of course, the first nerd I met in Colt Valley turned out to be a total jerk.

I was proud of myself for not turning around.

I charged from the house and toward the car. There were ground lanterns around the driveway that led the way.

Jenny followed and unlocked the car. "Wow, that was intense."

"He's a jerk." I shivered as I got into my heat. "How could he do that to her? Flirt with me right in front of her like that? That's so disrespectful. At least other cheats hide their lewd behavior."

"I agree. That was bad." Jenny started the engine. "I feel bad for Lilac."

"I hope his dick falls off."

She laughed. "If only wishes were that easy."

"You should have warned me." She knew what I was talking about.

She glanced over. "Sorry. I remembered how handsome he was, but I didn't know you'd be affected. After all, you're surrounded by beauty all the time."

That was true. My men were some of the most beautiful creatures on the planet, but Sirius had been a shocker. The familiarity I sensed in him didn't make any sense.

I looked back at the house.

It stood like a jewel against the black night.

Poor Lilac. I couldn't understand how she put up with someone who clearly wanted more. I didn't know her story, so I couldn't judge, but that didn't stop me from wanting better for her. She'd probably moved Sirius to the mountains, thinking she could finally have him to herself, but location couldn't change character.

"If he was single, do you think the guys would mind you dragging him back home?" Jenny asked.

"Nah. They've been hinting I should replace Wei as if one person could simply fill the shoes of another."

"I'd heard about the party," Jenny said with a lighter tone. "Some of the wolves at your house were talking about it when I came over. Apparently, the fairies plan on going as well."

I shifted to face her in the darkness. "But some of the fae have pointy ears. How in the world do they think this is a good idea?"

Jenny shrugged. "Maybe they'll try to pass the ears off as plastic surgery?"

"And maybe Sirius and Lilac won't call the police when they start groping them and talking to trees."

She giggled. "Oh man, now I definitely can't miss this thing. The guys will have to go. Someone needs to keep the fairies in line."

I threw myself back against the seat just as something shot out in the middle of the road.

The figure stopped when it got caught in the headlights.

"Stop!" I stuck my hands out as Jenny jammed on the break.

The figure ran away, and I got out of the car.

I looked around in the dark but couldn't see anything except for the space in the front of the car where the high beams glowed.

There weren't many streetlights in Colt Valley, and we happened to be on one of the roads without any at all. But I didn't fear the dark. Maybe that was because I'd learned to love and control the very things that haunted it.

Jenny got out and audibly shivered in the cold. "What did you see?"

I shook my head. "I don't know. Scared eyes. I think it was a man."

"A real man or a dead man because I didn't see anything."

"Dead men are real men. They're just … really dead." I walked around the car and stood where the guy had been. I didn't know what I was looking for.

The sound of the car engine was loud, but I tried to listen around it. Maybe someone was scared and needed help.

Jenny joined me and looked at the concrete and then out toward the meadows that spread deep on both sides of the road. "Did you want to look around?"

"Yeah." But not with my eyes. In fact, I lowered my lids and took a breath.

My magic felt just as cold as the wind. My skin prickled. My sense of spiritual awareness went out to hunt the dead.

I felt a tug in the direction from where we'd come and wondered what sort of dead my web of power had caught. Was it a vampire? A ghost? Some other undead thing that I'd yet to meet?

I tried to pull the creature toward me, but something blocked his path. I could feel my command wrap tightly around the form, but I wasn't strong enough to make it submit. It refused me but not by will alone. Something else separated us. There was a wall of magic that was impenetrable.

"Can we do this in the car?" Jenny's teeth chattered.

I smiled. "Yeah, we can go."

I melted under the heat of the car.

"Did you sense anything?" Jenny asked once we were clear of the area.

"Yeah, there was something out there, but it wouldn't come to me."

"Has that ever happened before?"

I nodded, even though I knew she couldn't see me. My thoughts were miles away. I was trying to remember what the man looked like. He hadn't looked translucent like a ghost, but he'd definitely been dulled by death. His skin, hair, and clothes had all been a ghastly white.

"The dead have refused me once. Remember the night I found you locked in that pocket dimension? I found Zane first, and he didn't want to come to me when I called, so I yanked him forward. It was almost like I had a leash on his soul."

"And you couldn't do that tonight."

"Nah. Whatever is at the end of that leash is being protected by magic."

Her hands tightened on the wheel. "So, someone is using magic against you?"

I didn't think the magic was personal, but I wasn't sure.

My fixation on the ghost vanished once I got back to the house. Dr. Shaw's white luxury crossover Lexus was in the driveway. What did the woman want now?

I'd barely taken a step into the foyer before Blair was on Jenny and me. "Please, you have to help me. I can't find my mother."

"Dr. Shaw is missing?"

I'm gonna take this moment to confess that the first emotion that hit me wasn't worry or sadness. The thought of never seeing Dr. Shaw again set off a flutter in my belly. I had to fight down the smile that threatened to break out over my face.

Blair's eyes narrowed slightly before she relaxed and returned her expression to something more professional. "Please, you're the only one who can help me."

"Why me? Why not another witch?"

She looked at my throat. "Your stone is connected to her."

I touched the necklace her mother had given me. "You mean she didn't give this out to other patients?"

"No, only you. I don't even have one."

Another happy flutter went off in my belly that was almost stronger than the first.

Dang it. Why did Blair have to go and tell me I was special?

But I wasn't special. Dr. Shaw was only around for the prophecy baby, and once the baby was gone, I'd never see her again.

Alan and Dimitri poured out of the living room.

"Where's Zane?" I asked.

Alan shrugged. "He said he was going out."

What was he up to?

I tried not to look for Ewan but found myself doing it anyway.

Maybe he'd changed his mind and decided I was more important than his people. Maybe he'd decided to come back because he was worried about me and couldn't keep away. I'd be the first person to admit that I had dependency issues. I was proud of Ewan for what he was doing, but that didn't mean I liked it.

"Does Zane know …?"

"That Ewan is gone?" Alan asked. "Yes, he was informed the moment he woke up. William and Willow were left with instructions."

"They were?" This wasn't my house, so technically I couldn't get angry about being left out of whatever meeting Ewan had with the commander of the wolves and the liaison of the Earth Court, but I had a feeling these "instructions" were about me and not about the house, so I was pissed. "What did he say?"

"He wants us to find Marco," Dimitri said. "You need to continue your necromancer training so that you can protect yourself. Until then, he'd like Jenny to keep practicing with you. He fears Corridan did not come through the portal on his own. There could be others around, and he knows how much you enjoy defending yourself."

The last words sounded like a dig. "I don't *like* defending myself. In fact, I wish I didn't have to, but if people are going to keep coming after me, I need to know how to fight. What's your problem?"

"Nothing." Dimitri turned on his heels and stormed out.

CHAPTER SEVEN

I had to steel myself against following Dimitri. Out of all the guys, he was the biggest and the moodiest. I had a feeling I knew what was bothering him, but I didn't have time to deal with it. There were other priorities.

I relaxed when Peter brought me a smoothie.

"Talk," I said to Blair as I wolfed down the smoothie. I was starving.

A fresh strawberry flavor burst in my mouth.

Blair licked her lips. "I don't know where she is. My mom went to visit a witch with an injured foot and never came back home. That was hours ago."

"Maybe she's with the patient."

"I called, and he said she wasn't."

"Maybe he's lying. Maybe they're together."

Blair narrowed her eyes. "Yeah, I thought so, too, which is why I went by to check. She isn't with the patient. She isn't anywhere."

My eyes widened. I hadn't been serious when I'd made my suggestion. When I thought of Dr. Shaw, I saw her as a sexless being, sort of like my parents. They were the last people I wanted to think about having sex with anyone, including each other.

Dr. Shaw seemed far too elegant to soil herself with such a baseless act as sex. I knew it was silly considering the product of sex was standing right in front of me, glaring. It was an expression I'd never seen on Blair before. I liked it.

Her eyes fell. "Please."

I sighed. "Look, I don't know how to help you. I can't locate anything but the dead. So, unless your mother is …"

Blair's face paled.

"I'm sorry."

At the first sign of tears, the smoothie felt like a lump in my gut, and the taste in my mouth soured. I handed the cup back to Peter. "I'm so sorry."

"You wouldn't have said that if you knew …" Blair closed her mouth.

"Knew what?"

"Forget it." She brushed her tears away and started for the door. "I'll find her on my own."

"Wait." I grabbed her arm. "I'm sorry, okay? I'll help you find your mom."

Blair shook her head and stared at my hand with all the venom in the world. She was being stubborn. "Let me go. I'll do this on my own." I liked the girl's sudden show of backbone.

I tightened my hold. "You came to me. Let me help you."

She jerked out of my hand. "You said you couldn't." She ran a hand through her hair, and it was right then I noticed that Little Miss Princess wasn't as put together as usual. She'd dressed in haste. Her shirt was wrinkled … bless my stars, she was wearing jeans. Her white sneakers were a clean that seemed morally wrong, but otherwise, she was a mess.

Her blond hair fell around her shoulders in heaps of curls.

She looked normal, less *Pretty Woman* and more *Erin Brockovich.*

"How do you expect to help me?" Blair asked.

I sighed. "Jenny is a geomancer." Geomancers pulled their power from rocks, sand, and other natural elements.

She knew a few location spells. She'd tried them on the soul stone to see if she could find Wei inside of it. It hadn't worked, but it might work for Dr. Shaw.

Blair looked at Jenny with hope. "Please. My mother keeps to a schedule. She'd have told me if she was anywhere else."

"Of course, I'll help you." Jenny gave her a soft smile before she looked at me. "I'll need the gem."

I touched the rock around my neck and hesitated. "Will I get it back?" Though the object had more in common with a house arrest anklet than an actual gift, I was protective of it.

It was mine.

Jenny nodded. "After all the work I did with Wei and your mother's soul stones, I know the spells by heart. It shouldn't take but a minute, but depending on how far she is, I'll need power."

"Mrs. Green is here," Blair said in polite reference to Marquessa. "I called her before I came here."

"Good," Jenny said. "But I'll probably need even more help than that."

I took off my necklace and gave it to Jenny. "Be right back." If it was going to be all hands on deck, then I needed to find my men.

I walked over to Alan and said, "I'm surprised you didn't follow him."

Alan shrugged and smiled. "You needed me more. Also, my beast enjoys his space." His beast. His pet name for Dimitri.

I loved how confident Alan was in his relationship with Dimitri. Naturally, he worried whenever Dimitri was upset, but there was the peace in knowing that once Dimitri calmed down, he'd come back around.

Alan spent years longing for Dimitri. Now, he was merrily in love with the broody male.

"I'm happy for you."

"I'm happy for all of us," Alan said. "It seems the old saying is true. The more, the merrier."

I laughed. "Yeah, and I think we've reached our limits."

He lifted a brow. "Don't be too sure. I'm all in favor of more eye candy."

I laughed again. Alan only had eyes for Dimitri and me. He was only saying that because he loved me and wanted me to do whatever pleased me. All the guys had echoed words of a similar message. They knew I missed Wei and didn't mind the idea of my replacing him.

That was a possibility I didn't want to think about.

"I need your help," I told him.

"You never need to ask for it."

I smiled and kissed him.

He wrapped his fingers around the back of my throat and placed the other on my hip. He pulled me in, and I moaned. A ball of need began to grow deep within me. He backed off. "We don't have time for this."

No, we didn't. We had a doctor to find.

Alan and I walked hand in hand to the sitting room. The fireplace was going and illuminated the side of Marquessa's face. The warm, plump woman gave me a strained smile as she kept her ear pressed to a cell phone. Someone on the other line was speaking. Finally, she sighed and said, "Well, you call me when you hear somethin' … Uh-huh … Okay, bye, hun." She hung up.

"Who was that?"

She'd called the other person hun, but hun could be anyone from one of the ladies she played poker with on Saturday nights to the president of the United States.

"That was Sheryl." Sheryl was not the president. Sheryl also didn't play poker. She was the woman who owned the big store in town.

I called it the big store because in comparison, Marquessa's was small, but Sheryl's was only a few feet bigger.

"Sheryl said she tried to call Ralph to speak to Margot, but Ralph didn't pick up, and Margot ain't home."

"What's that mean?" I was confused.

"It means Ralph and Margot aren't picking up." And that seemed to trouble Marquessa. I'd met Ralph and Margot, and Ralph had become local after Marquessa went on the hunt for witches. Only a handful of them had stayed in town after I was taken to the land of the fae. Most of them had assumed I'd died and that the prophecy had died with me, but Ralph, Margot, and Marco had stuck around.

That was what Marquessa had said at least, but I hadn't seen Marco since my return, and so I assumed he'd eventually left as well. Now, I wondered if Marco was missing and if he was maybe with Margot and Ralph as well.

And Dr. Shaw.

"Have you been able to find Marco?" I had to ask.

"No," Marquessa said. "And he's been gone for a while."

Blair fell onto the couch and stared at the fire. "So, my mother really is missing."

This was bad. My chest felt tight.

Alan tightened his hold on my hand, and I thought it was only to comfort me until a shadow moved on my other side. Dimitri. I was stunned to see him.

His brows were furrowed, and his mouth was set into a hard line. "We've lost enough. If there is a way I can keep that from happening again, I will do what I must."

I was glad he was able to see past whatever was bothering him. He took my hand, and I leaned my head against his shoulder as I turned to the room.

Jenny sat by her grandmother and placed my aura crystal and a map of the state on the table. Triangles and circles had drawn on the surface, and I couldn't help but think of how much Reikah would have approved of the meticulousness in the art. Reikah was a stickler for perfect lines and circles.

Jenny grabbed Marquessa's hand and then motioned us closer.

We formed a circle, and I asked, "How does this work?"

Jenny answered, "Dr. Shaw made the spell that's on the crystal, so all we have to do is trace the spell back to its maker."

For a while, there was only the sound of breathing and the cracking of the fire. The sweet fragrance of the burning oak made my eyes heavy. I closed them for a moment. Maybe more.

Someone's breath caught.

I opened my eyes as the crystal rattled on the paper. It pivoted and stopped.

Everyone leaned forward.

"It didn't move," I said.

"It did," Jenny countered. "It just didn't move far. That means she's in the area. Maybe less than five miles away."

"Great, so she's in town." That told us very little.

Blair worried her lip. "Does this mean she's still alive?"

Jenny nodded, and I unlocked my shoulders. I unclenched my jaw. I hadn't even known I was holding my breath until after Blair asked her question.

Jenny picked up the necklace and held it out to me. "It's hot."

She didn't lie. I dropped the hard stone between my palms until it cooled down enough for me to put on.

I studied Blair and watched as she trembled in her seat. No way she should be driving in her condition. "You can come stay at my house if you want."

Blair looked up and then around. Then turned back to me. "You're talking to me?" Her unadulterated surprise disturbed me; I hadn't been that cold to her, had I?

Maybe I had been. "Yeah, you can totally come over. It's the night I usually spend by myself, but you're more than welcome. We can stop by your house to get a bag and then head over to mine." The more I thought about it, the more the idea excited me. It had been a minute since I'd had a girl's night.

Blair hesitated and then lowered her gaze. "No, I'll be fine."

"No, you won't. This is what's going to happen if you stay home. You'll sit at home and stare at the clock for hours. Every minute will feel heavier than the next until you finally break under the weight and go crazy. Come with me. At least then you'll have something else to watch."

"What would I watch?"

"Me kick your butt at video games."

Blair cracked a smile. "I've played *Assassin's Creed* before. Just once. It wasn't so bad."

"Great." I turned to Jenny. "You in?"

She nodded. "But only to make sure you don't stay up all night. We've got training in the morning. If witches are actually disappearing, we need to be prepared."

She wasn't lying.

CHAPTER EIGHT

The Shaw family owned a house on the outskirts of town and in the opposite direction of my place. It was a grand two-story structure that I was sure looked beautiful at sunrise. It was tucked behind a line of trees and offered a great amount of privacy.

We'd taken Blair's mom's SUV since I wanted to eat on the way.

Stepping on the land was like stepping into a dream. My limbs felt light. Peace settled over me, and I knew it was magic.

"What is this disturbing happiness I'm feeling?"

Blair laughed, which was exactly what I wanted. "You would notice. Doesn't it feel great?"

It actually did. I started to think about my problems, the ones that felt like chains around my ankles that were dragging me down at every turn. The problems were still there, but they had no hold on my psyche.

I was free of the worry. I could think clearly.

Blair unlocked the front door. "You're feeling the wards my mom put around the property. She didn't mean for it to affect guests so much as criminals who were intent on robbing the house."

"Does it work?"

"We haven't been robbed yet." She used her body to prop open the door. "But this is Colt Valley, and Colt Valley is nothing like the city." She flicked on the light.

71

The first thing I noticed was the soft colors that flowed between the kitchen and the living room. Beige with splashes of gold with turquoise and other blues gave the space a beachy feel. Even without the wards, I would have been relaxed. "Where did you come from?"

"Richmond." She shut the door. "I'll be right back. Make yourself at home." She walked up the stairs, and I roamed the first level with excitement.

I knew absolutely nothing about Dr. Shaw except that she was an auramancer with a daughter named Blair.

I wandered into the stylish kitchen and ran my fingers against the pale granite countertops as I made my way to the framed photo on the fridge. I recognized Dr. Shaw and Blair. They were standing with a man who was probably Blair's father. The man had his arm around the two women at a fair.

I wondered where she got her blond hair since both of her parents had dark hair. Her father, Mr. Shaw, was tall and had very thin and long features. Blair's were round like her mother.

"Where's your dad?" I asked.

Her voice carried down the stairs. "He's a doctor oversees. He works with an organization that saves lives where poverty is high and people are too poor to seek regular medical care."

"Of course he does." Mr. Shaw was just as perfect as his wife.

"What?"

"Nothing."

I stared into Mrs. Shaw's eyes and felt a nagging at the back of my head. There was something familiar about the woman, but I didn't know what. It was like trying to remember a dream you forgot the moment you woke up.

It's lost forever, yet still, you try.

That was another thing that had always disturbed me about her. The list of things I had against Dr. Shaw seemed to grow longer every day.

"Ready?"

I spun around and grabbed my chest. My heart lodged itself in my throat.

Blair lifted a brow. "Are you okay?"

"You scared me."

"Sorry." She backed away. "Didn't you hear me come down the stairs?" There was a backpack over her shoulder. All her winter gear was in place. "Let's go."

In the crossover, she asked, "Did I really scare you?"

"Blair, I think I lost nine lives."

She laughed. "I think only cats have nine lives."

"Well, this is why."

She giggled. "Lorena, you're hilarious."

I crossed my arms. "Well, it's either laugh or cry, and I hate crying."

The next breath she took was a deep one. "Me too."

Looking her over, I couldn't help but try to figure out what sort of things Blair cried about. From the outside looking in, she seemed perfect. She'd showered before she'd come back down. Her hair was pinned high on her head in an elegant style that was more fitting to the woman I knew. But it dawned on me that I didn't know anything about her.

"It must have been rough switching schools in the middle of the year, and this is your senior year."

Blair shrugged and kept her eyes on the road. "It wasn't too hard."

"Didn't have a lot of friends?"

Blair looked like she'd be popular.

"I had friends." She clearly didn't want to talk about it, so I let it go.

"Is your dad a witch?" I asked.

"Yeah. Yours?"

"Yup. He's a mathmagician."

"Oh. My great grandfather was a mathematician."

"Really?"

She nodded.

I wondered about my great grandfather. I knew very little about my family history. For years, my father pretended like our family didn't exist. I'd only learned about his parents, Loretta and Jake, through the journals my grandmother had left behind, and I was only halfway through those stories.

My grandmother had been given a glimpse of the future and had seen herself exchanging vows with my grandfather, but I'd stopped reading after she'd decided to date someone else because Jake was mistreating her.

But clearly, they'd found their way back to each other because how else could I be explained?

"Is your dad traveling?" she asked.

"Yeah, for work." I was just glad he was no longer dragging me around with him.

As she pulled into my driveway, I couldn't help but compare my house with hers. My grandmother's place looked just as abandoned as when I'd first arrived. It was shabby and was clinging to the side of the mountain for dear life.

Blair shivered audibly and wrapped her arms around herself. "Something's wrong here."

I turned on her. "Don't talk to my house like that. My place might be old, and its wards aren't spellbound with happy aura magic, but ..." My words trailed off as I looked at the ghost in the back seat.

The man from the road was sitting in the car, and now that he was close, I recognized him.

Death had paled him. He stared out the windshield at my house. "I've been here before." He'd been to my house often enough, but he didn't seem to remember it.

"That's not it," Blair said. "I can feel something ... wrong here." She turned to me. "You know what? Maybe I should go home." She stared at me for a moment and then looked into the back seat. "What?"

"There's a dead man in your car."

Blair's mouth dropped, and then she shut it. "Why is he sad?" The fact that his sadness was the first thing she asked about told me this was not Blair's first time dealing with ghosts either. She didn't look frightened anymore. Instead, there was sympathy in her expression.

"I don't know." My voice cracked as tears blurred my vision. "He shouldn't be dead, Blair. Maybe that's why he's sad."

CHAPTER NINE

I reached out and touched Marco's hand.

The moment our connection was made, it solidified. His ghost pulled power from me and seemed to come alert. He was cold but started to warm at my touch.

Blair was staring right at him. "That's amazing. I can't actually see him, but I can see his aura. He's blue, very, very blue. Oh, you poor thing. Who is it?"

"Marco."

"Marco?" Blair hadn't met him, but I saw recognition pull at her features. "He's one of the missing witches, isn't he? Like my mother? Oh my gosh, Lorena. What if my mother is next?"

I didn't want to think about that right now. I didn't want that to be a possibility. If I let myself think it possible, I'd lose my mind.

Marcos' gaze sharpened like a blade as he glanced around. Then he looked down to where my hand held his. Then he looked up. "I'm dead, aren't I?" His creole accent made his words roll around in his mouth like he was making love with them. Even in death, he looked the proper gentleman. His ash hair had been carefully styled.

"I ... think so." I don't know why I felt so emotional over this. I hadn't known him long, but it still hurt to see him like this.

He, however, nodded like I had told him he had nothing more than a ketchup stain on his shirt. He accepted his fate like he knew it was bound to come. I wondered if that was because he was a necromancer. Would I ever become so cynical about death?

He cleared his throat a moment later as if he was embarrassed by his state of lifelessness. "Well, I should probably find out who killed me so my soul can finally rest."

"You think someone killed you?" I asked.

"Someone killed him?" Blair's voice rose in volume an octave.

I was barely holding on myself. I didn't need her anxiety to feed into mine. I tilted my head in her direction. "Hey, why don't you go wait inside?"

"No way!" She turned her body in the seat and crossed her legs. "I want to know what's going on."

"Then, I'm going to need you to find your inner monk and whoosah, because I'm trying to work here."

"You do this often?" she asked. "You help ghosts?"

"Uh, no. Most of the time, ghosts are helping me." Speaking of ghosts, I realized I hadn't seen Maahes. Where was that cat? I hadn't seen him in days. If he was alive, I would keep a closer eye on him since someone would have to feed him, but being dead had given her many advantages.

Maahes had been my grandmother's cat. He was an old tabby, stoic and curious in nature. He was more intelligent than any cat should be. I wondered if he was off helping someone else right now. Maybe he'd found Blackbeard's treasure or decided to take on the Abominable Snowman.

Or maybe he was just chasing ghost mice around.

Anything was possible.

I was no ghost whisperer by any means, but I knew Marco, and I wanted to help him.

"Could you share your memories with me?" I asked Marco. "Maybe I can find out who killed you." I'd spoken to the dead before. The former queen of the werewolves had contacted me to help her save her family. Now her daughter Evelynn led the people. It was the one and only time I'd ever helped anyone get to the afterlife.

But maybe this was my destiny. I'd been wondering about what I would do after the baby was born. I didn't think I'd want to be a stay-at-home mom, but nothing else had struck me either.

Marco brightened, not physically, but a light went off in his head like he had an idea. "I forgot you could read the minds of the dead. Let's begin."

"Bring it on."

He looked at me, and I immediately felt the pressure of his thoughts on my mind. It pushed until I felt like my head was going to explode. But I saw nothing but what was right in front of me, a ghost who was concentrating so hard he looked constipated.

I tried just as hard as he was, but something was blocking my magic. "Yeah, I got nothing." It seemed my ghost whispering days were over just as quickly as they'd begun. Thankfully, I was used to not having a job.

"What's happening?" Blair asked.

I plopped back forward on the seat. Suddenly, I was drained. My head felt like it had been trying to follow one of my dad's mathmagic spells. "I can't get his memories."

"Neither can I," said Marco. "I don't remember what happened to me. Perhaps I was run down by a wagon."

"Even in a backward town like this, I don't think anyone in Colt Valley is using a wagon."

"Wagon?" Blair asked, lost to the conversation. "How old is this ghost?"

"Old." He'd been frozen in crystal for years. "Can't you remember anything?" I asked him.

He shook his head. "And I must admit, I thought death would feel different than this."

"What do you mean?"

He looked at the hand I wasn't holding and then looked where my fingers touched his. "I've been roaming Colt Valley for days. I don't know how many. Numbers evade my mind when I'm not touching you."

"What are you getting at?" I asked.

"I mean, I lost my ability to reason until I touched you." Maybe that explained why he'd been wandering in the middle of the road earlier tonight. Not that he had to obey the law of traffic anyway. As an impalpable being, he wouldn't feel a car anyway, and no one else could see him but me.

"Why were you crossing the road?"

"To get to the other side." He smirked.

I laughed.

"What happened? His aura is changing."

I told Blair the joke. She giggled. She was the only person I knew who actually giggled the way a giggle should sound, light and airy. My giggles sounded like an angry llama.

She colored. "Well, I'm glad he's managed to find some humor in all this."

Me too, but I could hold his hand just to keep his thoughts agile. He was right. The ghost I'd met had kept their intelligence for the most part. Heck, every time I thought about testing back in to school, I wondered if I could get Maahes to help me get the answers.

There was something off, or I had a lot to learn about ghosts. Lucky for me, my grandmother's books of shadows was thick and probably had the information I needed.

Studying wasn't how I'd pictured my night going. I had planned to play video games and build a friendship with Blair, maybe even convince her to get me some Dr. Pepper.

Hey, a girl could dream.

But it looked like I'd be pulling an all-nighter with my grandmother's grimoire. Yay me.

I held Marco's hand as I unlocked the door. When Blair asked me why I was only using one hand, I explained the entire situation to her.

"We could suspend his animation for a while. That way, you can study without having to hold onto him, and he won't lose his mind." There was a small box on the front porch. She picked it up.

"You can do that?"

She nodded as she glided inside. She looked around as she put the box on a table by the door. I read the name on the front. It was from Dad. He'd been sending me little gifts from the places he visited. Sometimes, he even sent spells he thought I'd enjoy.

Blair explained herself as she took off her black gloves, navy-blue coat, and fuchsia scarf with great care. She hung everything on a tree by the door. "It's kind of like a hypnotic coma. His soul is part of the atmosphere now. Since I can change the aura of a place or a person, I'll be able to do it to a ghost as well."

I yanked my things off and tossed them up the tree. "Hypnotized a lot of ghosts in your day?" My question had been meant to tease.

But Blair's cheeks tinted, and she glanced away. "It should work."

I looked at Marco to get his permission. Even though he was dead, I still believed in fair choice.

Marco looked skeptical. "I don't enjoy being frozen in time. I've already been through this once."

I told Blair what he said and then went on to explain how I'd found Marco to begin with. A hag had kept him trapped in a crystal for years.

"Well, this is nothing like that. He'd actually be alive and alert in his mind. He'd be in a dream state. He'll be able to imagine himself anywhere, doing anything, and there's no chance of nightmares. The aura will keep him happy. I'll know how he's feeling based on the shade of the talisman I give him."

She'd definitely done this before. I'd barely turned to Marco again before he cut in with his verdict. He "That sounds lovely. I think I'd rather be alive there than like this." He could barely contain his giddiness.

I didn't blame him. Heck, I wanted to join him. What would it be like to imagine the best scenario possible?

I know what I'd imagine. I'd be with my men. Ewan, Dimitri, Alan, Zane, and Wei. We'd be together on a beach in some hot, tropical place. We'd soak up the moonlight as the waves lapped at our toes, and I'd make love to them, maybe all at the same time.

It backed away from the thoughts before they could grow pornographic.

"What sort of talisman do you need?" I asked Blair.

She moved to one of the shelves in the living room and grabbed a blue gem with golden flakes that was about the size of her palm. It was lapis lazuli. "Wow."

"Yeah, Jenny said the same thing when she saw it."

"It's very valuable. The stone doesn't only hold the power to control heart rhythms but helps with perception and can command energy flow."

Marco murmured, "The ancient Egyptians turned it into powder and dyed their robes to symbolize they were gods." He bowed. "I feel honored to have such a beautiful woman in command of my energy."

I glanced over and noticed the way Marco was watching Blair. I wasn't one to pull out words like "riveted" all willy nilly, but the man was riveted. I couldn't blame him. Blair was very pretty, and even in a pair of jeans, she could give Vivien Leigh a run for her money, though her looks were more Marylin Monroe.

I told Blaire the first part of what Marco said, deviated around the latter bits, and added, "The early members of Islam believed it protected them from the evil eye."

If there was one thing Jenny had taught me during my studies, it was everything about stones.

"This is perfect." Blair looked at Marco or what she could see of him. "Why don't you lie down?" She placed the stone on the couch and then backed away.

I walked Marco over to the couch and held his hand as he laid down. He straightened his tall six-and-a-half-foot frame on the couch that could barely contain his shoulders. Fortunately, the actual structure didn't matter. He was simply floating there with the stone located somewhere close to where his intestines should have been but weren't on account of him being dead.

"What is his full name?" Blair knelt on the ground and moved close. Her knee brushed mine.

Marco spoke in a romantic whisper, his mouth just inches from hers, "Tell her my name is Marco Laurant." He was still giving Blair that dreamy look, and I didn't need a crystal ball to know exactly what Marco would be imagining the moment it was lights out.

He'd be dreaming of Blair and what she looked like underneath her clothes.

He sighed. "I knew she was beautiful in the car, but she's even more striking in the light. She's like a goddess. Tell her she can have her way with me. Tell her she is in complete control."

"He said his name is Marco Laurant."

Blair said to him, "Open yourself to me."

"I am open to you," he purred. "It is you I wish would open for me."

I cringed and shifted around on the ground uncomfortably. I felt like I was caught in the middle of something I should not be present for.

Blair touched the end of the couch. Her fingers rested in his body. "He should be relaxed and at ease. Is he at ease?"

"I think if he got any easier, we'd have a real problem."

Marco smirked. "Tell her I'd be more comfortable if she got on top of me."

"I'm not saying that."

"What did he say?" Blair asked.

"I think I just said I wasn't going to repeat him."

Blair's brows knotted. "Lorena, this is important. I need to know how he's feeling through the entire process. Is he in pain?"

"Tell her I feel the pain in my ..."

I hurled a punch through my power and hit him square in his chest.

He stiffened and winced. Then he smirked. "Sorry. I'll be a gentleman now, but I must admit the other side has its advantages." He didn't just look at Blair. His eyes were glued to her in a way where I thought she should have noticed. I was surprised she couldn't feel it.

Another great thing about his hypnotic state was that he couldn't follow Blair to the room when she got ready for bed. He was acting like a full-blown creep.

"He's looking down your shirt," I said.

Marco's face was a mix of shock and intrigue.

Blair gasped and covered her chest. "Tell him to stop looking down my shirt."

Marco said, "Tell her to take the shirt off. That way I won't have to ..."

"You've got three seconds to apologize, or I'm going to let go of this hand and let you go play in traffic."

The threat straightened him out. He leaned back on the couch and closed his eyes. "I'm sorry."

"Let's get this over with," I said to Blair. "I have a busy night ahead of me and a busy day tomorrow. Hopefully, we can find your mother."

"I hope so," Blair whispered.

She closed her eyes and placed her hands back on the couch. Then she did the last thing I expected her to do. She pulled out a blade from her pocket and cut her palm with an X. X marked the spot, the place she wanted to trap him.

"Who's her mother?" Marco asked.

"Dr. Shaw."

Marco sat up and grabbed my arm. "Stay away from Dr. Shaw."

Fear made my skin crawl. "Why?"

He never got a chance to say.

CHAPTER TEN

When I'd first discovered that I was a witch, a few movies, shows, and comic book versions had come to mind, and I had to ask myself which witch was closest to my idol, Wonder Woman?

The first runner-up was the Scarlet Witch, not the Elizabeth Olsen version who got her powers from Loki's scepter, but the mutant who'd already been doing her witchy thing before she evolved.

She was pretty cool, so I accepted her and went around and assigned other celebrity witches to my friends.

I dubbed Jenny after Wiccan, only because Wiccan was one of the most powerful witches in Marvel history and a jack of all trades. She was capable of anything. I thought Jenny was capable of anything, so it fit. My mother, Connie, and Reikah had been the girls from *The Craft*. But then Reikah morphed into Agatha Harkness. In the beginning, she'd been a mystery and seemed to have her own hidden agenda.

Marco had been my Dr. Strange, Sorcerer Supreme. My hero.

Marquessa was Fairy Godmother. I know the fairy kind was one-off, but she has a wand, so I'll take it.

Dr. Shaw was both the Good Witch and the Wicked Witch from the *Wizard of Oz*, and my feelings for her were as tangled and convoluted as my feelings for both those characters.

The list went on and on from there. I'd had my pick of Buffy and even sweeties like Kiki, who liked to make deliveries when the witches had come to live with us last year, but what I'd never found was anyone to compare to any of the witches from my favorite film, *Hocus Pocus*.

Until now.

Blair's spell came out in a song that caused the same shiver to run down my spine as when Sarah Jessica Parker sang to the children of Salem. Blair's voice was just as sweet as her apparent nature. The tune was slow and reminded me of music that spinning ballerinas in boxes would dance to. I could feel the ancient power in my bones and at the back of my skull.

I watched Marco blink and then fall back in slow motion to the couch.

Blair's voice never grew, but the power did until it saturated the room.

I didn't know if I should stop her. I wanted to, but the magic was already thick, and I feared the consequences of disrupting it. What if Marco was lost to me forever because of something I did?

But he'd told me to stay away from Dr. Shaw. Did he want me to stay away from Blair as well? Did it mean Blair was a bad person?

What had I done? Who had I let into my house?

Watching Marco's body become opaque shut down my thoughts. He shifted until he was more comfortable on the couch. The cushions dipped underneath him and whined. Fingers that were usually coarse became as smooth as ceramic.

He firmed up into a pale-blue glass statue of himself. I let go of his hand so I wouldn't get stuck. His mouth froze in a pleasant expression.

Blair's song ended, and a second later, she huffed a breath and studied her creation. I knew she could see Marco because her eyes widened. "He isn't terrible looking."

No, he wasn't. It was unfortunate that he was dead.

"What did you just do? Why is he solid?" And was she going to eat his soul in order to stay young and beautiful? Hey, someone had to ask the tough questions around here.

"All sentient beings carry an aura. I just made his aura stiffen to form the shape of him." She touched his cheek, but the gesture didn't seem romantic, just curious. "He's beautiful. What sort of monster would kill him?" She didn't look to me for the answer, which was good because I didn't have one.

What if her mother was the killer? Did Blair know? I wanted to think the best of her, but my track record for choosing the right people to trust was lousy.

"How do I wake him up?" I asked.

"Just remove the stone from underneath him, but once you do it, I can't use the spell on him again."

"Why not?"

"Music spells have the same effect as playing your favorite song a hundred times. It starts out great, but eventually, you wear it out and it loses its potency. It won't have the same power without an extended break between plays." She stood and stretched. "Music spells, especially the ones that hypnotize, require a break. Or rather, the listener needs a break."

"I get it. I skip some of my favorite theme songs when I binge-watch. It's great during the first few episodes, but after a while, I want to bang my head against a wall."

She smiled in a way one of my old friends used to look at me. The expression said I was cute but also a nut. "I don't usually stay up late. Where should I sleep?"

I looked at the couch where Marco was stretched out and then back at her. "You can have my bed."

"What?" She jumped back. "No way. You're pregnant."

"Yeah, well, it isn't like I'm going to be getting a whole lot of sleep tonight anyway. I have the grimoire to dig into." And how was I supposed to sleep after Marco's warning? The answer was simple.

I couldn't.

What if I was next? Someone had killed Marco. There was ample chance that someone was taking witches in Colt Valley and that I had let the killer's daughter into my home.

I should have known something was off about Dr. Shaw's whole Mary Poppin vibe. I was going to take the gemstone around my neck off the moment Blair went to bed.

She had put up a good fight for a while and listed all the reasons I shouldn't be staying up, but eventually, we agreed to share the bed.

I showered after her. After she went to bed, I changed into my favorite Wonder Woman pajamas, tossed my hair into a messy bun, and grabbed my grandmother's book of shadows off one of the many bookshelves in the room before settling down in one of the overstuffed chairs in the corner.

For some reason, I felt more comfortable being in the room with Marco than I would anywhere else.

If Blair turned out to be the Hyde to her mother's Jekyll, I wanted to be with someone when the showdown took place. I know Marco was dead and even asleep, but it was like sneaking into your parents' room after a bad dream. I didn't really want to disturb him. I just needed to be close to someone.

Thinking of my current state of loneliness made me think of Ewan.

I wondered if he was okay. I wondered if I'd know if he wasn't. Shouldn't couples be able to sense if each other is in danger? Though we'd only been close for the last few months, those months had been intense.

I wondered who he could trust on the other side of the portal. His mother wouldn't kill him. She loved him in her own twisted way. She'd do anything for him.

But I also knew that Queen Titania liked to make decisions for him. Corridan said she had aligned herself with the Court of Fires. Would the queen make Ewan marry the daughter? What had she promised in order to negotiate such an alliance?

As soon as I found Dr. Shaw and the other missing witches, I was going after Ewan and Wei.

Having a set goal relaxed me enough to start reading.

I'd known where the pages on spirits were located since I'd done a little digging after Maahes opened a door for me a few years ago. He was a poltergeist, or a sprite, which was different than your everyday run of the mill spirit because Maahes could touch things and affect things past the atmosphere.

Sprites usually died with some sort of power already. Since I had a horse that could fly without wings, I wasn't surprised that animals could be enchanted, but I did wonder what Maahes had been capable of during his living days.

Most ghosts weren't sprites, so they couldn't interact with the world. Like Blair had described it, they were part of the atmosphere and could influence mood or temperature. They were sentient spirits who had died when their emotions were high.

This sort of ghost was usually referred to as a phantom. They disturbed the mind by imbuing their feelings into the air until they were impossible to ignore.

As a necromancer, I was able to deal with this pretty well, but for people who were unaware of the various planes of existence, a phantom could influence their emotions to the point of severe rage or depression. Not knowing what was causing the new, unfounded heightened emotions would lead to delusions and send them to the nuthouse.

Both sprites and phantoms could be controlled by necromancers because death was dark, and darkness was the necromancer's business, so why hadn't my powers worked with Marco if he was dead?

I flipped through the pages to read about the other members of the dead I was able to control.

There were only vampires and zombies left.

Vampires and zombies would be the same thing if not for the soul. Vampires were created in two ways. Either you were born a vampire, like Ewan, or you died a horrifying death and managed to have vampire venom inside you when it happened.

The venom trapped the soul inside the body so that when the vampire rose, he walked with any conscious and intellect he'd died with. Zombies were the opposite.

Without something anchoring the soul to the body, a zombie worked without one and thus lost all ability to reason for himself. The necromancer became the zombie's soul.

I had never risen the dead and couldn't say it was high on my bucket list anyway.

Marco had shown me what it looked like just so I'd be prepared for the sight. I couldn't help but think about all the hard work that went into funerals and the well wishes for the dead to rest in peace.

By disturbing them, they were no longer resting or in peace. Instead, they were puppets controlled by the necromancer to eat whatever their master willed and do their master's bidding.

The last was one Marco had told me about but had never shown me. A shell. They were like zombies, soulless puppets, but they could not be controlled by a necromancer so long as their maker was alive.

Shells were made from children who'd had their souls ripped from them at infancy. My grandmother's book didn't tell me anything else about them except that they were rare because only a few people knew the spell it took to make it happen.

I did some more reading on necromancers to see if there was anything that could block the connection I had with the dead. From what I read, the answer didn't exist. Either my grandmother hadn't been told the answer to the question, or it just wasn't a thing.

I probably should have asked Marco where he kept his grimoire before I let him go to sleep. I needed to solve this puzzle, and it was highly probable that the necromancer across the room held all the pieces.

Maybe my powers didn't work because Marco had been a necromancer, and necromancy canceled either other out.

There weren't many necromancers, so maybe that's why the book hadn't mentioned it.

The reasoning sounded plausible, at least to me.

Why had he told me to stay away from Dr. Shaw?

All the thinking made me hungry. I was barely a month into the pregnancy, and already, my appetite was voracious. It was getting so bad that I was *this* close to packing up my stuff and moving into the top shelf of my refrigerator.

Grocery shopping had never been my thing in the past, but as I stepped into my kitchen, I wondered if I'd left anything at the store for anyone else. Between the fridge and the cabinets, I'd probably cleaned out aisle five and six.

Snacks and packaged meals filled the shelves. I'd even gotten into hummus, which is what I decided to grab from the fridge.

I was grabbing the pita chips when something touched me. Not physically, but there was a knock on the doors of my power. The energy grazed mine, and before it could get away, I grabbed it. My power wrapped around it like fingers and pulled.

My first thought was that Blair had woken Marco up and had somehow hypnotized him into killing me. After that, I thought it might be Blair looking for a way to kill me.

But since I had no power for the living and Blair could only mess with auras, I was hooked onto someone dead. I hoped it wasn't Dr. Shaw. Even knowing she was dangerous had me crossing my fingers.

The spirit moved closer. I felt when it stopped on the other side of my front door. A robust knock sounded on the door.

I grabbed the cool knob, took a breath, and released it at the same time I opened it.

I threw up a wall of magic to protect myself but dropped it at the sight of Zane.

"Zane, what are you doing here?"

His body filled the doorway. Being close to him afforded me a better look at his sinewy arms and chest that he hid underneath his woolen sweater. Freedom looked good on him. He'd laden his body with muscle.

His skin was the warm shade of a freshly fed vampire. I knew the vampires were feeding on the house guests. Since my blood was off-limits, I hadn't had much choice but to allow the vampires to feed elsewhere.

The fae had volunteered, which was apparently a big deal as fae blood had power in itself.

There wasn't a long history of the fae and vampires interacting with one another. According to what I'd read in the library, this was probably the first time a group of so many had lived together much less depended on the other for substance. The men were high-rolling the bills for the groceries and letting the fae try every cuisine and strange fruit that existed in our world.

In exchange, the fae were letting the vampires take into a vein.

The trade had bothered me at first. Vampire bites were intoxicating, not just for the giver but for the taker as well. Vampires were known to go mad. But the fae had learned to turn their need toward each other, and my guys had gotten into the habit of only eating on the nights they were sleeping with me.

So, it worked.

That being said, it wasn't Zane's night to sleep with me, but his need bathed the air around us. He cupped my chin. The touch was electric, sending a zap through my blood. I lost my breath.

He leaned in. "I'm protecting you. Alan told me you were spending the night here."

"Of course." The men were very protective of me, even before the pregnancy that rotated watch duty.

Alan must have told him everything that was going on with the missing witches.

"Where were you tonight? Where have you been disappearing to?" I searched his mind for the answers, slipped my power inside of him to get a glimpse of where he'd been going these last few days. As I let my power drift through him, I was met with the same blank walls that Marco gave me.

An ominous thought pounded through my mind, traveling at the same speed as my heart. "Why can't I read your mind?"

Zane stroked my lower lip with his finger. The onyx ring around his finger caught the light of the foyer and gleamed. His copper gaze trailed his action. "Perhaps, you don't need to know everything about me."

Before I could respond, his mouth covered mine. His tongue swept into my mouth with the heat of a poker meeting flame, striking me right between my legs.

We backed into the house. He kicked the door shut with his foot and then picked me up.

My legs went around him, even as I fought to clear my mind.

But he was stiff between my thighs and already rubbing us together. My body craved what he was offering. I would get answers later. "My room and living room are inhabited."

He turned sharply to the kitchen, put me on the dining table, and took off my shorts.

I sat on the edge.

He dropped to his knees, and then his mouth was on me.

I pulled in a breath and held the scream that wanted to leave my lips. The stroke of his tongue over my clitoris had me mewling and panting and grinding against him for more.

He replaced his tongue with his fingers, worrying my wet flesh roughly. "I love how much you love my tongue on you. How much you need me."

"Yes," I hissed. "I need more."

He slipped his fingers inside and lowered his mouth back down. I threw my head back and reached for his head as pleasure drowned me. Then everything was gone. His touch. His heat.

I looked up, and he was standing. His pants were around his knees. His shaft was out. The thickness made my limbs quiver.

Then he scooped me up, shuffled to a wall, and slammed into me, planting himself deep.

I cried out, and he growled but didn't move. I could feel every inch of him inside me. I gripped his shoulders and squeezed myself around his length. "Zane, please." Sometimes, I wondered if he liked to hear me beg.

Maybe he did, but I also knew he loved being inside me enough to make it painfully slow. His need for me went deeper than the physical. His soul sought me as much as his body did. He explored underneath my shirt. His fingers traced around my stomach, and I felt him pause there. Then he moved up and massaged my breast. I hadn't realized how sore they were until his hands were on them.

"I need to see you," he whispered as he took off his sweater, using the wall to keep me upright. "I need to see all of you."

He didn't have to ask me twice. There wasn't a single self-conscious bone in my body, not where this was concerned. I was comfortable in my nudity, especially with Zane. I flung the shirt off my body, and his gaze worshipped me as it always did. My body was impaled by his. The sight of my pale skin next to his deep, rich tone was beautiful. My fingers marveled at how chiseled he was.

"Beautiful," he whispered. Then his hands were on my thighs again, and he was moving. He was shooting forward with a hunger that heightened the desire in my blood. Zane pounded into me, and I couldn't hold back my whimpers.

We were probably going to wake Blair. But that was the last thing on my mind.

Zane was great at helping me forget everything but him. Dr. Shaw and others faded until all that remained was him and the feel of his strokes against the walls of my core. There was never enough room for disappointment and fear when Zane was inside me.

He held my eyes as he surged inside me. His strong hands dug into my butt and kept me splayed for his assault. His warm breath mingled with mine.

I arched my back, and he gave me what I wanted without me having to ask.

He kissed me. My tongue met his fangs. I pricked myself, and the power that surged through me was enough to make my muscles lock as I came.

I clung to him through the aftermath. When my heart slowed, he set me down on my feet. Then he fixed his pants, put his sweater on me, and picked me up. He carried me to the living room and sat down with me on his lap.

I rested my head on his chest. I was used to the lack of a heartbeat. The silence had stopped disturbing me long ago. He wrapped his arms around me, and I wished he could hold me through the night, but I knew he'd leave for his own room. Falling asleep anywhere the sun could enter was dangerous.

"How many hours until sunrise?" I asked.

He rubbed my back and my thigh. "We have some time. Winter nights are long."

I looked up. "Why can't I see your thoughts?"

"Do you need to?"

Did I need to? I sat up. "That's not the point. Usually, I can, but not today. Why is that?" Was I losing my power? Was the baby weakening me as I got strong? My next statement was one I never saw myself saying. "I need to speak with Dr. Shaw."

"I'm sure you're fine," Zane said. "Perhaps, you're just stressed."

"That can't be it. I'm great under pressure. I fight best when stressed. Something is wrong with me."

"Nothing is wrong with you. You're perfect."

Was he just saying that because I was his girlfriend, or did Zane know something I didn't? At the beginning of our relationship, Zane had kept secrets. He'd dated my sister, and he'd believed he was in love with her until the love spell he'd been under was broken. After all of that, I'd had to learn to trust him again, but could I?

"Zane, what's going on?"

Zane's body took on the motionlessness people associated with the dead. It was the stillness that came without blinking or breath. "Do you trust me, Lorena?"

Why was he asking me that? Why had he said my name like that?

Slowly, I crawled out of his lap and stood.

He didn't stop me. His hands moved to his knees. His expression remained stoic. It disturbed me.

"What's going on? Tell me right now." Power burned in my chest, but I hesitated to release it. What if I failed?

He got to his feet very, very slowly, like he didn't want to frighten me away. "I'd never hurt you."

"I don't know that."

As if possible, his body went stiffer than ever before, and even without using my powers, I knew my words hurt him. But I refused to take them back. I couldn't trust people who kept secrets from me. "Are you seeing someone else?"

The question had clawed at the back of my mind for weeks now. Maybe he was doing a whole lot more than feeding on one of the fae. Zane was very handsome even more so now that his body had filled out. Maybe being part of a team wasn't working for him anymore.

We stared at each other. The silence grew more disturbing by the second. Anger and pain laced itself thought my heart. "So, it's not a *no* then."

He took a deep breath, which was unnecessary, considering he didn't actually need to breathe. "I can't even believe you'd ask me that." He lowered his brows. "After everything we've been through, after everything I survived so that I could get back to you, I can't believe you'd ask me that."

Guilt pricked my chest, but I put it aside. "Well, we've been through a lot, Zane. I want an answer. Tell me the truth." I sent my power out. It had built until it could no longer be contained.

I searched Zane's mind for information, just a little. I saw his emotions. Was his anger genuine, or was he hiding shame?

I got nothing.

"Lorena." He reached for me.

I pushed him back, and he flew across the room and hit the wall. His mouth twisted in rage.

So, my power wasn't completely broken; it was just my necromancer specialties that were acting wonky. "If you can't give me a straight answer, then you can leave." I tossed off his sweater and threw it at him.

Zane straightened off the wall. "I've been faithful to you."

"Then where have you been going?"

"I can't tell you, and I've taken measures so you don't find out."

"So, you're purposefully hiding your thoughts."

He shrugged and swept his sweater up off the floor. "If I were a human male, you wouldn't be able to read my thoughts. Do you trust men so little that you must monitor everything that pops into their heads?"

"No, but you're keeping secrets about me. What have you done to me?"

"Nothing." He pulled on his sweater. "I'll watch the house from outside."

"No, you're not. You're going to stay and answer my questions." My power hooked him in place.

He turned around and glared me down. "I can't tell you any more than I already have."

"Then I guess we'll be staying like this for the rest of the night." I crossed my arms. I meant every word.

I'd let him go an hour before dawn, but he'd be chained by the time we woke up.

He cleared his expression. "I have done nothing to tamper with your magic."

"Then what is happening to me?"

"As I said, there is nothing wrong with you. You are as perfect as the day we met, Lorena."

I tried to ignore what he was trying to imply. He still loved me even though we were currently fighting.

"I can't let you go until you tell me what I want to know."

He looked at the door. "No matter what happens, I want you to know that you can trust me." He didn't break from my hold. Instead, he walked away from my power like it was nothing more than an annoying spider web.

He hadn't stopped because I was holding him. He stopped because he'd wanted to.

"Zane, stop!"

He did the opposite. His body moved in smooth motions. He opened the door and walked out.

He never looked back.

CHAPTER ELEVEN

I wasn't ready to get up when my mind became alert. Slowly, I opened my eyes and found Blair sitting in the corner of the room with my grandmother's grimoire in hand. She wore a long, blue dress with black heeled boots. Her blond hair was pulled back into a style I still thought was too mature for her, and her posture held a refinement that only came from lessons and lots and lots of practice.

She looked up and smiled. "Good evening." I glanced at the clock. It was three. Blair must have just gotten out of school.

I moved my limbs around before I started to sit up straight in the bed. "Hey. Did you just get out of class?"

"Yeah. It was the last day of school. I'm officially on winter break."

"Cool."

"I saw this book open by the chair in the living room. I hope you don't mind if I read it."

I shrugged. "Have at it." I'd rather wake up with her reading than trying to kill me.

And she could have if she wanted it. I hadn't planned on sleeping as hard as I had, but something about the fight with Zane had drained me.

I couldn't believe he wouldn't tell me what was going on or that he was involved in it. He said he'd taken measures to keep this secret from me. What measures? Why couldn't I control ghosts or make Zane obey me anymore?

Blair settled back into the grimoire. "I made you breakfast." She gave a dainty nod to the nightstand.

I looked and saw a pink smoothie and croissant sandwich. "Yum. Thanks."

As I ate, I watched her and decided that no matter what Marco had said, I refused to think Dr. Shaw was actually Dr. Evil. There was no way the woman would hurt me. I couldn't let myself believe that, and I wouldn't stop looking for her either.

Call me a glutton for punishment and disappointment, but I believed Dr. Shaw actually had my best interest at heart. With everything else going on, I needed to believe that. I needed to believe in someone.

So, once I had finished eating, I said, "Let's go find your mother."

Blair brightened. "Really?"

I nodded and got out of bed. "Let me shower, and we'll go to the library and ask for a map of Colt Valley. Then we'll take it to Jenny and see if we can narrow down your mother's location." I had never been to Colt Valley Library. The library at the mansion had every book I could possibly want or need, but it didn't have a map of the town.

"Thank you, Lorena. Thank you for everything."

I saw the worry in her blue eyes and wondered if she'd slept at all. I wouldn't know. I'd been knocked out and drooling.

"Is Marco still in his trance?" I asked.

She nodded. "I checked on him this morning. He's still on the couch."

"How long should your power hold him?"

She shrugged. "I've never held a ghost longer than a few days."

That answered my question. This hadn't been Blair's first time doing what she'd done to Marco. "How many ghosts have you met?"

She played with her earring. "A few."

I wondered why the question made her uncomfortable but decided to leave it alone. I did have another question, though. "You plan to study medicine, right?"

She dropped her hand and straightened her back. "Yes. I'll be joining a pre-med program come fall."

"Have you ever thought about going into music?" I stretched. "You're really good."

Again, she got nervous, but this time she rubbed the cover of the book. "I thought about it. Maybe it's something I could do after I get my Ph.D."

"That's a long time from now." I found myself asking, "Do you even want to be a doctor?"

She shook her head. "No, but it's what my mother expects."

"And your father?"

"He doesn't care."

"So, why not study what you want? Why are you letting your mother choose?"

She looked away. "It's no big deal. I can always pursue my dreams later."

"Why later? Why wait? Would your mom really be that upset?"

"I just don't want to upset her."

"I understand your feelings. I've been in the same position before. I spent years doing everything I could to not upset my father, but it was only after I finally did something for myself that I felt free. And now, my dad and I are finally building a real relationship with one another. It isn't perfect, but it would never have gotten this far if I hadn't taken the time to figure myself out."

Blair turned away. "It's not the same thing. She's ... different, Lorena. She's different from your dad."

Different like she'd killed Blair if she disobeyed? And maybe she killed Marco? I really needed to wake up Marco, but I couldn't if I didn't want to hold his hand for the rest of the day. I didn't want his soul to wander away, and until my powers were back up, I couldn't hold him.

So, Marco would be staying behind and was now another man in my life who was holding a secret.

I showered and scrubbed, but no matter how much I attacked my body, I couldn't get rid of the memory of Zane's touch. I cried underneath the falling water. I don't know how long I stood there, drowning in my feelings, but eventually, the water ran cold and forced me out. I got dressed and followed Blair from the house.

I knew the Colt Valley Library wouldn't be big. I'd been prepared for it to be the size of a house. What I hadn't been prepared for was the library actually being inside someone's house.

The pretty yellow home with its picket fence looked like it had come straight out of a 90s movie. I easily imagined a family of five with a golden retriever living here. The youngest son would be a problem child, mischievous in nature. The older daughter was a drama queen. The father was a workaholic who still never missed a little league game and the mother head of the PTA.

It was the home dreams were made of.

It was owned by Lady Annie. That was how she introduced herself, and since I wasn't sure if her first name was Lady-Annie or if she was a titled woman, I decided to be on the safe side and curtsey. She accepted the gesture like someone who was used to it and ushered us inside.

We walked past a lovely front room with Queen Anne chairs and a coffee table that held needlework and a few doilies, through a hallway that had portraits of a family that looked exactly as I'd picture it, only instead of a younger son there were two daughters, and then through a door to the back of the house.

The house was bigger on the inside than it had looked on the outside. The room was yellow and white, with a ceiling fan that circulated air. There were rows of books, more books than I thought there would be, and a few plaques about photos on the wall.

"This is actually my private library. My husband and I built the public one the town had, but when the place fell into disarray, the town had a vote, and everything was moved here. I keep it open to the public for the same reason I donated to the old place.

"Reading is a power I think everyone should possess." Reading was one of my favorite hobbies. For years, books had been my closest friends and got me through the long bouts of loneliness when my father moved us around.

"And there's more downstairs through that door. Just bring up what you need, and I'll set you up with a library card and check you out." Lady Annie left Blair and me alone after that announcement.

The shelves were labeled. The first floor was all fiction and even had a children's corner with colorful chairs and stuffed animals.

Seeing that made me like Lady Annie all the more, and I knew I'd be bringing my baby back here once he or she was born.

We went downstairs, and I saw the map on the adjacent wall. Hopefully, there was a book with that image as well.

We walked down metal rows until we got to the map. The very last row was all about Colt Valley. There were periodicals and news clippings dating back almost fifty years. A wedding registry caught my eye, and I grabbed Q before I could even think about it.

I searched for Quinn and saw my very first image of my grandfather as a young man. He was in a suit at a wedding with his bride on his arm.

My dad looked like him. They both had dark hair and green eyes.

Jake Quinn was definitely my grandfather, but what threw me off was the picture of the blonde on his arm. The woman was not my grandmother. I looked like my grandmother. This woman looked nothing like me.

I looked for the name.

Missy Morton.

I recognized the name. She was the woman my grandfather had started seeing before he finally dated and fell in love with my grandmother. I hadn't finished reading my grandmother's journals, but this made me want to go back immediately.

What happened?

I flipped the page and saw a wedding photo of my grandfather again, but this time Grandmother Loretta was on his arm. Marquessa stood at her side as a bridesmaid. Both women were beautiful.

I checked the dates between the weddings. Jake had only been with Missy for three years before he married my grandmother.

That was odd.

Back then, divorce was taboo, and I was sure it was even more taboo in a small town like this.

Maybe Missy had died.

I found myself looking for the obituaries when Blair said, "I found it!"

I walked over to the book in Blair's hand and looked down.

Colt Valley looked larger on paper. The map was drawn in black and white and included the meadows, forest, and pastures that had only distributed by nature.

It was thirty years old, but it would work.

We took the book upstairs, and I signed myself up for a library card. While Lady Annie checked me out, I asked, "Did you know Missy Morton?"

She smiled at me. If Dr. Shaw was Julia Andrews from *Mary Poppins,* then Lady Annie was Julia Andrews in *Princess Diaries.* She had a regal disposition and kind gray eyes that matched the short, ash curls in her hair. "I recognized your last name, but I didn't want to jump to conclusions. You look like Loretta. I knew Missy. She was my friend."

I didn't know if it was appropriate to ask any more from this woman. I wasn't sure I would like what she had to say, so I let it go. I know my grandmother didn't like Missy, so if this woman had been Missy's friend, then she probably hadn't been Loretta's friend.

But she surprised me when she said, "Loretta was such a kind woman. I'll never forget what she did for Missy."

"What did she do?"

"She helped pay for the wedding. Missy had the time of her life."

"She did?" Now, this was starting to sound crazy. There was no way my grandmother gave another woman the means to pay for a wedding to the man she loved. "Are you sure Loretta paid for it?"

"Oh yes. She went with Missy and me to pick out the dress. I saw her pay for it. She worked long hours at the diner to make it happen. Missy had the wedding of her dreams, thanks to Loretta."

The woman clearly had my grandmother mixed up with another Loretta, but she recognized my name and said I looked like her. In a small town like this, it would be hard to get people confused.

I thanked Lady Annie and walked back out into the stuttering cold.

Blair's car blasted heat within seconds. "Now, where to? The mansion or back to your house?"

"My house." I needed to get my hands on my grandmother's journal. "I'll call Jenny and make sure she meets us there."

My grandmother had been gifted with the ability to see the future. She'd known she would marry Jake, so maybe that's why she'd let Jake marry someone else, but it still didn't make sense. She'd been so upset when he'd asked Missy out, so why help the woman at all? Why had my grandmother taken Missy dress shopping and worked so hard to make sure Missy got whatever she wanted?

Was it blackmail? Did Missy know something? Maybe my grandmother hadn't loved Jake at the time, but I doubted it.

Blair was quiet during the drive, and I noticed she hadn't said anything to me since we'd left the basement at the library. Her pinched brows reminded me of the reason we'd gone to the library at all. This was about finding her mother and other witches.

"Sorry if I got distracted back there."

"It's … okay."

"We'll find your mom."

"I know." But she was still worried. "Why do you think your grandmother wouldn't pay for that other woman's dress?"

"Because my grandmother hated her. Jake was supposed to be with my mother. She saw it in a vision."

Blair's eyes rounded. "Your grandmother was a seer?"

"Yup."

"Well, I hear visions don't always work out the way seers think they should."

"Yeah, I guess that's what happened." I didn't know what to think about that.

Jenny and Marquessa got there the same time we did. I barely said hello before I asked Marquessa, "Did my grandmother pay for Missy's wedding?"

"Who told you that?" Marquessa had grocery bags in her hands, and my stomach did a happy dance. She was planning to cook something, and it was going to be good.

"Lady Annie." I quickly opened my door and helped her inside.

We went to the kitchen, and Marquessa set everything onto the table. Jenny carried in the rest.

My grandmother's oldest friend kept her back to me as she spoke. "She did."

"Why? Did Missy blackmail her?"

Blair slipped into a chair at the kitchen table Zane and I had used just last night. I couldn't look at it without imagining his head between my legs and those lips bringing me to the edge of orgasm. His lips could do many things ... including lie.

Jenny sat down beside her, and I did the same.

Marquessa pulled a chicken, carrots, and potatoes from the bag and then opened a cupboard for a cutting board. "We'll eat, and then we'll hunt. No one should go huntin' on an empty stomach."

Jenny said, "Grandma, maybe you should stay home. We'll look for your friends."

"Nonsense, girl." Marquessa glared. "I dragged these witches here, and now they're gone. Findin' them is the least I can do. Now, don't pretend like it wasn't me who taught you how to use magic in combat. I'm coming whether it cramps your style or not."

Jenny pursed her lips but said nothing.

I wanted to argue for Marquessa to stay home as well, but I feared everyone telling me I should stay home as well on account of the pregnancy. Therefore, I kept my mouth shut and knew that if things got tough, I'd get Marquessa out in one piece. "So, blackmail?"

Marquessa turned on the oven. "There wasn't any blackmail."

"Then why did she do it? I thought she loved my grandfather."

Marquessa pulled out the cutting board and went to the sink. "Loretta did love Jake, but when he started dating Missy, she started dating my cousin, Richard, to make Jake jealous. I told her it was a bad idea, but ..." Marquessa shrugged. "Being a seer isn't easy. Knowing the future and not knowing how it will unfold can be a very hard pill to swallow."

Who was she telling? In the beginning, I hadn't known how the prophecy would work. I thought I'd fall madly in love with one vampire, get married, and have a baby.

None of that had happened. Instead, I had fallen for five vampires, married none of them, and was pregnant with one of the four's children.

Fate had thrown me the curveball of the century.

I remembered reading about Richard Green. "Where's your cousin now?"

"He got married to another woman. He was always in on Loretta's plan to make Jake jealous." She scoffed and shook her head as she scrubbed potatoes to an inch of their life. "That didn't stop Richard from falling for her."

"I didn't know Uncle Richard dated Lorena's grandmother." Jenny tossed me a grin. "We were almost family."

I laughed and took her hand. "We are family." I'd never had a closer friend than Jenny.

She squeezed my fingers back.

Blair asked, "So, what happened? How did Lorena's grandmother go from hating Missy to being her friend?"

Marquessa finally joined us at the table. "They were never friends. Loretta never liked Missy."

Now I was completely lost. Up was down and down was to infinity and beyond. Nothing made sense. Part of me wanted to know more, but the other part of me wanted to throw in the towel, admit defeat, and try to forget the incident ever took place.

I threw up my hands. "Be straight with me, Marquessa. What happened?"

CHAPTER TWELVE

Marquessa took me seriously and got straight with me.

"Your grandmother saw Missy's death in a vision."

Blair stiffened. "What?"

Marquessa nodded. "It's all in the past now. I'm not sure you'll find that confession in any of her journals, but your grandmother knew Missy would die and wanted to give her a few years of happiness even if that happiness was with a man Loretta loved."

"Wow." That was big of my grandmother. I don't know if I could have done the same, even knowing Missy would die. "What did Missy die of?"

"Lupus."

I'd heard about the disease before. It attacks the immune system. Some people live long lives with it, while others can die very quickly once they're diagnosed. "She couldn't fight it?"

"Technology and science weren't what they are today. Today, you have a better chance of fighting it."

"A better chance, but anything is possible," Blair whispered before she lowered her gaze. Having two doctors for parents meant she'd know more about this stuff than me and maybe even Marquessa.

"How quickly did she die after the wedding?" I asked.

"It was about a year and a half later. When the symptoms got worse, she left Colt Valley. She didn't want Jake takin' care of her at the end." Marquessa shook her head. "We heard about her death sometime later through a friend of the family. Missy's parents left soon after their daughter disappeared."

This was not the story I'd been expecting at all.

I tried to imagine what it must have been like for Missy, my grandmother, and Jake. The situation had been very complicated. I wondered if my grandmother had told Jake anything about the prophecy or if she'd let it play out.

How long did Jake wait before he started seeing Loretta?

Jenny got up to use the bathroom. When she came back, she asked, "Why is there a statue of Marco in the living room?"

Blair and I shared a look. We'd completely forgotten about Marco. I'd been so wrapped up in the past that the present had eluded me. "Come sit down."

Marquessa had moved to the stove, but at the tone of my voice, she gasped and ran to the living room. There'd be no sitting for her.

I got up. "Wait."

"No!" Her cry came from the other room.

Marquessa was crouched by Marco's body. A hand was over her mouth. She rocked on her knees as tears fell down her cheeks. "No, this can't be. What have I done?"

"It's not your fault." I moved over and sat next to her. "I'm the one who brought Marco here."

"But I asked him to stay. Oh." She looked at me. "What if the others are dead?"

Blair gasped from the entrance to the room.

I looked at her and said, "They're not. We're going to find them."

"How do you know, Lorena?" Blair asked. "My mother could be …"

I didn't want to tell her what Marco told me, but I felt like his words were a clue to what was going on.

I decided I was going to keep what I knew to myself. "Let's eat. Then we'll find out where your mom and the others are."

Darkness had fallen by the time we'd gotten the table clear of everything but the map and my gemstone positioned at my house.

The four of us grabbed hands, and Jenny began to chant.

The black stone jerked and then moved south before it stopped in the middle of a field. Since the map was old, we had to use modern GPS to find the right coordinates. I pulled out my phone, and everyone looked down. We started at my house and then moved the view south.

"There's the mansion," Jenny said.

Blair's mother was located somewhere in the field behind the mansion, on the other side of the forest that was now a treehouse.

I stiffened, and Jenny grabbed my arm just as I said, "I know where your mother is."

"Where?" Blair asked.

"This is where Colt Valley's newest residents live. Sirius and Lilac."

Marquessa slammed her hands on the table. The object rattled as she stood. "Let's go."

We piled into Blair's car because it was roomie, newer, and would heat in a blink.

I called Alan on the way, and he picked up on the first ring. "Hello." There was a lot of noise behind him. I could hear a heavy beat pounding through the phone. The electric music wasn't something Alan usually listened to.

Even still, his voice purring into my ear never failed to affect me.

"I'm on the way to the new neighbor's house with Jenny, Marquessa, and Blair," I told him where the house was. "I need you and Dimitri to meet us there. Sirius and his girlfriend might be holding Dr. Shaw hostage."

Alan fell quiet and then asked, "Are you sure she's here?"

"Here? What do you mean? Are you at the mansion?"

"No, I'm where you are heading, at the neighbor's house. Sirius has a soirée. I'm here to assist in keeping the fairies in line. Someone had to make sure the fairies didn't get too drunk."

I'd forgotten all about the party. Leave it to Alan to call an EDM event a soirée.

I hung up and turned to Blair. "Is it possible your mother is attending a party?"

"What? No. Why?"

"Because the neighbors are hosting a party at their house."

Everyone saw exactly what I meant before we were even close to the event. There were white tents set up around the glamorous house, and as our car pulled into the driveway, a valet approached the car and offered us a ticket in exchange for the keys.

The event occupied the house as well as the tents. I saw people through the windows of the house and moving through the tents. The door flaps fluttered open whenever someone came out.

"Should we split up and spread out?" Jenny asked at the front door.

I wasn't sure. I'd seen enough horror movies to know that splitting up was a bad move. It made it easier for the antagonist to pluck them off one by one.

But at Blair's tense expression, I relented. "Yeah, let's split up. We'll cover more ground that way."

The front door was opened by a staff member I hadn't seen during my last visit. They took our coats, and then we all separated.

Blair stuck with me. "I don't think my mom is here." She was studying the crowd.

I looked around the house. With the dark party lights and the foot traffic, the glass castle looked different. If anyone had asked me before tonight, I would say the design had been for show. In my head, there'd been a big red sign that said, "Look but don't touch."

White furniture always seemed sacred. It reminded me of cats, the ones that walked around like they were royalty with their nose in the air. They'd scoff at the idea of a human petting them. White couches were the cats of furniture.

But people were everywhere, sitting on the couches with their feet on the coffee table, relaxed. Everyone was also dressed just as casually as me in jeans and boots. We were a bunch of country folk in a palace.

If Sirius and Lilac had been expecting a different crowd, they should have lived in the city.

"Lorena, you made it. I didn't think you'd come." Sirius approached and took my hand before I could stop him. He rubbed my fingers possessively as he held my eyes.

I'd almost forgotten how beautiful he was. In the dim lights, his hair looked darker, his eyes more potent of foreboding. His expression would be pretentious if he weren't so good-looking.

He'd never gotten this close to me before or touched me. His fingers were rough and large. They stroked my fingers like he was trying to memorize their size.

He was tall with shoulders wide enough to block the sight of everyone else around him. And I was just as drawn to him as I'd been the first time we'd met.

Was he a fae? Maybe I was being enchanted.

But he looked so human, and his palm was so warm.

I snatched back my hand. Good looking or not, the guy was a sleaze. "Where's your girlfriend Lilac? I want to introduce her to Blair."

Sirius smiled. "Lilac isn't my girlfriend."

I hesitated. "Since when?"

He lifted his eyes to think and then dropped him. "Lilac and I dated briefly in college until we realized we were better off as friends and partners. That was almost five years ago."

Five years?

Blair cut in, "I'm going to the bathroom." She rushed away before I could stop her. She was concerned about her mother, and here I was talking to Sirius. We were here on a mission. We needed to find Dr. Shaw.

But maybe Sirius could help.

"Lilac told Jenny and me you were dating?" I asked.

"Did she?" Sirius stroked his jaw. "Are you sure?"

I opened my mouth and closed it when I realized that Lilac hadn't told us she was dating Sirius at all. She'd acted jealously, that could not be denied, but hadn't introduced Sirius as her boyfriend or even moved to stand by him when he'd come into the room. "She still wants you."

"That's not my problem, and neither is it yours." He grabbed my hand again. "Come. I want to show you something."

I almost snatched back my hand, but I was curious about what it was that Sirius wanted to show me. I needed to find Dr. Shaw, and my search would look less suspicious if I let him guide me off somewhere.

Maybe he was planning to trap me wherever Dr. Shaw was.

As he guided me through the party, I tried to catch the eye of anyone I knew, but the fairies were all occupied with the humans. I noticed more than a few of the fairies already had their tongues down someone's throat.

"Uh, you should be warned that things might get a little frisky around here." And by frisky, I meant pornographic.

He dipped his chin and smiled. "I hope so."

"Wow. I was talking about my friends. You're bold."

"There is a quote that says, 'It's only by being bold that you get anywhere.'"

"And you're trying to get into my pants?"

"Amongst other places." Again, my mind wondered what that bread would feel like on me, stroking my inner thigh.

"Wow." Shock was becoming a preeminent state around him. "Look, you should know that I have boyfriends. *Plural*. And I'm not in the market for another." And Sirius didn't strike me as someone who liked group assignments. Everything about him said, "solo."

He opened a door in the hall. A dark, ascending staircase was on the other side. It was different than the one that was out in the open on the other side of the house. This one seemed to lead to a private room. He started up the steps and looked back. "I'm not really into labels. We could find this thing between us as a mutual attraction."

I looked back and caught Alan's eye. He gave me a slight head nod. He knew why I was here, and now he knew Sirius was taking me to the attic. I'd be safe.

I joined Sirius on the step and tilted my face back to look at him. "You assume I'm attracted to you."

Sirius didn't move, but as he lowered his voice, he felt closer. "I assume your panties are wet."

"They're not." But his words had set off a tingling in my body. "I'm dry as burnt toast down there."

"Mind if I check?"

My lower muscles clenched. "Mind if I knee you in the balls?"

He smiled. "I like you, Lorena."

I took my hand back again. "I like me too. Now, what is it you want me to see?"

He chuckled and motioned for me to go ahead of him. "I want to show you my work. After you."

I walked ahead of him, completely aware that his eyes were on my butt. Oh well. He could look all he wanted. He'd never get a touch.

The attic was very attractive, with an exposed wooden panel theme. The lighting was warm and calm. There were diagrams and a blue map on the wall with swirling white lines and dots. It took me a moment to realize I was staring at the galaxy. I moved forward and took in the stars. Each and every one of them had a name.

The handwriting underneath the stars was small, but the strokes were strong enough for me to know who'd written them in. "What do you do?"

"I'm a mechanical engineer, but my calling is astronomy." He moved in close but didn't touch me. "The heavens hold the answer to strength, love, shadow, health, foresight, and hope. And you." He pointed at a star named Daphne.

"That's not my name." Few things were more embarrassing than telling a guy he got your name wrong.

He smirked easily. "I know, but it's what your name originates from. Without Daphne, there would be no Lorena."

"Really? I thought my name was about a bunch of twigs and leaves folded together to make a crown."

"The laurel wreath. Yes." His gaze moved to the stars. "But before it became a symbol of academic achievement, it was a symbol of love."

I just stilled myself from rolling my eyes before I said, "Go on."

He motioned me over to a book that was sitting on a table. I walked over and was fascinated by how ancient the pages looked. The book had a worn look that only came with age, great use, but also great care.

There were drawings in the pages of people in togas in summer fields and clouds, fighting, talking, or making love.

He turned the page to a depiction of a strong man who was chasing a woman with deep curves. "Apollo and Daphne," Sirius said. "Apollo had teased Eros for using an arrow for love and not war."

"Apollo is the god of war." I knew that much.

"Exactly. He thought himself more important than Eros, so the god of love shot him with an arrow made of gold and forced him to love the nymph, Daphne. Then he shot Daphne with an arrow made of lead and forced her to forever hate Apollo."

"That's not good."

"No, it's not. Eventually, Daphne begged to be away from Apollo, so she was turned into a laurel wreath."

"I knew there was a reason I didn't like Greek mythology. Why did Daphne have to be pulled into that mess with Eros and Apollo? Why not turn Apollo into a tree?"

He smiled. "It's no secret the Greeks favor men."

"The world favors men."

His hand landed on my hip. It was hot enough to burn through my clothes. "I favor women. You're very beautiful, Lorena."

I backed away. "Beauty is fleeting."

He followed. "'But a thing isn't beautiful because it lasts. It's a privilege to be among them.'"

I hit a wall, and my hands shot out. "Wait. I know that line. Did you just quote *Vision?*"

He smiled. The black earring winked with the same fire of his blue eyes. "You watch Marvel movies?"

Was this guy serious? "I prefer DC comics. Wonder Woman specifically, but I'm an all-around geek."

"Princess Diana." His gaze dropped to my feet and then slowly climbed back up. "I could see it. You favor her but in a softer way."

One of his hands remained on my hip while the other rested beside my head on the wall. Around his wrist, he wore a braided leather wristband. The bracelet had symbols pressed into the material.

I recognized witchcraft when I saw it.

My hackles rose. My power gathered in my palms and heated the air around me. My senses heightened, and in the distance, I could hear someone screaming.

"Who are you?"

His eyes darkened. "I'm the man you're going to fall in love with."

"What makes you say that?"

"It's written in the stars." His mouth began to descend.

I whispered, "Here's another movie quote for you. 'Hulk Smash!'" My knee went up and found its target.

Sirius fell over, and I pushed him to the ground before I ran out, following the sound of the screaming that sounded like it was coming from everywhere and nowhere at the same time.

I heard it in the back of my head more than my ears, yet my body felt sure of the destination.

At the bottom of the stairs was Dimitri. He grabbed my shoulders and started to talk, but I wasn't listening.

The screaming was louder. It was like a game of Marco Polo, and I was getting closer.

Which way should I go? Another door right next to the one that led to the attic. I tried to open it, but it was locked.

Dimitri set me to the side, threw his fist back, and slammed into the door. The wood splintered and broke. If I were wrong about what was downstairs, we'd have to pay for that. Dimitri unlocked it from the other side and opened the door.

There was a stairway to the basement.

The screaming in my head was louder. It pulled me down. I kept my power pressed to me as my foot found one step at a time. "Can you hear it?" I asked Dimitri.

"Yes, I can hear it through your mind."

"What?"

He touched my chin. "You're talking to me in my head." He turned away. "She's this way." He leaped down the stairs, and I felt very human as I ran on two legs.

A light was cut on by the time I reached the ground level. The walls and floor were cement and covered in symbols written with a red ink I knew had to be blood.

There was no one in the room, but the screaming was coming from down here. I was sure of it. I looked around for a door but saw nothing.

Dimitri's breathing caught my attention, and I stumbled back at the sound of bone cracking. His bones shifted as his beast exploded from the confines of his flesh. His arms and thighs were twice as thick. His skin went as white as snow. His ears shifted up and pointed with a splash of fur decorating the ends.

I stumbled back and remembered the way he'd attacked me last year in the library. I hadn't seen him like this in a long time, and any time he did shift, he was hard to control.

I called for Alan, not with my voice but with my power. Only Alan could help keep Dimitri under control.

But my power pulled on everything and everyone dead. My necromancy poured from the room and spread out. I felt many in the house that belonged to me. The thought was possessive, but that was how my necromancy worked. My power had an acquired taste for the living dead and didn't like to share.

I felt my men in the rooms upstairs, but I also felt others, unknown bodies tied to me on the metaphysical plane where reality made war with the unknown.

I put up a wall of magic between Dimitri and me.

His ears twitched. As if sensing my fear, he rotated his head. He bared his teeth. His fangs looked like they could saw through the cement wall. Anger blacked his already dark eyes. His curls fell over his face. "Still don't trust me, necromancer?"

He then dashed away and crashed into the far wall. The building shook, and some of the cement gave. He turned to me, and I dropped my walls. He wasn't trying to attack me. He was trying to help me find the voice.

A stampede was heard from upstairs. Alan came down, followed by Zane, William, Sirius, and Lilac.

Lilac took one look at the wall and screamed. "Stop!" She reached out her hand toward Dimitri and closed her fist.

Dimitri howled in pain before he dropped to the ground. He didn't get back up. He didn't move.

The world shifted underneath my feet. The shouts around me ceased to exist as my mind tried to back away from the scene in front of me.

Dimitri was dead, and I had no way to deal with this.

Actually, there was one way. I tossed out my magic and flung Lilac into the wall. I would have the blood for the blood I'd lost. I would maim her. I would kill her slowly. I would carve her heart out just as she'd carved out mine.

I would have my revenge. I would take justice in the form of her flesh, a pound of every pound I'd lost from my beautiful Dimitri.

I was on Lilac before anyone could stop me. She came to with my hands around her throat. My hands weren't big, but neither was Lilac. I didn't want to use magic to kill her. I wanted her to know it was me who did it. Lorena Meredith Quinn, who took everything from her.

I sputtered in fear, and I dug deeper.

"Lorena!" someone shouted.

But it was too late.

Have you ever had a bone break? Well, I'd had plenty of broken bones over my life. I was not one people would call a girly girl. I wasn't really a tomboy either. I was just me. Awkward and impulsive. I was accident-prone.

But what happened to me next was no accident.

Lilac showed me her hands. It looked like surrender.

Until she closed her fist.

My forearms snapped.

At first, I didn't feel it. All I noticed was that the bones were in the wrong position.

Then the pain crashed over me. It was so great that I ended up vomiting all over Lilac. I got one moment of victory, watching her shout in rage before I passed out.

CHAPTER THIRTEEN

Someone was stroking my hair. The fingers were soft and light, so I thought it was Alan. I felt great. The bed I was sleeping in was soft and had that smell of detergent. I loved that smell. The sheets were warm, and I was snuggled next to something soft.

I smiled as the fingers stroked around the edge of my hairline and then into my locks of hair. For once, I was glad I hadn't cut it. I was used to wearing it short. Then Ewan had taught me all the many uses for my hair when worn in a braid.

Yeah, Ewan brought the freak in me out. Honestly, all my men did.

The sharp knock on the door disturbed me.

As did the sweet feminine voice that responded to it. "Come in."

"How is she?" That was Zane. I could hear the guilt from all the way across the room. He felt bad.

Good. It served him right to keep secrets from me. "And the baby?"

I stiffened at that question, and the fingers in my hair stilled.

"The baby is fine," Dr. Shaw answered. She resumed her menstruations, and I relaxed. "The child is strong."

I fought back my smile. I didn't want Zane or Dr. Shaw to know I was awake. I wasn't ready to get up and face the real world. I wanted to stay in this tender box where people as pretty as she cared for crazy, damaged, girls like me.

Her voice came from over my head, which told me that the soft place I was feeling and smelling was actually her dress. I was resting on her lap.

I heard footsteps and then Zane's voice. He was closer. "I'm going to turn in." His hand landed on my shoulder. He bent down and kissed my lips.

I fought the urge to press closer and wrap my arms around him. I was angry with him, but I still loved him.

He pulled away too soon. "The men and I will check on her again when she wakes up. We also request that you ask her to stay in this world until we've talked to her."

Why would I leave this world? What had happened?

Dang it. Now I'll have to get up.

But ... not yet. I'll ask Dr. Shaw what Zane is talking about in a few minutes, maybe an hour.

"I'll make sure she hears your request."

There were more footsteps, but these retreated. The door closed, and the room went quiet.

Dr. Shaw sighed. "Are you ready to get up?"

"No." My throat was dry. I cleared it. "I'm still tired." I was.

"All right." She didn't sound bothered in the least. She was patience reincarnated.

No one had ever cared for me the way Dr. Shaw did.

My eyes burned when I realized how much I wished my mother had been this way with me. My mother had raised my sister, Connie, and I couldn't help but wonder if she'd stroked Connie's hair when she'd been hurt.

My mother didn't strike me as the tender sort. I couldn't picture her wrapping me up in a towel after a long swim in the pool or making me turkey sandwiches with the crust cut off. I couldn't see her meeting my eyes in the mirror as she brushed my hair.

She would never have done any of that for me because she'd hated me. She'd hated me for being a necromancer. She'd hated me for being born.

I broke into the sort of sob I did best. The ugly sort.

Dr. Shaw gathered me in her arms like a mother hen would do to a baby chick, even cooing as my sobs racked my body. I tried to keep my face away from her so she wouldn't see me and get turned off or push me away, but she was having none of that.

She wiped my face with something and then said, "Tell me where it hurts."

If only she could fix my stupid heart, but she couldn't. My parental issues were beyond repair. That part of me was better off being taken to the city dump and buried away until the end of time.

I didn't know how anyone put up with me. Maybe she hated me because she knew how screwed up my life would be.

"Who?" Dr. Shaw asked.

It was only then I realized I'd spoken out loud. I sniffed and kept my eyes closed. "My mother." I didn't want to see her pity or watch her face change as she realized I wasn't worthy of the tenderness she was giving me.

Instead, Dr. Shaw tightened her arms. "This doesn't sound like the warrior princess I know. Where's my strong Lorena?"

My eyes began to leak again. "You know about Wonder Woman?" I looked at her through watery eyes.

She smiled down at me. "Only vaguely until I met you."

Wow. The woman was even trying to get to know me more than my mother ever had.

"I'm sorry I give you such a hard time," I found myself saying.

She shook her head. "Peter and I have had some conversations while I helped prepare your meals. I know a little bit about what you were forced to survive. Anyone who knows you would be proud of the woman you are. Why else would all these men adore you?"

I sniffed. I was feeling bad for myself and throwing a pity party of the century with streamers, balloons, and a ten-foot ice sculpture of my weeping face included. "Because of the prophecy?"

"Lorena, you're already pregnant. If any of them only wanted your womb, they'd be gone by now."

That was true. I was pregnant and carrying the child of the prophecy. There was no other reason to stick around unless … they actually loved me.

I smiled. "You're right."

"Oh, what a beautiful expression. You were meant to smile, Lorena."

She hugged me, and I sighed with relief when her arms went around me. "I'll probably lose my temper later today. I want to keep you informed."

She laughed and patted my back. "That's all right. I've seen your strength and know what you'd be willing to do for your friends. I couldn't imagine having you for a mother. You're going to do very well."

I pulled away.

I was in my room in the mansion.

Dr. Shaw put the box from my dad on my lap and said, "Blair thought you'd want this."

I picked up the box, shook it around, and stiffened. The slushing noise gave it away big time. I knew what was in it. Did Blair know? Did Dr. Shaw?

She smiled. "Go ahead. Just this once."

I laughed and opened the box. Inside was a carefully wrapped bottle of Dr. Pepper. I let the soda settle from all my shaking and then cracked it open and took a sip. Sweet bubbles of vanilla filled my mouth and had me moaning and drinking down half the bottle before I knew what I was doing.

It was then I also noticed my arms were whole.

Reality crashed down on me, but thankfully I wasn't alone when it happened. Dr. Pepper was with me. "What happened after I passed out?"

Dr. Shaw sighed. "So much."

"How are you here?"

"You and the others found me." She got up and started straightening things that didn't really need to be straightened and dusted my gems with a cloth. She struck me as that sort of person. If she was going to fidget, she was going to be productive. "I was beyond the wall in the basement."

"Why? Were Sirius and Lilac planning to kill you?"

She shook her head. "No, they kidnapped me to save Lilac's sister, but she might have eventually killed me because there was nothing I could do for the girl."

"What's wrong with Lilac's sister?"

"I don't know, but she's been suspended in a state of stasis for many, many years. Lilac won't tell me what happened. Neither will Sirius. Lilac is also unstable."

"What kind of witch is she?"

"One that people fear more than you." She put down my Funko Pop! Wonder Woman figurine and met my eyes. "She's a carnomancer, and she's very, very old. I could sense it in her aura when we first met. Her power had age to it."

Carnomancers were the exact opposite of necromancers. While I controlled dead flesh, Lilac could control living flesh and manipulate it any way she saw fit. "She doesn't look old."

"She uses her power to keep herself young. I'm not even sure her face is the one she was born with. Either way, she should be dead. The human mind can only take so much before it corrupts. I'm sure she didn't mean to become what she has, but longevity and sadness can make a person neurotic."

Not just humans, I thought, but others as well. I'd seen the psychotic side of some of the fae and vampires like Vlad. I wouldn't live forever, and I was glad about that. Harvey Dent got it right in *The Dark Knight* when he said, "You either die a hero or live long enough to become the villain."

"Where are Lilac and Sirius now?"

"Your men put them in the basement with the former Mr. Corridan."

"Corridan is dead?"

"Lady Aisling killed him."

"Hold up. Aisling is here?"

"Yes. Apparently, she followed Corridan into this world and chased him down while he was chasing you. Then she was captured by Sirius and Lilac the night you were attacked."

"Why? What did they want from her?"

"The same thing they wanted from me. Help. Margot and Ralph were there as well. They'd been there for weeks before I was taken."

"I hadn't known. Are they alive?"

"Yes. A little shaken but alive."

I wondered what was wrong with Lilac's sister. I took a breath and asked my next question. "Was Marco there?"

Dr. Shaw sat on the edge of the bed. "I didn't see him. You could ask Margot. She's still awake. The other witches are asleep. However, Margot is kind of busy. She said she had some time to make up for."

"Meaning?"

"She's copulating with any fae in the house that will have her."

"Let me guess. She's got bodies lined up around the block." Margot had a timeless beauty. She also had charms, both in the flirty sense and the magical sense. Margot was half-fae.

"She's taking a few at a time." Dr. Shaw's tone was so composed you'd think she was saying Margot was putting pills in her mouth as opposed to hard shafts in soft lady parts. "You might have to wait for a while."

Then that was exactly what I was going to do. I looked down at my arms. Last time I'd seen them, they'd been as broken as Humpty Dumpty's shell. "Who do I have to thank for putting me back together again?"

"Not me. I don't possess the sort of gift that could make that happen overnight. I assisted Margot."

I got out of bed and held her gaze. "Thank you."

She smiled. "You're welcome, Lorena."

"Why are you so nice to me?" I had to know. Half the people who smiled at me wanted me dead. I couldn't forget Marco's warning. He'd told me to stay away from Dr. Shaw, but everything inside me wanted to do the opposite.

Dr. Shaw thinned her lips and pulled in a breath. She looked down at her lap, and I knew right then and there she was hiding something from me. I just didn't know what. What was she hiding? When she finally lifted her head, she said, "I care about you, Lorena."

"Why?"

She stood and straightened the bedsheets. "I'm not your enemy."

"What are you then?"

"I'm here to help you. That's all."

"Why? Because Marquessa called and asked you to?"

She said nothing, and I shook my head. I was going crazy. "Sorry. You're just being a doctor. You're being professional, and I'm being a suspicious dork."

She walked to the bathroom. I needed to shower and do something to clear my head.

Her hand stopped me right before I crossed the threshold. "I'm not just being professional, Lorena. I actually care about you." Her eyes were like sapphires or stars twinkling in the sky.

"For how long? Until the baby is born?"

Her eyes softened to sadness. She tucked my hair behind my hair and cupped my cheek. "For far longer than that, Lorena."

My heart raced. Who was this woman? Why did I always feel so much when she was around? Her face was like a suspended memory of the dog days. Only, I'd never had dog days. My life had been hell, but my heart recognized her in a similar way that my power recognized the vampires.

I felt like we fit, which was crazy.

I'd had a mother, and no matter how much I enjoyed Dr. Shaw's mothering, I was too old for foster care, too hard to be nurtured, and had seen too much to be looked after.

"Don't make promises you can't keep," I whispered, completely aware that I was once again trying to drive her away. Again.

She dropped her hand and stepped back. "I won't be around forever, Lorena, but I vow to be here as long as I'm allowed."

"You're allowed to stick around but keep your hands off my Dr. Pepper."

She bobbed her head and laughed. "Deal. I'm off to bed now. I'll see you in a few hours."

I shut the door. My grin was big as I showered.

Peter was waiting for me as I climbed down the stairs. He had a smoothie in his hand. I took it, thanked him, and walked to the sitting room.

The conversation died on my arrival. Willow and William were by the fireplace.

"What's up?"

Willow cleared her throat. "Nothing. We were just discussing going into the fae world. Has Dr. Shaw cleared you for travel?"

"Not yet, but now that we've found Margot and Ralph, I don't want to waste any more time. I need to find Ewan and finally get Wei out of the stone." The stone was currently with my mother's stone at my house. I'd have to go get that.

They got quiet again.

"What?" I asked again.

Willow had braided her red hair onto a crown around her head and found a white, lacy dress that looked ancient enough to have come from one of the trunks from the attic. She looked like a bride, and for a moment, I wondered if I was interrupting something.

William said, "Sirius and Lilac wish to go with us."

"No way. They murdered Marco." I didn't have the proof, but I was starting to piece everything together.

Willow gasped. "Are you sure? Did they confirm this with Aisling?"

"No. Wait, where is Aisling?"

"She's interrogating them in the basement," William said. "They probably won't survive until the morning."

I hesitated only a moment before I sprinted for the basement door.

CHAPTER FOURTEEN

"Stop!" I called down to the basement before I descended the stairs at a neck-breaking pace. Don't worry. I held the rail.

At the bottom was Corridan's body. His throat had been cut, and his body pierced with the many stars he'd tried to kill me with. He'd probably tried to kill Aisling with them as well.

Looking the dead man over, I had to admit, I didn't think Aisling had it in her.

In horror films, faces were often caught in a petrified state, but in reality, only Medusa could freeze a face in terror. Instead of twisted horror, Corridan's face was slack with rest. The only thing that gave off the sense that he'd feared for his life was the stench that told me he'd lost the fight with his bladder.

I covered my nose and skipped over the body.

The second thing I noticed about the basement was the improvement to the air quality. Away from Corridan's body, my lungs no longer felt suffocated by magic. My limbs were no longer weighed down by the curse Titania had placed over the space. The spell had been broken.

The basement was a large space packed with antiques, cages, and even a few medieval torture devices. I had a feeling the guillotine had been brought over by Vlad himself.

Vlad had "villain from a cheesy movie" written all over him. During my first encounter with the man, he did that thing villains always do where they lock up the protagonist and then tell them their plan in novel-length details.

I could see him rubbing his hands together and chuckling as his victim screamed for the mercy that would never come.

Around an old Japanese room divider, I found them.

Aisling had Lilac and Sirius tied to a chair. Lilac's hands were spread on her thighs, which kept her from using her trick.

Sirius noticed me first, and he unfurrowed his brow. He was wet from sweat. His red hair looked brown as it clung to his forehead and face. He looked at me like I was bringing succor, like I'd come to alleviate his pain, to rescue him. His eyes cleared like a summer sky after a storm.

The expression tripped me up. I didn't understand why he thought I'd save him after what he'd done.

Then Aisling lifted a blade, and I didn't know where it was going. I didn't even know if she planned to use it violently, though I didn't see any turkeys for carving in the vicinity. I don't know how to explain why I did what I did next, but I did it.

I flung her hand back with my power and watched it smack into a nearby mahogany column. The blade dropped. My aim was getting better. I specifically only aimed for her hand, and I got it on the first try. Go me!

"Ow!" She winced and shook her hand. "Lorena, whatever would lead you to make such an offense to me?"

I'd almost forgotten how uppity the chick could sound when she talked.

Strangely, I loved her outfit. She looked like Black Widow, especially with her blood-red hair. Her black leather covered her slim feature like a second skin. She looked like she'd been dipped in dark licorice. The black shined blue in the light. Her boots were kickass. I wanted to know her tailor. Considering all my recent crime-fighting, I think I deserved it.

There was a bow and arrow attached to her back. A knife holster was snug around her waist.

"First things first. Why do you look like Black Widow?"

She slapped her hands onto her hips. "I'm here to avenge myself, find my brother, and gather troops to end this abhorrent war. Why does everyone continue to compare me to a spider?"

Sirius snickered. I fought back my own laugh. I refused to agree on anything with him, which included our sense of humor.

I crossed my arms. "No one is comparing you to a spider. It's a character from a Marvel Comic. She's an assassin. She's really good."

Aisling straightened and smiled. "Oh. Well, that's less revolting than a spider."

"I tried to tell you," Sirius muttered.

I rolled my eyes. "I take it back. You look like Selene from Underworld."

Sirius's mouth sneered. "No, she doesn't. Selene wore a coat that made her look like she was wearing a cape."

"She would take the coat off. Duh."

"Well, Selene's hair was black and cut blunt, unlike Black Widow or this deadly creature." He motioned his head to Aisling.

Aisling gasped with pleasure. "Am I the deadly creature?" You would think he'd said her hair was shiny.

"Fine," I said, exasperated. "She looked like Black Widow, and you're about to look like the victim caught in her web."

Aisling raised her hand. "I thought you just said—"

"Never mind what I said, Aisling. I didn't mean an actual web."

She put down her hand. "Ah, well, then, why did you stop me from killing him when I had the chance?"

"I don't know. I just … can't let you hurt him."

Sirius smirked.

"But I can." I walked over to him and slapped him.

He grunted and murmured, "Usually, I sleep with a lady and don't take her number before she slaps me."

I hit him again.

He smiled. His lip was cut. "But I'd never do that to you, sweet Lorena."

I shook my head. "The first hit was for Dr. Shaw. The second was for Marco, and there's more where that comes from."

He stiffened, and his smile fled. "Marco was an accident."

I knew it was his fault, but the confirmation hurt all the same. "Why? Marco was a good man."

"Aye, he was." His voice was different, no longer American. Now it was Gaelic. "I'm sorry, lass."

I grabbed his throat, and he lifted his chin to give me better access. "Why?"

He gave me nothing.

I looked over at his partner in crime. I wasn't sure how many other ways she was his partner since, according to him, they weren't dating, but that didn't matter. "You've been suspiciously quiet?"

Her hair hung around her face. "I haven't read or seen any of the pop culture references you've mentioned."

That was as good a reason as any. "What's wrong with your sister?"

Lilac didn't bother to hide the hate in her eyes. She also didn't bother to answer my question.

And that bothered me.

I let Sirius go and straightened. "You want help waking up your sister? I'll do it for you." I made my voice unnaturally light and gentle.

Fear twisted her face. "No! Your necromancy will ruin her."

It would. She'd wake up a zombie. "You wanted Marco's help, didn't you?"

"That was for something else."

"What?" I asked. "What did you want him for?"

"Please. Leave my sister out of this. She hasn't done anything wrong. She was only a little girl when it happened."

"What happened?"

Lilac's head fell forward. Her sobs sounded just as rehearsed as a Jerry Springer guest.

Aisling came around to the front, lifted the woman by her chin, and punched her in the face.

The smack cracked the air.

Lilac's breathing changed and grew heavy. "Curse you, bitch!"

Aisling hit her again. "I'm not a bitch, you changeling. I'm the Black Widow."

I grabbed Aisling's shoulder before she could hit Lilac again. "Woah there, Natasha Romanoff. Let's calm down."

"I want them dead." Aisling's green eyes glittered with the shine of epic reprisal. "I want this floor painted with their blood and innards. I want their heads on poles, and I want them forced to watch goblins eat their gouged eyes."

I didn't think now was the time to tell her that Lilac and Sirius wouldn't be able to see anything if their eyes were gone. Also, they'd be dead.

But Aisling was clearly on a roll, and one never stopped someone who was on a roll even if that roll took a sharp turn to Looney Tunes Land.

She lifted her hand, pinched her thumb and forefinger together, and made a dipping gesture. "I want to hang them from their toes over a pool of lava and slowly lower their screaming faces into ..."

I squeezed Aisling's shoulder. "Hey, get a hold of yourself." What the heck had they done to her? From what I could see, she still had her limbs, but her body was covered in leather. Did she have scars underneath? Had they touched her inappropriately? Had they done an experiment?

Suddenly, I was upset. Yeah, I know. Me? Upset? No surprise there. But I couldn't let them die. Not yet.

Her nostrils flared and looked down at a stubborn Lilac. The woman's face looked smashed in but not bruised. And was it just me, or did her nose look twisted? Where was the blood? Was this what changelings were capable of? Was she, in fact, a changeling?

"You were going to kill me. Now, I shall kill you."

"No one is killing anyone until I get answers." I wasn't even entirely sure I'd let her kill them after I interrogated them. I wasn't big on murder. I cut Aisling off. "Upstairs. Now. You've had enough. You need to cool down."

"You can't tell me what to do!" she fired off in my ear.

I rounded on her. "Yeah, I think I can, seeing as this is my boyfriends' house. Plural. That means if I say go cool off, I mean find a bath of ice and take a timeout. You're done here. So, make like a UFO and pack it up and go."

She elbowed Lilac in the face hard enough to send the metal chair back. Lilac was out before it rattled to the ground. Aisling stormed from the basement, and I was kind of disappointed her costume didn't come with a cape. This moment had been cape worthy.

I moved to check Lilac. Yup, she'd be out for a while, but she wasn't dead. Being a necromancer made me more accurate than a heart monitor.

"Now that Natasha's gone, it's just you and me, lass. I often thought of myself as Superman."

I rolled my eyes. "You're confusing universes."

"Sorry. You've got my mind all muddled." His gaze did that tracking thing where he was clearly undressing me and a whole lot more. "You're a sweet distraction."

"Keep looking at me like that, and I'll let Natasha feed your laser eyes to the goblins."

He spread his thighs as much as the ropes around his waist, feet, and hands would allow. He was bloody, and still, his shaft pressed against his jeans, making his arousal very evident. "You know you can't resist the Man of Steel."

"Sorry. I don't mess with men who finish as fast as the speed of light."

"Ouch. I'm wounded."

"And gross." He wasn't gross. He wasn't gross at all, but I wished he was.

Every time I got near him, I only wanted to get closer. My fingers itched to touch him everywhere, staring at his wide shoulders and sliding down to discover the chest I knew would be solid. I'd stroke his abs. My mouth would take over the journey after that, heading south to his … "Fae."

"Guess again," he teased. He had to be a fae. That was the only thing that made sense.

"Witch." Maybe he'd spellbound me somehow. Maybe it was the water Lilac had given me at her house. That made sense.

He shook his head. "I'm not a witch."

"The bracelet."

He hesitated. I smiled and started forward.

"Wait." His jocular inclinations died. "Wait! Don't take it."

I moved around and crouched. I grabbed his bound wrist and tried to untie the leather, but it was impossible. "How do you take it off?"

"Get my name right, and it unravels itself from my body."

"Rumpelstiltskin!"

He shifted his head to look back at his wrist. Then he tsked. "No. Sorry, lass. Wrong riddle."

"Maybe I should cut your hair. Maybe that's your weakness."

"Oh, we're going biblical, are we?" He chuckled. "Very well, give me a kiss, and I'll tell you."

"What story is that?"

"The kiss of betrayal," he said gruffly. "I'll betray myself for that pouty mouth." He bit his lower lips, and I imagined those teeth on my own.

"Tell me how to undo the leather."

"I'd rather tell you how to undo my pants and then what to do once that's done."

"Is your mind always in the gutter?"

"As a matter of fact, it's a permanent resident. Lucky you."

Lucky me? I really wanted to hate this guy. I wanted to be around him and feel nothing.

"Tell me about the bracelet."

He shook his head. "Lass, why ever would I tell you such a secret?"

His face wasn't far from mine. I moved in closer. "Because I asked nicely?"

Sirius pulled in a deep breath, and I had the feeling he was trying to breathe me in. "Come up here and sit on my lap."

"Then you'll tell me?"

"Why don't you come up and see?"

It had to be a trick. I just didn't know what kind. What did he really want from me? I knew what I wanted from him. The place between my thighs was on fire and not in the urinary tract infection sort of way. I was hot for him.

I moved without thought and swung my leg over his.

I felt his stiffness and paused. Was he really that hard? This was an interrogation. What was wrong with me? I grabbed his face. I'd never touched a beard before. Every man I'd ever kissed had been clean-shaven. "Tell me what I want to know."

He leaned forward. "A kiss first, and you better make it good."

He wanted a kiss, did he? I'd had plenty of practice.

I didn't tease him. I just went for it. His tongue met mine, and I melted from the inside out. He jerked forward, and my hips started to rotate on their own. I'd given an old boyfriend a lap dance before, but this was so different. I could barely breathe. I didn't want to breathe.

All I wanted to do was feel. More of him. More of his tongue. More everything. I couldn't get close enough. My skin ached. His mouth was like manna, and I loved the beard. The combination of soft skin and coarse hair heightened the experience.

"Untie the rope," he panted. "I won't attack you."

"I know you won't." I gyrated my hips right over his manhood, rubbing it against my slit. I'd started off this game wet. Now, I was soaked. "I know what you'll do if I let you go."

He wouldn't kill me. He'd take control of my hips and take my body right here on this chair. I'd forget that he was a killer, my enemy. He chased my mouth; then, I'd pursued his. He tracked my every move to the point that I was starting to think I was the one in restraints, and he was the free one, free to do whatever he wanted with me.

He jerked his hips forward. "I need to be inside of you, Daphne."

"I'm Lorena."

"You're the brightest star in my universe."

I slowly pulled away. "You don't even know me."

"Are you sure?"

My heart beat like the drums that signaled war. I was lost in the meaning of his words and the beauty of his face. "Who are you?"

"Can't you feel it, necromancer?"

I cupped his face. His warm, beautiful face. "Vampire."

He smiled. "It only took you four guesses to get it right."

"Three," I corrected.

"There was a Rumpelstiltskin in there somewhere."

My mind was blown. He didn't look anything like the other vampires. Maybe Ewan, but he said he wasn't half-fae. His skin wasn't as pale as the others. He also didn't possess that strange stillness that sometimes came over Alan and the others. He had a heartbeat. His cheeks had color and life.

He could be lying. I wasn't ready to believe anything that came out of his mouth except for the fact that he wanted me. I could feel the evidence of that stabbing me in the nether regions.

"How?" I asked.

"There's so much I want to tell you, Lorena." Large hands grabbed my hips. They were his.

My life flashed before my eyes. There were so many things I hadn't done yet. I'd never been skydiving, though I never wanted to until this moment. I hated heights, but everyone should skydive before they die, right? Also, the baby. I was carrying a baby, and I didn't care if the child was the answer to the prophecy. The child was mine, and I loved it.

Now, we'd die together.

He rubbed my hips soothingly. "Shh. Calm down. I won't hurt you. I'd never hurt you, Lorena." I loved the way he said my name with that accent. I didn't know why he hid the Gaelic. It was a lovely dance in my ears.

But I could barely hear it over the rushing of my heart. "How did you break the rope?"

"Lady Aisling can wear whatever costume she wants, but she's not Natasha Romanoff."

"So what? You've just been sitting here, pretending to be tied up?"

"Pretty much."

"Why? Why let her torture you?"

He glanced away. "Because I deserve it."

The confession twisted my gut. "Did you … hurt her?"

"No, but Lilac would have. I tried to tell her to stop collecting powerful beings, but she won't listen. She's determined and has lost the ability to control her anger."

"So, you didn't kill Marco?"

"Nae. Lilac did it, but I should have stopped her from taking him to begin with."

"Why didn't you?"

He didn't answer, so I assumed it was because he loved her or at least still had feelings for her. What sort of person built a home with their ex? I remembered the way Lilac had gotten territorial that first day. If she'd been a pitbull, there'd be bite marks on my ankle.

"Why are you in Colt Valley?"

"Isn't it obvious?" His smirks were the dirtiest thing I'd ever seen on a man and having worked in fast food, I'd seen a lot. "I'm here for you. I came here for you."

"Why?"

"Because I'm the last one."

He wasn't making any sense. "What?"

"The ancient points of magic. I'm the last point." He flashed his teeth, and suddenly there were fangs where there hadn't been before.

Pentagrams had five points. I had five boyfriends, including Wei. Was he saying I wouldn't get Wei back? Was he here to replace Wei? I shook my head. No one could replace him.

"You think you complete the star?" she asked.

"Aye. I've been reading the stars, Lorena. I know all about you."

Was he saying Wei was dead? I didn't like that. I needed my Wei back. Not having him wasn't an option. "You're a seer?"

"Yes. A sky teller. I read the stars. It's my gift." His fingers kept stroking up my hips and over my stomach and back. "Amongst other things."

"Your ex-girlfriend is lying on the ground right next to us."

"*Ex,*" he emphasized. "I haven't touched Lilac in decades."

That didn't mean the witch didn't want him to.

I got off his lap. He reached down toward his ankles.

"Wait! Just because you're a vampire doesn't mean I trust you." I could go on and on about the people, including vampires, who'd already tried to kill me. The names were all in my head with bullet points in Times New Roman twelve-point font. Double spaced. "Until I know everything, you're still the enemy."

I saw the moment he made the decision to test me. I slung my magic with the precision of a slingshot. It knocked him in the chest, and his metal chair rattled as it hit the ground.

He wheezed between breaths. "If you … wanted me on my back … all you had to do … is say so."

With all the time my irises spend rolling in the back of my head, you would think I'd be able to paint the interior of my skull by now.

Moving around him, I crouched closer to him than I should. "How do I get the bracelet?"

He lifted his fist, and the leather fell away.

I didn't know what I expected to happen. Actually, I did. I expected his face to change into something less appealing. I was still convinced his beauty was an illusion, but all he did was pale. His heart still beat. He was still handsome.

"Was this one of Lilac's tricks?"

"Perhaps." He grinned, and I saw it. The fangs. "I smile a lot. The bracelet allows my smile to pass for human."

"Have you tried not smiling?"

His reply was to grin brighter. "I'm a happy man."

"Vampire."

"Your favorite." He grabbed me and settled me on his chest. "I'm sorry I was too late to be the father. That honor belongs to someone else." He stroked my stomach.

I closed my hand over his. "We're not having sex."

He rolled his eyes. "You'll be thinking about me all morning."

And speaking of morning ... "How are you able to be awake?"

"I was created ... differently than others."

"Meaning?"

"I am not a son of Vlad."

He tried moving his hand again, but my power held him back. Still, it took a combination of my strength and my magic to keep his hand still. What was happening to my magic?

He leaned up. "In case you're wondering if I'm holding back, I am."

I jumped off of him.

He untied his ankles and picked up the chair before he stretched.

I backed away farther.

"I'm not going to hurt you."

"Why can't I control you?"

He twisted his lower back and then rotated his arms. "You ask a lot of questions for this only being our first date."

"This isn't a date."

He grunted and scratched his belly. "You're right. Usually, on a date, you get fed. Where could I get a snack around here?"

"Do you live off blood or food?"

"Both."

"Just like Ewan."

He nodded. "Aye." He started for the staircase.

I looked at Lilac, who was still out.

I turned to him. "What are you doing? You can't go up there."

"There's only one way to keep me down here, and you're not ready to give that up." He moved Corridan's body to the side and started climbing.

I sprinted around him and held out my hands. "You're not coming up here."

"Oh? And who's going to make me stay?"

"We are." William stood at the top of the steps. Three other werewolves were behind him, and they all looked ready to fight.

Sirius stared them down as if contemplating whether or not he could take them on. Then he nodded and retreated a step. "I suppose the basement isn't all bad."

I climbed up. I was done talking to him or allowing him to make me feel the way I was. I shut the door behind me. "Thank you," I said to William. I guess it was a good thing they'd all decided to stick around.

William bowed his head. "There shall be guards at the door at all times." This was the only exit from the basement.

I liked the idea of the door being guarded as opposed to me being trailed all the time. "Great." I left feeling lighter.

My enemies were finally all in one place.

Except for Queen Titania.

And King Oberon.

But they didn't count. They were in the middle of a war, and I was likely the last person either of them cared about.

CHAPTER FIFTEEN

Aisling was in the dining room with a few of the fae. She stood at the head of the table. A large map covered the surface. She was pointing as she spoke to the two dozen who'd gathered in the room, most of them werewolves. Willow was also there. Some were sitting, eating. Some were standing around. No one acknowledged my entry.

"The most stealth fighters will come with me. We'll drop in at night."

"What's going on?" I asked.

A plate was put in front of me, and I dug in.

"Thanks to Corridan, I have Oberon's portal key. It will drop us right in front of the main gate."

"That's both convenient and risky."

"Indeed." Aisling sat, and even in the leathers, she moved with courtliness. "So, we'll need to find a way to get the guards not to kill us upon arrival. Well, naturally, they won't kill me. I'm far too valuable dead than alive. At least I was before my brother returned to our world."

"Why does Ewan change your value?"

She lifted her chin. "I was the heir while he was gone. Now, according to your people, Ewan has returned, and our mother has always loved him most."

I always felt the same about their family dynamic, but I'd decided to keep my opinion to myself. Titania did speak of Ewan fondly and all but waxed poetic about her love for him. While Aisling always just seemed to be there.

"I don't fault him for that, by the way," she added. "That was our mother's choice. Nevertheless, if it's a choice between Ewan and me, I know who she'll save." Or, more specifically, let die.

"I would presume Lilac and Sirius are still alive."

"You would presume correctly."

Someone stood so I could have a seat at the other end of the table.

"I'm all for strategy, but maybe we should wait until the men wake up."

"Why? They can't come," Aisling said. "They'll slow us down. In fact, I don't think you should come along either."

The words burned a hole through my chest. "That's not your decision to make. I'll go with or without you." I leaned forward. "And you should note, I'm already leaning toward the latter option." Who did Aisling think she was? This wasn't her house, and already she was thinking of taking my people to the fae world. I know, technically, they weren't *all* my people, but the werewolves and fae were here for me.

"I thought I instructed you to cool down, Aisling," I whispered. "Maybe you'd like someone to escort you to a room?"

The werewolves shifted toward Aisling, ready for my command. She may be a princess in the fae world, but I was more or less the queen of his house.

Aisling's emeralds flared. "Wait!"

"Maybe it's you who we'll leave behind."

"You don't understand. You're somewhat of a hot commodity in the fae world. Everyone is aware of what the child you carry can do. The trees have spoken."

"I wasn't aware the news of the treehouse had traveled that far."

She shook her head. "Lorena, your child didn't just make a treehouse. He made a fae, like the Old One who gives magic to my world."

Willow said, "This is how your child will restore the magic."

"Great." I played it off like I wasn't losing my mind when I was. "So, is magic back?"

"Not yet," Willow said. "The tree still sleeps. He is locked away until ..."

"Until?"

She shrugged. "I don't know. The story of the Old One is one that was never shared. He has no name because he was made during a time when there were no names. When the humanoid fae began to populate the kingdom, they forgot all about the trees."

I could see it all exactly like she's spoken it. I saw the Old One and watched a blank world shift and form around him. Grass and rain. Wind and climbing mountains in the distance. It moved like time-lapse footage. The sky faded from midnight blue to burnt orange, then purple, and finally a blue as clear as the Mediterranean sea before it faded and did it all over again. The suns and moons passed one another, dancing around the stars in the sky.

A branch broke and then took on arm and legs before taking the form of a gray woman.

She loved the Old One.

They had more trees together.

Trees grew around them and then around the world.

Animals moved in. Birds took to the blue skies and made his branches their dwelling place. Then the humanoids came and cut them down. They built homes and roads. They burned it for warmth. The Old One didn't mind. He enjoyed watching the fae use what he could provide. Then eventually, a group of fae arrived who decided they wanted to be close to the Old One. So, they formed their homes from his roots, and the population of the Earth fae spread.

Eventually, when the war came, they became the Earth Court.

The images stopped, and I grabbed my stomach.

I stood and felt the familiar tug from the outdoors, but this time, I knew who was calling me. The tree.

Peter met me at the door and helped me into my coat. I refused the gloves and walked across the fountains and toward the giant gray structure that looked darker in the late morning against the pale winter sky.

I placed my hand on the arm, and my fingers locked onto the wood just before I felt a blast of rage.

The tree was upset. My skin burned. I tried to yank my hand back but couldn't.

One of the male wolves moved forward to help me, but Willow held him back. Then she knelt, and everyone else did the same.

Pain coursed through my body, and my knees buckled underneath me.

"It took you long enough to realize who I am. Now you come to me?"

The pain vanished, and I pressed my head on top of her large roots. Hell hath no fury like a woman scorned. This tree was female. Her voice was in my head and rang through my bones.

Fear crawled up my spine. "I'm sorry, your ... majesty?"

Coolness slipped into my blood next, and I was immediately filled with relief. I took a breath.

"Day after day, I called you, and you did not come. Then when you finally did, you forgot me."

I swallowed. "Well, I'm not really outdoorsy, but that could totally change. I'll pick back up on *Pokémon Go*. I'll be the most outdoorsy nerd ever."

"Never mind that, witch." Her highness was as temperamental as me. *"You will listen and do as I instruct."*

"The sass is strong in this one."

"Don't mock me. I rest, yet I am still powerful."

"This is you at rest?" My fingertips started to burn again. "Sorry! Sorry! Habit."

"It is time you left for the fae world, Lorena. My brother is in need of help."

"Your brother?"

"The Old One. The Court of Fire threatens him. You will go to the Court of Water and gain their alliance."

"Can't your brother talk to the Court of Waters?"

"No, it must be you. You have what they need."

I could feel her voice pulse against my fingers, but I couldn't see her face like I could the other tree. "Oh yeah? What's that?"

"They will tell you once you arrive. Now go. Take your vampires with you. The journey will be long. Once you return, I will wake, and magic will once again flow in his world."

"Wait, but ..." I leaned close, so Aisling wouldn't hear. "The vampires have to sleep during the day. I'd probably travel faster without them." What could I say? The snooty princess had a point.

"Your new mate will help you with this."

My new mate? I didn't have any new mates. Alan and Dimitri had been with me since the beginning. Zane came right after them. Ewan was kind of new, but not really. If anything, I'd spent the most time …

"Oh …" It hit me then. The new mate was the guy I was still convinced wasn't my mate at all. "You mean Sirius. Are you serious?"

"As a heart attack."

"Haha."

She let me go. Strings of sap came away with my hand. A brown glob of it covered my palm. I tucked away my disgust and turned to the house so I could wash my hands.

But I was stopped by the fae before I could get too far. One of the male fae stepped forward. His hair was every shade of blond that existed. The curls fell to his brow and around his sculpted chin. He grabbed my hand and stuck my finger into his mouth.

His blue eyes held mine as he swirled his tongue around my finger.

I snatched my hand back, but by then, he was already moaning with pleasure. His eyes glowed.

"Woah." What the heck was in the sap? Meth?

More people moved in, swiping their fingers against my hand to get more of the goop, but Willow moved them back, or at least she tried, but they were fighting to get close.

"Lorena, eat the gift, or they will."

I sniffed the goo, and then I took a lick.

It was actually pretty good. I liked it. It was gone faster than I realized I'd eaten it, then a rush swept through my blood. Power pulsed in my veins and in my head. My vision sharpened, and the iridescent magic thread showed up everywhere and hummed with power. They were stung through the air and rested on the frozen patch of dirt and beyond.

"How long will this last?" I asked.

"Not long," Willow said. "The gift is meant to be given."

But who could I give this to?

I thought about Wei in the stone. What if I could open the soul stone now? Then Wei would come to me, and I'd be happy.

But the world around us would still be in danger.

Quietly, I set that dream away and focused on the present. I needed to get a hold of myself.

The tree, who was much like the Old One, hadn't bothered to give me a name, and said Sirius could help me.

So, I went to the basement.

Aisling was walking close. She watched me, but I could tell her thoughts were heavy.

"Question. If I'm such a hot commodity in the fae world, why did it take this long for Corridan to come after me?"

"First, he needed to get a key to come here. Second, he needed a seer to find you. Third, you spent most of your time indoors, so whenever he got close, you'd go back inside, and he'd lose you. Colt Valley was the last place I thought you'd be."

"Sorry."

"No matter. What did the tree tell you?"

I stopped in front of the door to the basement. "You should stay up here." No one needed to deal with her temper and mine. I needed Sirius alive, and I couldn't deal with her threats right now.

Aisling was staring at the door. "Give me the woman, and I'll back down."

"You'll back down, or you'll be escorted to a room. I was once held in one that had no windows and no doors. It could only be opened from the outside. Perhaps, you'd like that accommodation."

Aisling crossed her arms and tapped her foot. "Very well. I'll wait here. You'll go deal with the witch and her dog." Now she was the one giving commands, and since they were my wishes as well, I couldn't throw them back in her face.

"He's not a dog." That's all I had at the moment. I'd probably think of some snappy come back later, but by then, it would be too late. The joke would have grown cold.

I swung open the door, and it flew off the hinges and remained in my hand. The solid wood felt light as a feather. Whatever was in that sap had cranked up my physical strength.

I turned to my audience and passed the door to William.

Two of his wolves closed in behind me and became the new door once I started down the steps.

Sirius's voice echoed in the black. He'd turned off the lights. "I hope you come bearing gifts because I'm famished." He'd returned to his North American dialect.

"No gifts. No food."

"Doesn't matter. I'm sure I can find something else to eat." He bit out the last word. I waited for fear to hit me like a linebacker but instead … dammit! I was kind of aroused.

It was impossible to see anything in the dark, but the magic was still beating like an EDM song, so in a blank, the threads came up, and I was able to make Sirius out in the dark. The magic took on a neon shade.

He hadn't released Lilac. She was still strapped to the chair.

Sirius himself was only a few feet away from me. When he reached out for me, I didn't stop him.

Being a creature of the night, he didn't need light. He was nocturnal. Or, at least he was supposed to be. I didn't know anything about him except for the basics. His name. He was a vampire but not by Vlad. Once upon a time, he'd been in a relationship with Lilac.

And according to Her Majesty the Tree, now he was supposed to be with me.

He wrapped his fingers around my wrist and then slid his hands to my waist.

I shoved him away, and he stumbled back.

"You're stronger." His surprise penetrated the dark.

"Yeah, I am." I looked over at Lilac. "You didn't pick her up."

"She's asleep. I thought it best I let her rest. She hasn't slept this well in half a century. I don't want to disturb her."

I still didn't understand this guy's deal? Why live with the ex? Why come for me? Had he really seen us written in the stars? I supposed if werewolves, fairies, and vampires could be real, then anything was possible. "You're going to come with me."

"I like this idea already," he growled.

"Upstairs!" I shrilled. "You're going to come with me upstairs, and you're going to answer my questions the first time I ask them. Do you understand?"

"I do."

"Great. Follow me."

"To my death," he promised.

We went up to the game room. The space reminded me of Alan and soothed me. I pictured the place how it had been the night I'd returned from the fae world. The entire mansion had looked like someone had taken wrecking balls to every room. This was the room that had pained me the most.

Aged games and precious crystals from Alan's past had been destroyed. Card games that had once been worn and used gaily had all been tossed, and the room redesigned with pieces he'd found at auctions. The entire room had been redone but not reimagined. If you ignored the electric lights, stepping into the game room was like stepping back into time.

Some of the tables, games, and chairs were from the French Revolution. All of it had cost him an arm and a leg.

There was only once space that threw everything left.

For me, Alan had done something special. A large TV was set up on the back wall with every game system ever built, including Atari.

He'd shared this special place with me, making me feel at home.

Which explained why I said what I said next, "Break anything, and I'll break you."

The wolves escorted Sirius upstairs. He had to be the most confident prisoner I'd ever seen.

He winked and sat in a high wingback chair across from the ornate couch I took for myself. There were a few leathers on the other side of the room, but I didn't want to take him deeper into the space than we already were. The air smelled like Alan, his scent calming, and alluring.

Aisling sat down beside me, twisted to the side, and crossed one ankle over the other before tucking them back. I didn't know if she was aware of her good posture. Was she doing it as a means to intimidate him with her good pedigree? It could be both, I realized. This was the way Aisling had acted before we had formed our temperamental friendship.

"Where are Jenny, Marquessa, and Blair?"

"Sleeping upstairs," Aisling said. "The witches decided it best that everyone remains together."

I liked the idea of everyone staying close. It would lower the chances of anyone going missing before we could formulate a plan of action, and as Testy the Tree had declared, we didn't have much time.

Willow sat on my other side. She was graceful but, in a way, very different from Aisling. While the princess of the Unseelie moved in a way that denoted nobility, Willow moved with a sense of awareness that was closer to a cat. She moved like the room had been made for her, like every step would be written down and logged into a book.

But both of the fae women sat rigidly in the cushion and looked ready to pounce at a moment's notice.

I wondered what Willow was capable of. She was just as sweet as candy I couldn't imagine her ever going sour.

I sat with my legs spread and my knees resting on top. The power inside me was so strong that I was sure I could move nothing more than my finger to knock someone out. I felt like I'd gone into Starbucks and ordered a venti in every flavor. I could feel it jolting around in my mind, sparking like a live wire. I needed his stuff out of me and now.

"How are you awake right now?" I spoke again before he could say something stupid. "Don't waste my time?"

His gaze deemed. Then he pointed to his ear or, more importantly, the earring. "Lilac enchanted it for me. It changes my biology. Makes me ... less dead."

No wonder he moved like a human.

And why my power could recognize him but was stunted at the same time. I couldn't read his mind any more than I could read anyone else who wasn't a vampire. He no longer recognized me as his master. My necromancy was muted.

"Great. I need her to do it ... four more times." I needed an object for Alan, Dimitri, Zane, and ... My thoughts ran out when I thought about how odd Zane had been during our last confrontation. "You already gave one to Zane, didn't you?"

"Aye. I gave him my ring." He rubbed his thumb over the empty finger. I usually keep two objects on me at all times, just in case someone gets the clever idea to remove one during the day.

I remembered the black ring Zane wore. He'd told me he was hiding something. Now I knew what he was hiding. Sirius. He'd known about Sirius for weeks. Why would Zane help him? What was going on? Those were questions I had to put on hold, seeing as my brain would explode at any moment from all the power.

"So, if I took your earring out …"

"I'd be all yours."

"Or you'd burn to a crisp in the sun," Aisling said.

He met her eyes and her challenge. "Exactly."

"No one is dying." And more than ever, I was glad I'd saved Lilac's life. Apparently, she was part of this prophecy as well. Oddly enough, it felt good to know I wasn't alone in this. For a long time, the focus seemed to be on me and my womb. Now, there were others involved. We were assembling like the Justice League.

I stood, needing to move around the room. I was aware of the eyes that followed me, mainly Sirius. The guy was a walking boner. "We need to wake up Lilac."

"We also need Marco's corpse," Sirius said.

I almost tripped but managed to catch myself on thin air. "What?"

"The spell requires the bones of a necromancer."

The power burned my skin. "Wait. Did you …?"

He held up his hands. "I had no intention of killing him. We just needed a few bones. Lilac regrew them, but the process was long."

"How could you?"

He pushed onto his feet. "Lorena …"

I shoved him with my magic. He cried out and looked down at his chest. There was a burn hole in his shirt, and his skin was charred.

I nearly threw up and spun away.

"Lorena!" Willow cried. Her fingers trembled by her lips.

"What?" I turned to the gilded mirror by the windows in the room and saw it. I looked like Johnny Storm. My hands were on fire, but they didn't burn me. I took a deep breath and tried to call back the power. The flames extinguished, but the power surges were still inside me.

"We're not touching Marco without his permission." I turned back to Sirius.

He now stood a distance away from me. The only sense of pain in his face was his labored breathing.

"What did you do to Marco? Why can't I control him?"

He struggled to speak. I'd burned the blithe right out of him. "His corpse wears one of the objects we created from his bones with a confusion spell on top. The confusion spell only works for a time."

That had to be the most twisted thing I'd ever heard. He'd killed Marco and then used his own bones against him. "Stay away from me."

Sirius closed his eyes and nodded. "As you wish."

"Where's the body?" I asked.

"We buried him behind my house."

I worked to fight down my anger and the sickness that kept rising whenever I thought about my lips on his. I didn't care what Lady Tree said. He was not my lover, and he'd never be. "I have to go see Marco and ask his permission before we do this."

"He's confused," Sirius reminded me. "He can't give permission."

I didn't bother telling him that the touch of a necromancer had cleared Marco's mind. He didn't deserve to know, and he wouldn't get another thing from me. I avoided his eyes as I left the house.

I got into my old powder-blue VW Bug and gunned it for my house.

I was pretty sure there were people who'd wanted to come with me. I was pretty sure some of them followed me in their own transportation. I hadn't even told anyone what to do with Sirius while I was gone.

And a part of me didn't care what they did to him. Aisling could go back to using him for a pin cushion for all I cared. He'd taken bones against someone's will so that he could walk in the sun. I couldn't get past that. I didn't think I would.

And Zane was in on it?

I had to reevaluate my feelings for Zane.

I pulled up in front of my house and noticed another car in the driveway.

"Dad!" I sprinted to the door and ended up blowing the wood right off the frame. "Dammit!"

I chucked the door into the yard and found my dad in the living room, staring down at Marco.

The first thing that hit me was the suit. My dad, while a businessman, only wore a suit on special occasions. I'd been ready to see him in his khakis, button-down, and comfy loafers. This man before me didn't look like he knew what comfy loafers were.

His dark hair was pushed back. The gray was more defined than when I last saw him. Everything about him was sharper like in HD. The black suit was custom built for his average size but made him stand out in a way that made him foreign to my eyes.

He rubbed his hands idly at his sides, and I noticed something poke around from around his feet.

"Maahes." I'd barely said the tabby's name before he was walking toward me. "Have you been with dad this whole time?"

He rubbed his soft nose against my fingers, and I picked him up.

Dad spoke, and his voice was the only thing I recognized. "What's wrong with Marco?"

"He's dead." I rubbed my tabby's back as he purred in my arms. The sound. The slight weight of his body. The motion of my hand was all familiar. They grounded me as I faced off with this stranger that looked like my father.

His demeanor had changed. It too was sharper. More distinct. His power levels were just a few pegs lower than what I was rocking.

"Did someone die?" I asked. "I mean, someone other than Marco? You look like you're going to a funeral."

His face softened. I didn't really look like my dad, but when we stood together, people said they saw the resemblance. I don't know if they were just saying that to be nice or if it was true.

"No, I've moved up with the company. I wear a suit now."

"Cool." I didn't know if that was cool or not. I didn't know if dad liked wearing the suit, but I was happy about the promotion.

"I'm sorry about Marco," he said. "I know how much you'd grown to care for him during the months that you trained with him."

"Thanks, and thanks for the Dr. Pepper."

"I'm glad you liked it." He remained across the room. He'd never been big on hugs. I was used to it. We'd grown closer in the last few weeks. He called me sometimes and sent me those care packages, but I couldn't remember the last time we'd embraced. "You can have my car if you want. I got a new one."

Dad's car was the same; it had always been except for the model. This VW was newer. He was a VW guy. "I also paid off your debt." Dad cleared his throat. "It's the least I could do."

"Well, I'd wondered why the creditors had stopped calling."

Willow and Aisling walked in behind me along with Jenny and Blair. My friends looked like they'd just rolled out of bed. None of us had slept for long, but I was wide awake thanks to her majesty.

"Is Sirius still alive?" I asked.

"For now." Aisling moved around me to stare down at Marco's body.

Dad asked, "What have you been up to?" Was this his version of small talk, or did he actually care?

"Oh, you know. I've just been … trying not to die. Same 'ole, same 'ole. You?"

Aisling touched Marco, and I could already feel the twinge of anger rising. Ghost or not, she was invading his space and annoying the heck out of me.

I let Maahes down and then walked over to Marco.

Sadness struck me again as I thought about what his life had become. He'd stayed in Colt Valley for me, and now he was dead because of me. The least I could do was make sure he rested in peace. I reached underneath him and took out the lapis lazuli.

I grabbed Marco's hand and felt his body reanimate. Then he opened his eyes and turned his head to me. I started to tear up before he smiled.

"Lorena."

"I have a favor to ask you. Know that you can say no." My voice was cracking like bloodied knuckles. This whole conversation hurt.

His voice was kind. "There is still something I could give you? Name it, and it is yours."

CHAPTER SIXTEEN

Never in my life had I ever wanted to be the sort of person who enjoyed talking about pleasantries and dancing around the issue more than that moment. I wanted to talk about mundane things like the weather and what Kardashian was doing what, but the truth was the truth, and I couldn't dance around it. "I need some of your bones."

Marcos's eyes fluttered close. "Ah. The bones of a necromancer. They are a powerful thing. Make sure you protect yours, Lorena."

"I hadn't even thought about using my own for this. Maybe I should …"

He shook his head. "No. Use mine. They are older and more powerful. They've aged and soaked in magic for many decades while yours, though powerful, are still young."

"Oh. Then okay. Can we use yours?"

I heard my dad release some pent-up fear. He hadn't wanted me to do it, and it was only then I realized I couldn't have done it anyway. My baby needed my bones.

Thankfully, Marco said, "I'd be honored to know that part of me goes on."

I rode in the backseat of my dad's car since I would have ended up in a ditch on a count of my watery eyes. I was also still holding Marco's hand. Until we got one of the talismans off Marco, I wouldn't let him go.

Maahes rode on my lap, and I couldn't help but think he knew I needed the comfort.

Marco didn't say anything until we were walking along the side of Sirius's house. Frozen snow crunched underneath my feet. "So, my vampires will wear my bones. That means we'll forever be close."

I smiled at him and asked, "Why did you warn me away from Dr. Shaw?"

"I remembered that Lilac was looking for her before she killed me. The trance Blair put me under helped me remember everything my traumatized mind had forgotten."

His mind opened to me, and I saw it. He was in a cement room with Lilac. But likely wasn't moving. I stared closer and realized it wasn't Lilac. Marco's memories told me this. The life-size doll was Lilac's sister. She was creepy looking and identical to Lilac in every way.

Her name was Rosalyn. She sat in a chair, frozen in her youth.

Marco concentrated on the sightless little girl as Sirius sawed off his foot. He didn't feel any pain. A spell to numb pain had been written on his leg.

His body was strapped to a hard surface with a bright light hanging over his head.

Sirius was talking. He promised Marco he'd walked out of the room alive once he was done. He told Marco he was being used for a greater purpose. He talked about the stars and their arrangement and the return of magic being dependent upon the gift Marco was giving.

I wanted to throw up.

Sirius took the foot and promised Marco that Lilac would take care of him. Lilac stepped into the light. Unlike her villainous partner, she wore a smile as she spoke to Marco. She enjoyed torturing him, but she made sure to hide her hate from Marco. She didn't want to heal him, but she'd do anything for Sirius.

Her tone turned condescending when Sirius left the room. Lilac wanted him dead. She believed his life was hoarding power from the universe. She said the less magical people there were, the more power there would be for her to resurrect her sister.

She was crazy. At least, she sounded crazy. I wasn't sure if she was right. I knew that magic was a form of energy, and it depended on energy, but I figured it was more kinetic. The more people who used it, the more available it became. That was my philosophy, but I didn't know if it was right.

I wanted Lilac to be wrong, but my own thoughts quieted when Marco's memories took over again.

Lilac washed the numbing spell away. Then she lifted her hands, and the pain came like an avalanche. Marco was smothered by it to the point of fainting. He screamed as Lilac regrew a portion of his foot. Muscle knit around the new bone. Then she stopped, said she was tired and would continue tomorrow.

She left him like that. His foot looked mangled by a beast. Sirius didn't return. The pain remained.

Marco bled out and died. He died alone. Cold and in pain.

"Sirius said it was an accident," I said.

"Sirius believes it was an accident, but Lilac killed me on purpose," Marco said. "I was a ghost when he returned. Lilac completed my foot after I died."

"How? I thought she could only deal with living things?"

"She took parts of me from other places that Sirius couldn't see. Part of my brain was used to replace the muscle, and my back was plied away to make skin for my foot."

"She's one twisted puppy."

"Yes, a bitch," he clarified. The word had never been more appropriate than in that instant. "And very obsessive about healing her sister. I believe Sirius feels an encumbering amount of guilt over her passing."

Part of me wondered if Sirius had been intimate with Rosalyn as well.

We made it to his grave too soon. There was no marker to indicate where his body was buried, and I realized that Sirius never told me where to look. He'd said the body was behind the house and he knew I would find it. The bones of the necromancer called to me.

I looked around at the party who had accompanied me. Dad, Jenny, Blair, Willow, and Aisling. No one had brought a shovel, which meant I was going to have to raise Marco.

I'd never made a zombie before, and Marco was one of the last people I wanted to do this to.

He seemed to sense my thoughts. "It won't be me."

"I know."

"I'm standing right next to you. What comes out of that grave won't be me. Do what you must do, just like I showed you."

I took a breath and closed my eyes. With another breath, I shut out everything around me and focused on the ground. I reached out with my magic and felt the bones of the dead slap against my necromancy like a magnetic.

The feeling of the dead-dead was different than the living-dead. While my men felt full of life, these bones felt empty. There was a craving for fullness, for wholeness that could only actually be filled with a soul. This made sense considering what I'd read about zombies. Their craving was a hunger, and they would feast gluttonously until they got what they really wanted.

Sadly, souls were hard to come by and even harder to infuse with the dead. Marco had told me the story of an older necromancer, the only one he'd ever known to have taken a body and the soul of a living person and infuse the two.

The implanted soul went mad and killed himself in less than a day.

I felt the dry bones underneath my feet and even the ones that were spread out in the meadow. Many people had died in these mountains, and I wondered about their story. Had there been a war in Colt Valley? The bones were too old to belong to victims of Lilac, then again, maybe not. How old was Lilac?

I focused my search for the freshest bones in the ground and commanded them to rise.

Nothing happened.

Marco, at my side, grasped and let out a funny but wondrous laugh. "I can feel that. Try again. I'll let you in this time."

"It probably won't work with the talisman still on you."

"No, it will work," Marco promised. "I'm giving you control."

I concentrated again. The body twitched down my line of magic. Then it lifted his hands and began to dig.

It was pretty silent for a while. In the movies, the ground shakes, and the amplified music makes the entire experience more grandiose than it actually is.

"Can you feel what your body is doing?" I asked.

He shook his head. "No, I lost the connection once you took control. I can't feel anything anymore." His voice fell on one of the last words.

It had to be odd being on the other side of this. The necromancer has become the necromanced ... or whatever. Either way, it was an experience I hoped never to have. When I died, I wanted to be left alone.

Eventually, the sound of shuffling underneath the earth grew louder. Then fingers broke through the ground. More digging went on, and then a head came out and shoulders.

I didn't want to look, but I had no choice. Marco's body was bloated and ashen. He was nothing like the elegant man from the bayou I remembered.

Grief hit me like a freight train, but the emotion wasn't coming from me but the ghost at my side.

"Oh." He covered his mouth. "I'm dead. I didn't ... This is ..."

Tears fell from my eyes. The truth hit differently when you came face to face with it.

Marco's body was cringeworthy. His eyes were sightless, and his body remained motionless as it waited for its next command.

If I let him do as he wanted, he'd go hunting for a soul. He'd try to eat everyone in the field, but so long as I kept him on a leash, he'd do anything I said.

I heard a gasp from behind me, and my eyes met Blair's. Jenny had her head down but couldn't fight the urge to keep looking up. Aisling was wound tight and kept her features composed, but her eyes betrayed her. She was disturbed as was Willow, who took a step back. What I was doing probably went against something she believed. She dropped to the ground and touched the grass. It seemed to help.

Dad was staring at Marco's body like he was a monster, which in a sense, he was, but then Dad looked at me, and with it came all his repulsion at what I'd just done.

And honestly, I didn't blame him. I didn't like this part of my magic either. It was dark, which meant I was dark. I had the power to turn your wildest nightmares into reality, but in theory, so could any other gift. It was all about how you used it, and I had no plans of using this gift to curse others.

I didn't blame my dad for hating what I did, but it hurt. I didn't like being a part of this prophecy any more than anyone else, but I was sure I had my ability for a reason.

Marco whispered, "I don't want her to see me like this."

I didn't know who he was talking about until I followed his line of sight.

Blair was pale and holding her mouth in the universal sign of trying not to vomit.

I yanked the cord on the mythical energy to Marco's body. His animation ceased, and he dropped to the ground.

Marco and I walked over to his body, and I looked for the object that was keeping him from my complete control. I found it in his ear. A black hoop hung from his ear. I took it out and pocketed it.

Marco took a breath as I gradually let go of his hand. "How do you feel?"

"I feel … free."

He looked at his dead form and then back at me. "Thank you, Lorena."

A hard thumping started in my chest, traveled up my throat, and pounded in my ears. "Are you leaving now?"

He nodded. "Yes, I feel like I should. I'm getting the impression that I'm needed elsewhere."

"Are you sure? You could always stick around like Maahes? I could use a ghost sidekick. You could be my Robin."

He touched his shoulder. "This is goodbye. I am forever glad to have met you, friend."

I said nothing else before the sorrow in my throat had expended to the point that air couldn't pass through.

He turned away and looked at Blair.

He walked over to her and kissed her kiss.

She shivered and looked around. "He's by me, isn't he?" Her abilities made her sensitive to spirits.

I placed my hands on my hips. "He is, and he's going to be on his best behavior."

Marco murmured. "You know, there's something familiar about her."

"Maybe you knew her doppelganger many years ago."

Marco tilted his head. "No, I mean her energy. There's something special about her, Lorena." He turned to me. "Watch over her, or I'll come back haunt you." He winked and vanished.

Blair's eyes flickered with weariness. "What did he say?"

"That I should look out for you." I left out the threat.

Blair looked as perturbed by his words as I felt.

Jenny shivered but not because she was sensing a ghost. "Can we grab something to carry the body so we can get out of here?"

My dad got up into the house. I noticed his magic was more fluid. Where once there'd been doubts and hesitation clouding his brow, I saw acceptance. He was a man who'd run from himself and had been in hiding just as much as he'd hidden me. He hadn't trusted the witch inside him. Instead, he'd harbored fear and hate.

But as this man in the suit held up his hands to the electric lock and moved in his fingers in forms of symbols and numbers, I got the sense that I was genuinely looking at another person.

I was riveted even as I wished he'd move a little faster. The cold was starting to get to me.

I heard the fancy lock beep, the lock slid open, then Dad tried the knob and pushed his way inside.

He held open the door, and we all rushed inside. I shook the frost and mud from my boots and sighed at the warmth in the house.

"This is a nice place," my father said as he walked deeper into the house.

"Yes, I agree. It's lovely." Aisling walked to the kitchen and looked around. "What do you wrap a dead body in?"

"There might be some plastic bags in there."

Jenny said, "I'll check the garage for larger bags."

"I'll get blankets," Blair said, going in the other direction.

Dad roamed away, seemingly more interested in the house than the reason we were inside. He was acting strange, but I could only deal with one strange person at a time, and at the moment, my dad was the least deadly of the two.

I walked over to the other side of the kitchen counter and braced my hands on the cool marble top. I watched Aisling for a moment and realized that no matter how great she looked in the leather, she also looked out of place. Now that I knew my dad had paid my debt, I really needed to find her tailor. I decided I would try to reach out to Aisling again, just like I did a few months ago.

"What's up with you? You're different."

Aisling looked up from where she was crouched by a cabinet. "Different? I didn't know me then, and you don't know me now."

"And yet, here I am still trying to be your friend."

She paused and caught my eyes. "The man I loved not only turned out to be my half-brother, but he also tried to kill me."

"Yeah, that would hurt."

She shook her head. "And not only did he try to kill me, but he would have done it in the most humiliating way. I'd have been executed for a crime I didn't commit, and all of fae would have known and cursed my name." She swallowed and turned away. "That sort of hate … I will never understand what I did to cause it."

She'd done nothing. I was learning that fact myself. Crazy couldn't be defined with reason. Crazy was crazy. But what I feared most was Aisling turning into The Punisher.

The Punisher was often seen as a superhero when, in reality, he was just as much the villain as the men he murdered. He took justice into his own hands and was willing to risk the lives of anyone who got in his way. His journey began with pain, and in the comics, it always ends the same.

Maybe I had my own screws loose for constantly trying to reach out to a woman who looked more ready to stab my hand than shake it, but I was who I was.

"You didn't do anything, Aisling. Corridan is responsible for his choices. He wanted power and recognition. And honestly, he probably just wanted his father's love, but Oberon deprived him of that when he rejected him and his mother." Corridan's mom had been a servant the king had carried on an affair with.

Aisling grunted and peeked at me from around her shoulder. "He wasn't the only one Oberon ignored or disregarded. He wasn't the only one he underestimated either." She checked another cabinet and pulled out a roll of white trash bags. "Corridan could have told me, Lorena. He should have trusted me." Her eyes saddened. "But instead, he betrayed me when he knew he was all I had. So, excuse me if you believe I have been altered in some moral capacity because I have."

"How did it feel?"

"What?"

"Killing Corridan?"

155

She stroked the counter with her fingers. "I didn't kill him. He fell down the stairs and broke his neck."

"Have you ever killed anyone?"

She shook her head. "But I wanted to kill him." When her gaze caught mine again, there were tears in her eyes. "And as wrong as it may sound considering our kinship, I wanted him to tell me it was all a lie. I wanted him to say he loved me. Even though we could no longer be what I'd hoped for, I wanted to know his affection had been genuine."

I walked about the counter and grabbed her hands. "You know who loves you?"

"Who?"

"Ewan. He's gone because he went looking for you."

She scoffed. "No, Lorena. Your fiancé doesn't care about me."

"That's not true. Yes, he talked about saving the kingdom and even your mother, but I remember the first words that left his lips before he told me he was leaving. He said he was leaving to find you. Those were also his last words. He couldn't stay with me because he thought you were in danger. He loves you, Aisling. You two may have always been at odds, but he cares."

Her eyes watered, and then the tears broke. She threw her arms around me, and I hugged her back. This was far from the reaction I'd been expecting, but if it made her feel better, I'd take it. I let her sob into my shoulder. We stayed together long enough for the rest of the gang to join us and find us still locked in an embrace.

Blair and my dad returned together, and I could tell they'd been talking about me as they came around the corner. Blair couldn't meet my eyes and kept her chin tucked into the large blanket in her arms.

Jenny had found large black trash bags, so we wrapped the body into two of them, placing one at the feet and other at the top and then folded Marco into the blanket before heading home.

I sat next to my dad on the drive back. Marco was bundled in the back. I wanted to address the strangeness I was getting from my dad, but I was drained from my conversation with Aisling.

I ended up napping instead. While the walk from the house to the mansion could take thirty minutes if you cut through the field, it was a little longer via the road.

When we arrived, I felt a little better.

"How are you liking Dr. Shaw?" he asked. "When we talked, you were at odds with her."

Dad had called me last week to talk about Dr. Shaw. He was worried about my health, and until that morning, I thought he was one of the few who actually cared about me and not just the baby. Now I knew Dr. Shaw cared about me as well.

"We buried the hatchet. I like her."

"You do?" His shock didn't surprise me.

I might have gone on at length about my rivalry with Dr. Shaw. "She's nice."

Dad shook his head and chuckled. Then he grabbed my hand. "I'm glad you're getting along."

"Was that what you and Blair were talking about at the house?"

He nodded and opened his door. "I was a little worried."

I stopped him from getting out. "Hey, so … what was that you did to the door back there? I thought you could only write your spells on paper."

He shrugged. "I've been working on my magic. I had someone help me understand how to cast my spells onto the threads of magic. It came easily. You inspired me to grow, Lorena."

My mouth fell open, and I swore that if it weren't blistering cold outside, I'd have been catching all the flies. My dad felt inspired by me. He'd never said anything like this before. "I'm glad I could help. Is magic how you got your promotion?"

His face colored. "More or less. Yes, I've been using magic."

"Hey, you're still doing the mathematical work. I'm proud of you." I don't think I've ever said those words to my dad.

He squeezed my hand until it nearly broke. His face was tense. Then he rushed from the car and traipsed toward the house. I was tempted to go after him, but the sound of the back door opening got my attention.

William and a pointy-eared fae named Asher were getting Marco from the back seat. He wasn't Unseelie and, therefore, just as affected by the cold as Aisling and me. He was bundled up in a hoodie and sweats.

I barely saw Asher. He was usually off somewhere screwing one or more people.

He winked a crystal-blue eye at me before he turned back to William.

I went inside and stopped at the vision I hadn't prepared myself to see.

Zane was up and walking during the day. Technically, nightfall was only an hour away, but this was just another example of the secrets he'd been keeping. "I suppose you know the truth now."

William and Asher walked past me with Marco's body, and everything I'd experienced in the last few hours came rushing back. "How could you be a part of this? How could you do this to Marco?"

He stepped forward. "Can we discuss this in private?"

"I can't talk to you right now."

He grabbed my hand, and I pushed him back. A touch of power pulsed through me, and he shuffled back but managed to catch himself before he fell. "Lorena."

"You lied!" I shook my head. "You're always lying to me."

He winced and hung his head. "I didn't lie to you, Lorena. I just withheld the truth."

"It's the same thing."

"No." He looked up. "There are things I can't tell you." He looked pained. "I want to tell you, but I can't."

"Why not?"

"It isn't time. Things must happen the way they are happening for a reason."

His words sounded like a reiteration of someone else's words. And there was only one seer in the vicinity that I was aware of. "Sirius told you to keep it from me."

"Yes," he confessed. He stepped forward. "Everything that I do is for you, Lorena."

"How can I trust you?"

His dark eyes held so much sorrow. It took everything in me not to fall prey to his display of emotions. Then he touched my stomach. "I'm the father."

My body stiffened, and my brain stopped working. My thoughts abandoned me. I tried to reboot my mind, but it quit on me every time.

Zane was the father?

He moved in. The space between us shrunk until there was almost nothing left. His nearness did things to my mind and my body. He stroked my hip and lowered his head. "I've been more or less trying to figure out how it happened and how best to protect you," he whispered. "I've never been a father before, and until this prophecy, I never thought it was possible. Children were only for the living."

I understood his confusion, but that didn't excuse the secrets. "I'd never been a mother before, Zane. You should have come to me. Instead, you kept this from me."

He reached for my face, and I smacked his hand away, knocking his ring against my knuckle. Pain ricocheted up my arm. I stared down at the offending object and felt genuine hatred for it.

"I didn't know the bone came from Marco," he said. "I only knew that I had to wear it to keep you from knowing what I know."

"Are you keeping anything else from me?"

"Yes."

"And you're not going to tell me?"

"Fate cannot be interrupted."

"And you think I'll do something to throw it off," I concluded.

His knees gave from underneath him, but he caught himself. "I know you will, Lorena."

"Why?" How bad was the future? What was going to happen? Did I die? Were Zane and the guys going to raise my baby without me? "Tell me."

"I can't."

"Then, don't talk to me again."

He backed away, and I watched acceptance cover his features. "All right, Lorena. As you wish."

That was it? That was all I got?

The hurt I felt was fathomless. The bottomless pit of blackness spread through my chest and hardened my heart. "I'm not going to let you hurt me again. I won't keep you from the baby, but we can't be together anymore."

I saw a single tear fall down his face before he turned away. "You may reject me, but I will always be yours, and you will always be my queen." He left in a rush, flying from the room in a blink.

CHAPTER SEVENTEEN

I became aware of my audience a moment later. I'd just broken up with one of my boyfriends in front of everyone.

I ran up to my room and fell onto my bed. I bounced once and grabbed my pillow. I buried my face and screamed as I cried. My sobs were bone-chilling but quietly trapped in the fabrics of the cotton. I cried for a long time. I cried for my baby and me. I cried because my child's parents were now at odds, just like my parents had been.

I wanted better for my baby. I hoped Zane was wrong about being the father, but I also hoped he wasn't. While I couldn't be with him, I did want his baby. At least a part of him would always be mine.

I was tempted to forgive him and just put on a front of happiness, but I didn't have it in me. Lorena Meredith Quinn deserved the truth, and Zane had hurt me too many times to accept anything less.

Hours ago, my anger for Sirius had been unforgivable, but now it was murderous. He'd taken Marco, and now he'd taken Zane from me. He'd tried to take Aisling, and he'd taken Dr. Shaw as well. Who else would he steal? How much loss would I suffer until I put an end to this?

I flipped over when the need for oxygen grew too great to ignore. The air crawled into my lungs. I held back another sob.

There was a light knock on my door.

"I didn't give you permission to come in," I shouted as the door opened. A second later, I sat up.

Half of Alan's face was visible between the crack.

I looked out the window. Night had arrived during my mourning. I didn't want to get up. I didn't want to talk to anyone. I didn't want to be around anyone or to have anyone around me.

"May I come in?"

I nodded the affirmative.

All right, so maybe I did want someone around me.

Alan came in, and I smiled as I took in the fancy top and dark breeches he was wearing. The clothes were a familiarity I needed right now. While his hair had been chopped to a length that I was still getting used to his smile was everything I needed. The white lace billowed around his slim waist as he moved closer.

He was memorizing to watch in motion, like a pale dream.

He stopped beside me. I turned my legs to hang off the bed, and he stepped between them before settling his hands against my face. His touch was cold, but his presence heated me enough to melt the block of ice that had formed around my heart.

My bed sat high enough that Alan and I were still the same height.

My angel lowered his mouth to mine, and heat in my chest unfurled through my blood and right between my thighs.

I moved closer and clutched his shirt.

He drove his tongue into my mouth and licked away the doubts and pain.

I wanted more. I moved closer to the edge, and he took the hint and settled himself against me.

He knew what I wanted. I loved that he knew my craving for oblivion was strong. I needed the high to escape this low, if just for a little while. He whipped my shirt over my head and rubbed his expert thumb over the nipple that poked out through my bra. He knew what to do with me, so I stayed out of his way and let him. I cupped his manhood as his mouth descended on my other breast, inflaming my blood with his clever lips and rough tongue.

"More," I whispered, clutching him.

He groaned against my skin, and his lips trembled. "You shall have what you ask for."

He helped me out of my jeans, taking my panties with them. I ripped my bra off, and his mouth returned to playing with my flesh as it eagerly tipped underneath his rough tongue. I undid his breeches and shoved them down.

He stuck up proudly between my thighs and used his hand to guide me backward. I lay down, and he climbed over me. Foreplay was done. He knew I didn't want it or need it. I was wet and ready and aching for him to fill me.

I threw my legs around him just as he entered me.

We moaned in each other's mouths. I pulled in his essence and felt him accept mine just as I readily accepted his shaft. He skipped right past gentle and took me hard.

"Yes!" I arched my back and threw myself at him. Our skin slapped. He stroked my hair back with hand and stroked my walls as he pounded into me.

When he took me like this, I was in heaven. The first time he was rough, I was shocked. He called Dimitri his beast, but those animal senses had rubbed off on him. I stopped thinking and just felt him as he filled my aching heat.

I'm comfortable letting him be the point of my existence. I feel free as a cry for more. My words weren't coherent, but he understands them and obeys me in a way that doesn't require magic, only skill, and knowledge.

With one hand braced by my head, he rubbed my clitoris with the other, and I came. Pinned to the bed, he fed my hunger and his own, used me. His eyes glittered, and I felt him tip over right before he crashed. Like a wave, my body was consumed, and I came again. The release was so unexpected that I choked on my next breath, and my eyes watered.

He rested his head on my shoulder, and I laughed.

"Thank you." I was sticky and sweaty in the best way possible.

His body, a combination of soft and hard, filled me with nostalgia. He was like a knitted quilt, a timeless gift that I held precious. He lifted his head, and I wrapped my fingers in his golden hair.

I'd barely spoken the words, "I want it longer," before the locks began to extend in my hand. I sat up and watched his once glorious mane return to its full length and volume. It seemed more illuminating than before, but maybe that was just because I'd missed it.

He grabbed at his hair and chuckled. "You never cease to amaze me, darling."

"I didn't know I could do that." The hair felt softer and slipped from my fingers like feathers, but again my mind could be playing tricks on me.

"It makes sense that you could. You are my master. You rule the dead."

"Yeah, but I thought hair was alive."

"Technically, it's dead, but that's not the point. You're alive, and you're inside of me just as much as I'm inside of you." He wiggled his hips and winked.

My laughter bathed the air, and happiness filled me. I felt it bloom from the place Alan was inside of me, not from his shaft through. That made me happy as well, but this came from my heart.

He kissed me and pulled back. "They sent me to get you."

"They?" I asked.

"Yes. Dimitri, Jenny, and everyone else. They're waiting downstairs for you."

The sight of his lean body held some of my anger back. I wanted to lick the contours of his pale skin, but duty called. "Is Zane down there?"

He took my hand and helped me up. I bounced off the bed and onto my feet. The wood was cool.

"Zane is present with the others."

"I don't want him present with the others. I don't want him present anywhere. I don't want him around."

Alan locked my arm through his and walked me to the bathroom in the same manner he'd have walked me to a gala. We were naked and heading for the shower, but I could almost swear I was in a ballgown and him in his vest and lacy shirt.

He stopped me at the shower and made me face him. "My darling, Lorena, he's the father of the baby."

"Our baby. The baby belongs to all of us."

He grinned. "Of course, but the fact remains. He's the father. He promises he won't touch you until you give him permission."

"I'll never give him permission again." I cut on the water, and Alan stepped in with me.

I noticed his silence and asked, "Are you taking his side?"

164

He reached for my shampoo, poured it into his hands, and lathered my hair. "I'm not taking any sides. I love you. I admire Zane. He hasn't always had it easy. None of us have."

I washed his body while he worked at my roots. Then we switched. He was trying to take care of me, but I wanted to take care of him as well. The hot water beat against my aching muscles and relaxed me.

I thought about all the crappy things Zane had survived, including being changed and drained and having my sister and mother mess with his mind and use him for their own gain.

"You sound like you're taking his side."

He wrapped his arms around him and positioned us both under the fall of water. If I blinked rapidly, I could see his eyes. "I don't want to fight, Lorena."

"Well, I do."

He smiled. "I know." He kissed my nose, and I turned away.

He slid his hand up my butt, and I ignored it. Then his hands gripped my waist, and he pulled me in. I struggled to pull in a breath. He was hard again, and I was hot.

I bent over, and he needed no further instruction. I gripped the wall. He took my shoulder and easily slipped inside my hungry slit. "Alan, you feel so good."

He grunted and stilled himself as he ran his hands over my hips and up my sides. He cupped my breast and pinched my nipples, which triggered a quivering in my mound.

He shuttered.

"Don't stop," I whispered as my muscles locked around him.

His voice was heady. "You shall have what you desire." But he didn't move.

"Now, Alan!"

He bent forward. His breath bathed my shoulder then I felt the prick of his teeth right before he drove in.

He held me still and finally, finally gave it to me good. Pleasure radiated from both of the places he penetrated me. I arched my back and cried out as stars overtook my vision. This time he was slow, gliding in and out of my dripping hole in a pace that made the ache worse even as it heightened my awareness of everything else.

With his teeth, he didn't take any blood. Instead, he gave me his essence, that dark, spirited fluid that gave him life.

He licked my wounds as the shower turned cold. We got out, dressed, and walked hand in hand back to the basement. The wolf guards parted for us.

Downstairs, I looked around at the people who'd gathered. There were the people I was starting to think of as the Usual Suspects. Jenny and Marquessa, my main gang, were there along with Dimitri and Zane who's direction I avoided entirely. William and Willow, who were starting to become as dependable as my right and left hand, were standing with the wolves who stood behind Lilac and Sirius. With a snap of a finger, they'd kill them both. I could feel that murderous energy pour out of them like wild waves. It crashed into me.

They were the deadly sort of sanguine. Lilac's hand was like the infinity gauntlet. A twitch could have us all calling for the paramedic. And she had Thanos's manic rage to match it.

I saw the hate that simmered in her eyes even as I suspected she wouldn't kill me. Maybe I was the sanguine one. Maybe I was foolish. It wouldn't be the first time.

The new recruits, Blair, Dr. Shaw, and Aisling, stood close to me.

There was a metal table in the room with small ivory objects spread out. They were rings, dozens of them made out of Marco's bones with stones of different shades in each one.

Runes had been drawn with blood on the table underneath them.

My shoulders tensed.

"His purpose in this life had been fulfilled."

"Shut up!" I scream at Sirius. "I don't want to hear any more from you. Talk again, and I'll have someone gag you."

He shut his mouth, took a deep breath, and pinched his lips.

I turned to Lilac. "Where's the body?"

"How should I know?" she asked.

"We gave him a proper witch burial," William said.

"Good." I didn't know what a proper witch burial was, and I prayed I never found out. Next witch to kick the dust better be me and hopefully not for a long, long time.

"What do you need from me?" I asked.

Lilac picked up a blade that had been sitting on the edge of the table and cut her palm. "I hear you're holding a great reservoir of power."

"I'm so full I could piss myself."

She cringed at my purposefully distasteful comment. Her discomfort pleased me.

"Why are there so many rings?" I asked.

"What if you decide to whore yourself for ten more vampires?" she taunted. "This way, you don't have to keep digging up wrinkly old Marco." She had the nerve to offer me the blade right after that little speech.

Zane stepped forward, and I held up my hand. I knew he no longer took commands from me, but he obeyed. I didn't need him to fight my battles any more than I needed anyone else to do it.

I took the sharp object and considered the best way to stab her back. "William, remove Sirius's earring."

Sirius stiffened but let the commander of the wolves do as I asked.

The connection clicked into place once the object was free.

"Take it back," I told Lilac.

She tittered with laughter. "Marco is better off dead. I got tired of all that screaming."

I yanked Sirius's mystical chain, and he shuffled forward. I didn't open my mouth, just my mind. Sirius saw exactly what I wanted him to do and was no longer able to resist.

Discarding the blade, I leaned against the table and felt him come up behind me. Then I tilted my neck and watched Lilac's eyes widened as his mouth settled on the special patch of skin between my shoulder and my neck.

I shuddered at the feel of his rough beard. The hair scraped me, and then his tongue licked me.

Briefly, I closed my eyes.

Sirius locked his arms around me and got carried away.

I decided to let him, but only for a moment as I spoke to Lilac. "Do you think Sirius likes screaming?" He bumped me with the muscle between his thighs, which caused me to bump the table. The rings rattled, and I moaned. "I think you're right, Lilac. I could use more boyfriends."

Another hand landed on my hip, and now I was really putting on a show as I turned my mouth up for Dimitri's kiss. I turned to him but didn't get far without Sirius. I was sandwiched between the males. Dimitri ate my face and reminded me of what he could do with his tongue while a hand dipped into my pants. I arched to give whoever it was better access.

"All right!" Lilac shouted. "You made your point!"

Her high wails pulled me back, and I managed to untangle myself from the magic that had fallen between us. I was embarrassed by my audience, especially Dr. Shaw. I could barely recognize the woman who'd just put on that show, but I did recognize the humming between my legs. Alan had left me swollen and sore, and yet my appetite was back.

I managed to peak around and noticed more than a few of the men in the room were now sporting a stiffy.

Oops.

I returned Sirius to his position and allowed him to take his earring back from William. He winked at me as he put it back in.

I rolled my eyes and picked the blade up again. "Let's do this." I cut my hand and felt the power boom through the room and rattle the house right before Lilac covered my hand with hers and began to recite words with a Celtic tongue.

The rings rattled against the metal.

The blood on the table deepened in color until it was ink black. Then it swam and sought the rings.

The runes sifted power from my blood. My heart weakened, and my eyes clouded.

My knees dipped. Dimitri caught me.

I managed to stay awake until the end.

Lilac had not. Sirius caught her, and I tried not to notice the tenderness he used to hold her unconscious body. My emotions were all messed up.

When I was strong enough, I straightened back onto my own two feet and picked up one of the rings. The sapphire reminded me of Alan's eyes, so I held it out to him.

Alan approached me and held out his hand. "I do."

I laughed and slipped it into his left hand.

He cupped my cheeks and kissed me.

I did the same for Dimitri. I gave him a ruby to match his passion.

He kissed me more fervently than Alan had. I was almost ready to let him throw me onto the table, but I remembered our audience this time and whispered, "Later." The boyfriend calendar was off-kilter, and I didn't know where to start arranging it again.

Jenny handed me a black velvet bag, and I put the other rings inside and counted them. There were ten left. Silently, I thanked Marco for his gift as I held them to my chest.

I didn't want to think about what Sirius said, but the words snuck up on me anyway.

His purpose has been fulfilled. I only hoped Marco felt the same way.

Fate was a wicked DJ who was changing the tempo of the music at every turn. I didn't know what was going on half the time. One minute, I was sure I knew the steps, and the next, I was spinning around in circles and looking for the quickest way off the dancefloor, but the music never stopped. The bass grew heavier by the day, but I could tell we were close to the end of the night.

Everyone but Zane met in the dining room when it was time to eat. I was glad he didn't join us. It had been hard being in the basement with him. I needed time away from him. Thankfully, we were planning to leave for the fae world in the next few hours. I was ready to see something outside of Colt Valley. Living here was starting to feel too much like *The Truman Show*.

Dad joined us for the meal, but he couldn't stay after. He'd only stopped by to visit on his way to DC. He was doing big things now. "Stay safe, Lore."

"I will."

"Promise me." The worry in his gaze made my chest tight.

It hit me that I was all Dad had in the world. Now that he was back on the road without me, he had to be lonely. Even though I could still feel the distance of past hurts and failures between us, at least when we'd been together, there'd been someone in the car to share the radio with.

Now it was just him and the concrete.

"I promise to be safe. I'll also try to be back in time so you can meet your grandkid."

His face softened. "I'll be on the first plane back." He squeezed my hand before he strolled out of the dining room.

I heard the door close and felt the urge to call him back and beg him to stay. The thought savagely ripped through my mind. I should stop him.

But I didn't.

After we ate, we went to the living room to work out the final details. I told them what the tree had told me. We needed to get to the Court of Water, where I would give them something that they wanted in exchange for their help in the war.

Aisling didn't see how the Court of Water could compete with the Seelie or the Unseelie armies seeing as their people were water-based and mostly healers, but she didn't argue. Apparently, even she knew to respect the trees.

Aisling had two keys, Corridan's, which actually belonged to Oberon, and the one she'd stolen from the palace.

We were trying to decide the best route to the Court of Water. Corridan's eye would take us to the front of the Seelie Castle while Aisling would take us to the Unseelie Castle.

The Seelie Castle was closer to the Court of Water but more dangerous to approach.

"They'll trail us to the Court of Water if they don't kill us first," William said. "We should go to the Unseelie castle, where you can hide us." He pointed his finger at Aisling, who narrowed her eyes.

Aisling didn't care for William or his opinion. William, while tall and broad in every way, was the most average looking guy in the room. His face seemed normal, guy-next-door.

Putting his lumberjack appearance to the side, I could see someone like him working a regular nine to five and mowing his grass to precisely two inches off the ground every Sunday morning.

When I was surrounded by so many people who looked like they'd been crafted by Michael Angelo, it was nice to see someone who was simple, like me.

Her voice was sprinkled with condescension. "Look at the map. The route to the Court of Water is long. That is why Ewan and Lorena's wedding procession went through the entire world before it arrived at the Seelie Court. You've never been there. You don't understand. Walking through the Court of Fire will be dangerous," Aisling countered.

"Then we'll go around them," William said, pointing at the map Aisling had brought with her. "There are villages along this valley route. Are these people friendly?"

The princess pursed her lips. "Yes, but that will take even more time."

"My priority is Lorena," William said with cool-blue eyes. "I do not care how long the journey will be. I care about her safety and the child she carries."

Aisling fisted her hands. "This could take months."

"So be it," he growled.

Her eyes blazed.

I stood and slapped my hands on my hips. "Am I going to need a whistle to referee you both?"

"He started it!"

"She started it!"

They spoke at the same time.

"Enough!" I held up my hand to silence them. "Her Majesty the Tree had said the journey would be long."

"Maybe she meant it wouldn't be easy," Aisling said.

William rolled his eyes. "Or maybe she meant exactly what she said. The journey would be long because it would take a long time."

Aisling pouted. Everyone seemed to be leaning toward William's plan, but honestly, I wanted to confront Oberon as well. Now that I knew he had the secret to getting Wei back, I needed to speak with him, but William's plan seemed safer in theory.

I looked down at the map on the coffee table. It seemed like a fragile antique that shimmered every time it updated. It pulsed with life. Apparently, the map was her mother's.

The fae world was spread out before my eyes.

There were continents and a vast ocean, but that was about the end of the similarities with Earth. For one, the Court of Airs were a cloudy mass hovering above the landmass closer to the Seelie camp when I distinctly remember it being farther west over an island in the sea.

The Court of Fire occupied the second biggest landmass next to the Unseelie. With the goblins, trolls, and aggressive attitudes that lived there, I supposed they'd need space to spread out.

What surprised me most were the black shadows that seemed to spread over half the Unseelie continent. I remembered the ominous twisting forest that surrounded the castle but not this blackness or the volcanos for that matter. "I don't remember this," I pointed out.

Aisling smirks. "It's my mother's little secret. The Unseelie Court holds the darkest creatures of all. Elves in the forest are enslavers. They catch other fae and enslave them and use terrible threats to keep them in line."

"Like what?"

"Like killing their children or killing the child's spirit. It's one of the reasons you weren't allowed outside the castle's premises. My mother likes to pretend that all is fair in the Unseelie homestead, but it's not."

"Does Ewan know about this?"

"My brother is aware. He doesn't like it, but you have to remember who my brother is. He'll never go against our mother," she said bitterly.

"He went against his mother by staying with me."

"Did he?" Aisling lifted a brow. "Are you sure? Because from what I remember, there was nothing more important than your union to Ewan."

"Only so she could control the future of her grandchild, but Ewan isn't the father's baby, and yet he stayed. He stayed because he loved me."

She turned away with a huff.

And I let her sulk because I knew I was right. If her brother didn't love me, then he'd have left and returned to mommy dearest with his tail tucked between his legs, begging for her forgiveness, but he hadn't.

"Well, we'd better hurry so you can reunite with your love," Aisling muttered.

"He went back for you."

She wouldn't meet my eyes, but I saw her doubt and resistance. She didn't believe me, or rather, history wouldn't let herself believe anyone actually cared for her.

I left her to her musing. Ewan would prove himself later. I was sure of it.

"Can I take Airgead?" I asked.

Aisling nodded. "You can ride him, but he can't fly. You'll be shot down on my mother's command. No one is allowed to take to the skies. I don't know if my father's lands have the same rules, but I imagine they do."

Well, I didn't want my horse shot, so flying was out of the question. And secretly, I was happy about that as well. I'd only offered flying as a means to appease everyone, but I hated heights. This worked out great.

I swatted my hair away from my face, and Dr. Shaw motioned me to sit so she could braid it. I let her with a big smile on my face. I had to keep from kicking my legs.

William and Aisling started debating again.

I was done with that. "Marquessa, can you open a portal like you did a few months ago?" She was a powerful witch and, at the moment, far more powerful than me, but that wasn't doing her justice on a count of my drained state. My power was poop right now.

Marquessa shook her head. "No, it would take me some weeks to build up the level of energy a portal takes. You were gone for a whole year before we managed to blast through this world and into the fae world. I had plenty of time then."

We didn't have a whole year. Her majesty demanded we leave soon.

I felt the urge to use the bathroom and excused myself after Dr. Shaw finished. I'd needed potty breaks more and more often since I'd learned I was pregnant.

In my room, I put the rest of the Marco rings in a satchel I was going to take, along with my wand and my mother and Wei's soul stones. I was taking it with me when we left.

When we got to the fae world, I would try to free them both, I decided. Even though my mother had tried to play Voldemort by overtaking my body, in the end, she was the reason I was alive, and I was willing to give her a second chance.

Or was this the third chance? Or the fifth chance?

Who was counting?

When I got back to the living room, it seemed a decision had been made. We'd go to the Unseelie Courts. It was a long way, but it was also the easiest route. No one would attack Aisling there, and she could cover everyone up and say we were a part of her new circle of advisors now that Corridan was dead.

Once away from the palace, she'd drop her identity and blend in as best as she could.

Everyone went upstairs to pack.

Dr. Shaw had originally said she'd remained here, but after some begging, mostly from me, she succumbed. She was the physician on our team, and though we hoped we wouldn't need her skills, it was better to be safe than dead.

The issue of clothing came up after that. Dr. Shaw had a unique style and would never blend in with fae natives. Neither would the rest of us for that matter. And finally, Aisling said she could have some clothes fashioned for our journey, and after some begging, again mainly from me, begrudgingly told us who her tailor was.

She sat poised in a chair by the window. "If you really must know … The birds made it for me."

"Birds?"

Her cheeks turned pink and added a depth to her green eyes. "Yes, the birds took to me when I first arrived. Actually, they were the ones who kept an eye on Corridan when I couldn't. Communicating with them is my gift. I talk to birds. Some bugs as well. Mostly, creatures with wings. Bats can be quite clever, but they're more temperamental." In her clothes, I almost forgot Aisling had wings, which was exactly what she wanted. She didn't want people to know she had wings. She called herself cursed because of them. They'd made her just as much a freak in the fae world as Ewan's vampire blood.

Ewan could turn into a shadow, something he'd inherited from his father, but I never thought to ask Aisling what she could do.

Her wings were beautiful. I wanted to tell her that but not in mixed company. It was obvious, she was still self-conscious about them. I was probably the only person in the room who knew why flying creatures adored her and thought she was one of their own.

"Could you get them to make clothes for all of us?"

Aisling nodded, undid the latch to the window, and pushed open the glass.

The cold crawled in with the sound of the night creatures. Then a black crow dropped down on the windowsill. It hopped on his feet close to Aisling and bent its head while she spoke to it.

It fluttered off, and the room was quiet again.

I was just about to move to the window when a flock of birds began to circle the room. Their wings beat against my arms and back. There were too many to count. It didn't hurt, but it was strange at the same time. A heard a scream, and Aisling said, "Don't move!"

My limbs locked as I closed my eyes. Have you ever been slapped around by birds? I'll tell you now if it ever happens, it's the most absurd feeling in the world. Eventually, the chaos ceased, and the last bird flew out of the window just before Aisling shut it. "The clothes will be done by sunrise. We'll leave then."

That was hours from now.

I didn't want to be alone, so I asked Dimitri to come to my room. Silently, I noticed his anxiety while we'd been in the living room and wanted to talk about it. He'd been so quiet. Sometimes he got into these moods, but this felt different.

I tried to get it out of Alan because I knew Alan knew what was going on, but my beautiful angel suggested the beast talk to me himself.

Dimitri sat on the edge of my bed and scrubbed his face and then his dark, unruly hair.

I walked over to him, and he spread his legs in invitation. He placed his head on my breast and breathed heavily. His arms went around me.

I wasn't sure how to start this conversation, but I'd never been one to walk on eggshells, so I didn't start now. "What's wrong?"

He shuttered against me and ran his hands up his back. "It's been so long. For years, I hungered for this, but knowing I would never be sated by this craving, I gorged myself on other things, mostly women."

"Okay." I patted his head.

"I laden myself in their soft curves. Choked on the perfumes of their heat. I broke them like mares and took their bodies like a well-earned bounty."

I pressed my lips together. He was working through something. I was sure he was going somewhere with this. I wasn't upset that he was talking about his past relationships. In fact, these didn't sound like relationships at all. I was sure he was used to women throwing themselves at his feet. Dimitri had a wildness that called to the very heart of me.

It also called to me in another place a little more south than my heart, the place I let him run free and conquer to his heart's content.

He lowered his hands to my butt and squeezed. "I never deserved you."

"Aw, that's sweet." I continued to rub my hands through my hair and tried to ignore how aroused he was making me. I mentally wagged my finger at my vagina and told her to stand down. This wasn't about me. This was about him.

"And now, you have given me another gift." He lowered his head, and I felt his breath at my lower belly.

My vagina perked up. Maybe we would get something out of this conversation.

"Sunlight."

I wrapped my arms around his head as I realized what this meant. Not only for Dimitri but for the other vampires as well. Not only were they free of my control, but they were no longer slaves to the dark.

I hadn't considered the fact that they could live normal lives now if they so choose to. They would wake up when they wanted, sleep when they wanted, and stay out as long as they wanted.

They could watch the sunrise and the sunset. The sun would no longer wound their skin but give them a warmth that had long been denied them.

I didn't want to admit it, but this fact did alleviate some of the guilt I felt at taking Marco's bones.

Sirius's voice reached my mind's ear again. I heard him talking about Marco's purpose.

I pushed the disturbance away and cupped Dimitri's cheek so he'd look up at me. He was a tall dude, so even sitting, there wasn't much lifting he had to do to meet my eyes. We were almost across from one another. "You, me, and Alan are going to watch the sunrise together."

His whole face broke out in joy. "We'll wake up in time for it. Tonight, I want to sleep in your arms like a living man."

"Okay."

"With the scent of your arousal in my mouth and on my manhood."

I shuffled from one foot to the other. "Okay."

He yanked down my sweats. "Your body shall weep onto my lips, and your screams shall fill my ears."

"I like where this is going."

He kissed me, picked me up, and tossed me onto the bed. "You are a meal that leaves me sated with a hunger that shall never die."

"Yeah, you too." My giggles ended when his mouth hit my clit, and then I was feeling his joy like he was shoving it into me.

We were still connected. I didn't stop being a necromancer to his vampire, but now he had to give me permission to roam in his mind. He opened to me as I spread my shaking legs.

Then he devoured me and sated us both.

CHAPTER EIGHTEEN

So, our vision wasn't obscured, we watched the sunrise from the treehouse. Alan and I leaned against a branch while Dimitri stood behind us both, big enough to engulf us in his embrace. I felt his body begin to shutter as the sun launched itself into the sky. Still hidden by the mountains, the sky paled first. Then the rays began to break. Soon pinks and orange light covered the snowy ground.

I looked at Alan and watched silent tears fall from his beautiful eyes. His pale skin reflected the hues of morning. Dimitri was sobbing into my shoulder.

I wrapped my arm around him even though I feared he'd miss his first sunset because of all his cries. "Look up."

His soft hair brushed my cheek as he placed his head on top of mine. "She's beautiful."

The sun.

The old girl finally showed her face, and I felt the guys stiffen for a long time before the tension left them.

I saw a shift on the corner of the eye and saw Zane standing a few feet away, but he wasn't watching the sun. He was watching us or, more importantly, me. He wasn't surprised to see the sun at all. He'd probably been watching it by himself for months. Yet another secret he'd kept.

Had he cried at his first sunset in so long? How did he feel now?

I knew how he felt about me. If his longing could control his legs, he'd be over here already.

I turned away and grabbed Dimitri's hand. I felt the ring I'd given him. The relationship felt more official somehow, though, in my heart, it had already been that way and set in stone.

I glanced over at Zane. He wore his ring on the right hand, and I remembered that for some other counties, that was the wedding finger, but it was also considered the widow finger in the states. How did Zane feel about us? Did he see us as dead? Divorce? Still together?

Alan leaned in my ear. "Do you want to talk to him?"

"I want him gone," I said loud enough for Zane to hear.

Zane straightened and left, almost like he would have if I still had some control over him.

When I could no longer focus on the sunrise, I broke away from Dimitri and Alan and told them to stay and enjoy the heavenly phenomenal while I went inside.

I snuck into the kitchen in the middle of a conversation between Dr. Shaw and Peter about the food in the fae world and what held the most nutrition.

Dr. Shaw looked at me, hesitantly. "Lorena, I don't think I should go."

"What? I thought we'd already discussed this." Already I hated this day. First, I saw Zane whose face did nothing but remind me of loss, and now Dr. Shaw wouldn't come with me.

Dr. Shaw patted the stool next to her on the island.

I sat down. "You have to come."

"I still have work I need to do here. People depend on me, and your journey sounds like it will take a very long time, Lorena."

"Please." My eyes were watering, and I hated it. I hated that I was begging her not to leave me. "Please, come."

She bit her lip and nodded. Then her warm hand was on my cheek. "All right, dear girl. I'll come." She hugged me, and I swear no one else's hugs felt like hers.

I knew my attachment to Dr. Shaw was coming from a place of brokenness within myself, but it wasn't something I wanted to deal with. Not now. Not ever.

She could take all the Dr. Pepper from me that she wanted, but I wanted her to come.

I turned my head on her shoulder and looked at the aura stone around her neck. Deep inside its dark depths, I could make out a blue color. Blue was the shade of tranquility but also grief. Was Dr. Shaw distressed about something?

I realized I didn't know her that well, and I wanted to change that. There was a long journey ahead of us, so we had plenty of time.

I left the kitchen feeling heavy, both in my belly thanks to the breakfast Peter had made me but also in my heart.

Marquessa's door was open, and I heard her talking to Jenny. They were going through a list of things that were starting to sound like a witch starter kit. They were getting prepared for anything.

When I walked into their room, Jenny held a tablet out for me. "Merry Christmas. I know it's a little early, but Reikah and I wanted to give you this."

It was a silver keychain with a book charm. I smiled. "Thanks."

Jenny laughed. "What's the password in 'Ali Baba and the Forty Thieves'?"

I'd read Arabian Nights. This was easy. "Open Sesame."

A cloud of silver poofed in my face, and I stumbled as something heavy filled my hands. The smoke cleared, and I saw that I was holding my grandmother's grimoire. The chain was gone.

I was flabbergasted. "How?"

"We'd been working on it for a while, especially after the fae stole you. We wanted to make you something that you could put on and always remember who you are."

I closed the book and cried full belly tears. "Thank you. My gift is going to suck in comparison."

"What did you get us?"

"I was going to name the baby Jenicah, a combination of your names." They were my closest friends. Who else deserved the honor?

Jenny's lips trembled then she burst into tears. "That's so sweet."

Her tears yanked the lid off my reservoir. "I know, but what if I have a boy? I can't think of anything."

We laughed and cried while Marquessa shook her head. "You two are a mess."

We huddled on the bed and video called Reikah so I could thank her as well.

Her pretty tan face filled the screen. Her dark eyes were tinted with warmth. "I am honored that you would think of me in the naming of your child. Names carry power and influence. I will try to live up with being worthy of his gift."

"Cool."

"I like that Dr. Shaw will be attending you on this journey. She can continue to address the state of your health."

I rolled my eyes. Reikah, who refrained from meat, had thought the world of Dr. Shaw when she'd first met her. Speaking of which, I turned to Marquessa, who was putting the last of her things in a bag. "Thanks for bringing Dr. Shaw to me."

She shook out a frilly, pink shirt with a scooped neck. I wondered if she remembered that Aisling was having clothes made for us. I wasn't going to interrupt her. "I didn't bring Dr. Shaw here."

Jenny and I had been laying on the bed and staring up at Reikah on the screen. Marquessa's words had me straightened. "But I thought you went to look for a witch doctor."

She grabbed a pair of khaki shorts that I knew she'd never wear. She always complained about her thighs rubbing together. But again, I let her pack it. "I did, but I didn't find Dr. Shaw. I was still lookin' for someone when the woman arrived. I thought you found her."

Huh? "Why would I choose a doctor I didn't like? I only let her stay around because I didn't want to be rude to you."

Marquessa put her clothes down and turned to me. "Well, I didn't know the woman until I met her here."

"Then who invited her?" Was Dr. Shaw actually Mary Poppins?

I looked at Jenny, who shrugged.

Reikah said, "Maybe one of the other witches found her."

"I'll ask them and then ask Dr. Shaw."

One of the witches popped her head in. Our resident, Marilyn Monroe. Her real name was Margot, but she was a Hollywood goddess in every way. "Hey, which wolves aren't coming?"

"All of them are coming," I told her. Our entourage was going to be huge. All of the fae and the wolves were joining us. That put the headcount at fifty, give or take. We'd been spending most of our journey on the outskirts of cities in tents.

"And the fairies?"

"They're coming too."

"Excellent." She squealed.

Before she could run away, I asked, "Did you or Ralph ask Dr. Shaw to come here?"

Margot tapped her dainty chin with a polished fingernail. "No."

"Are you sure Ralph didn't?" He was older, about Marquessa's age. Maybe Margot didn't know him that well.

She nodded. "I'm sure. We asked Dr. Shaw questions while we were all trapped in Sirius's house."

"What did she tell you?" I asked.

Margot tapped her fingers against the dresser by the door. "Let's see. She said she met her husband while in school in Massachusetts, but it's been many years since she's seen him. He hasn't come back to America since Blair was ten."

"You mean, Mr. Dr. Shaw hasn't come home for six years?"

"Apparently."

Not even for Blair? What was the story there? Maybe the marriage was estranged. Maybe Blair flew out to see her dad. Suddenly, I no longer saw Dr. Shaw as a doctor or a mom figure but a woman. I thought about the grief I'd sensed in her and decided I was going to ask her about it later.

"She's very proud of Blair," Margot continued. "She knows her daughter will be a good physician one day."

I knew Blair didn't actually want to be a doctor, but I kept that to myself. It wasn't for me to share.

Finished, Margot fled and left me with more questions.

Who was Dr. Shaw?

I said goodbye to Reikah and went upstairs to grab my things.

Three outfits were waiting for me on my bed. One of them was beige with brown leathers, a long, white tunic dress with a brown vest that came with a hood, and a black gown that shimmered. The last I knew was for a special occasion; the rest reminded me of something a Jedi would wear, which meant I loved it.

I put on the tunic and met everyone else downstairs. The foyer was packed.

We were all similarly dressed except for Aisling, who was wearing a red gown fitting to her station. It was something the courts would expect from her.

I looked around at the faces present and knew some of them wouldn't be coming back. These people were risking their lives for the people of the fae and me.

William stood at the top of the stairs and spoke. "Today, we leave this place behind to embark on a world that doesn't know we're coming. We don't know what challenges we'll meet on the other side, but as I look at you all, I don't see wolf, fae, vampire, or witch, but an alliance so powerful that all should fear on both sides of the portal."

The wolves growled and stomped in agreeance.

Their agitation heightened the power in the room and made me shiver. I took a breath and found feel the tension, hope, and dread, tasting it on my tongue. What we were doing was dangerous.

"Our top priority is to get Lorena to the Court of Water. Keep that in mind when dealing with the natives. Do not cause trouble or take on trouble that is not your own. Lorena's life takes precedence over yours."

I had a few issues with that. "I …"

Alan placed a hand on my shoulder and shook his head. "He's right. If we don't get you to the Court of Water, then we've failed everything and everyone."

"But what if someone gets hurt?"

"It's a war zone," Alan said. "Someone will get hurt."

I didn't like that. Even knowing he was right, I didn't like it.

I looked at Dr. Shaw. She was wearing a dark skirt and a pale top. As if feeling my eyes, she turned her head, and the corner of her mouth lifted. She was so pretty. I hoped I didn't get her, or Blair killed.

Blair was on winter break. I was hoping we'd be back before it ended.

That gave us a month to finish everything.

Peter stood in the crowd with Azalea in his hand. His tiny pink life partner was speaking to him. I didn't know he was coming.

I noticed Sirius and Lilac in the group and asked Alan, "Who said Lilac could come?"

"You said so yourself that Sirius must come, and he said he would not come without Lilac."

So, we were letting our prisoners make decisions now. Great. He'd betray us all.

Aisling finished the speech with some final notice about the fae world etiquette. Then she pulled out a golden key and stuck out like she was putting into a lock.

I heard invisible locks turn, and then she opened the door.

A white space glowed from the top of the steps. Aisling stood in front of it. "Ready?" She jumped.

CHAPTER NINETEEN

The air was cool on the other side. Night had fallen over the fae. Dry dirt was coming up at me, but a hand on each of my arms stopped me from smacking the ground. Dimitri and Alan kept me upright. The ringing of unsheathed metal had me looking around.

Our group was surrounded by fae guards.

The silver of their armor gleamed in the torch lights of the courtyard.

Aisling held up her hands. "Weapons down. It's just me."

The weapons stayed out.

Loud whipping sounded from the flags as the hard winds lashed against the fabric.

Aisling didn't bother to look around. She continued to face forward.

A large male with hollowed cheekbones and skin the color of coal came forward. He was hot in an elven kind of way. His ear struck back from his face. The points looked sharp as a blade. His voice was hard but also gentle. "Princess. I'm glad that you've returned. I trust your mission was a success?"

She held a bag up, and something dropped out. It hit the ground and rolled. I was in the middle of the crowd, so I couldn't see what she'd dropped, but I knew what was in the bag. Corridan's head. What I didn't know was how Aisling felt at this moment. There was the head of the man who'd once filled her heart with hope, the man she'd assumed loved her in spite of what she saw as her flaws.

Pride shown in the gray man's face. "You have fire in your blood, princess. I will enjoy putting that same fire inside your womb ... and other places."

Say what? What was he talking about?

Aisling bowed. "King Rolo. These are my guests and the people who helped me capture Lord Corridan."

King Rolo? I'd never heard of him before. I tried to think back to the list of people Titania had made me learn before the wedding procession. No Rolo came to mind.

"Put down your swords," Rolo commanded the guards. "It is late, but tomorrow we shall celebrate Princess Aisling's return. Let us make her friends comfortable." To Aisling, he said, "You will tell me all about how you slew Corridan."

That was a trick I wanted to witness. Aisling couldn't lie, which meant the story she'd told me was true. She hadn't killed Corridan. He'd fallen down the stairs.

"I cut his throat easy enough," Aisling murmured as she clung to the giant's arm. She must have cut him after he'd fallen. That was clever of her.

Clinking metal got my attention again. I looked through the slits in the metal helmets of the guards and noticed that only half of them were Unseelie. Members of the Court of Fire were present. Fairies, trolls, and goblins stood erect around the courtyard.

As the gates to the castle were opened, two by two, the guards took up a position behind us and marched us inside.

We went through another courtyard, and I saw more trolls and goblins of different sizes and heights strolling the open area. There were fire pits set out, and men laughed or fought around them.

I tried to still myself from looking for Ewan but couldn't help it. I missed my prince of shadows. I held back the urge to seek him with my power. I didn't know if there was anyone else out there who would recognize my power and give me away. I was so nervous. What if Ewan weren't here? What if he were here? He'd only been gone for a few days, but anything could have changed in that amount of time.

We were stopped by the door.

Dimitri's hand tightened on my arm. Being tall allowed him to see over heads. "They're checking everyone at the door."

"Meaning?"

"I don't know, but two of the guards are lifting hoods."

I'd be recognized if one of the guards had been around when I'd been around. Fear had me paralyzed but Dimitri was the only thing that was keeping me moving. Alan had let go, but then he grabbed me again. Dimitri grunted and squeezed me to the point of pain.

At the door, I dropped my head and clenched my gut. My hoodie was thrown back just before a guy lifted my chin.

Our eyes locked, and I recognized him. He guarded my door once. He knew me.

I held my breath. A minute passed before he let me go and started waving his hand. The pieces clicked into place right before I realized he'd let me go. Maybe the palace isn't looking for me, after all. Maybe I'm not such a hot commodity as Aisling claimed.

I fought for air as my heart slowed.

I hadn't missed his place at all. The castle was made out of various precious jewels all fit together and smoothed to perfection. The hall was obsidian and reflected everything to the point that it reminded of the glass rooms in a clown hour, creepy and hard escape.

The walls were lined with guards, and their gazes searched us in a way where I felt stripped. Did no one recognize me? I'd visited the Court of Fire. Sure, it had only been that once, but how many times had their princess attacked the fiancée of the man who hadn't even had the decency to visit her before outright rejecting the offer of marriage?

Yeah, it had been scandalous and something I would never forget.

I could feel power hovering around me. It gave me a spider web sensation. I fought the urge to beat it back for as long as I could, but eventually, I took my arm from Dimitri and tried to wave it away.

"Stop," the voice on my other side hissed.

I didn't detect Alan's French lyric in the words, so I turned and met Lilac's cold eyes.

"What are you—"

"Quiet! Unless you want to give yourself away." Lilac snarled in my face right before she turned forward and cranked up the charm for the guards. "And stop moving around so much. The masking effect has a delay."

Masking? She'd put a mask on me? No wonder no one recognized me. Now it all made sense, though not really. "Why didn't anyone tell me about this part of the plan?"

"Because I want to be near you just as much as you want to be near me."

True, but I hated the feeling that I was being left in the dark and handled with kiddie gloves. I wanted to rile on someone, and I would just as soon as we were in a private place. "Do you have to hold onto me?" I asked.

"Yes." Her fingers pinched me. "We're sticking together for the duration of our stay in the castle."

Oh, heck no. There was no way I was becoming bunkmates with this psychopath. She'd kill me in my sleep, eat my flesh, and use my bones to pick her teeth.

Even as I rejected the idea, deep down inside, I couldn't ignore the plan had its merits.

"Who's idea was this?" I asked.

Her smile slipped by about twenty degrees. "Like you don't know."

I knew who'd done it. Sirius. This was his plan. He was probably the only one who knew the extent of Lilac's abilities. This was probably the reason he wouldn't come without her.

She started to pout.

I wanted to pout, so I pouted too and even added a pursed lip.

This reminded me of those situations where parents made siblings hug it out. Only Lilac was a bonafide murderer and would likely stab me in the back if I thought to wrap my arms around her.

We were shown to a part of the castle I'd never been in before, the Emerald Wing, which was, you guessed it, emerald and cold. While I'd been a guest the last time I'd stayed here, Titania had kept me in the Pearl Wing. That wing had been closer to the queen. Close enough for her to constantly feed me her deceit whenever my mind tried to warn me that something was wrong. Close enough to trample on the memories of my former life whenever they rose.

The guests' wing had an open space called the receiving room, and the guards closed us in and left us alone after telling us to choose whichever room we wanted from amongst what was available. There were fifty of us—minus Aisling who'd walked off with Lord Rolo, maybe to her own room or maybe to Rolo's, so he could put that fire in her belly like he promised—and twenty rooms divided into three floors. People were going to have the share.

Once we were alone, everyone started to break out in groups. We'd planned for sharing. Otherwise, carrying fifty tents would have slowed the progression of our journey even more. The only people who were sleeping in my room were my men, and I planned to make that very clear very soon.

I snatched my arm from Lilac. "Go sleep with your assigned group."

"We're assigned the same room."

"No."

"Yes." She didn't look any more pleased than I felt.

Dimitri covered my shoulder with his hand and caressed my ear with his deep voice. "Nothing will happen to you. She knows what I will do if she even dreams of touching you."

I turned around. "You knew?"

"It wasn't a secret," he said in a calm manner like he was talking a small child out of a tantrum. "It was an idea that came up."

"An idea you knew I wouldn't like."

"This is why I couldn't tell her everything," Zane muttered from a few feet away. "She rejects sound ideas for her own plans and wishes." His dark gaze dared me to talk back and give him the fight he wanted.

My palm itched to slap him. "I am not rejecting the idea because I thought of a better one. The idea I reject is everyone treating me like a baby. I demand respect and to know what is happening to me. This is my life and not anyone else's. I'm all for a good plan, but when it involves me, I should be a part of it. Heck, I should be at the front of it, not just thrown into if afterward. It's disrespectful, and I won't tolerate it."

He didn't lower his gaze, but I knew I was right.

"And I thought I told you not to talk to me," I added.

"Tell her I haven't addressed her once," Zane volleyed back. "Talking about her and talking to her entirely different things."

I snarled because he was right. He hadn't been talking to me only loud enough for me to hear, which in a way was talking to me without having to admit that he was talking to me, and I hated that.

A glance around the room proved that everyone had stopped to pay attention. "To your rooms!"

The movement picked up again, and people started filing out in pairs or groups of three or more.

Alan came over with a meek expression. "I got us a room that has three beds."

"Good. I'm taking one for myself. You all can figure out how you're sleeping. In the room, if I'm in the mood, we'll discuss what other plans you have that involve me and I don't know about."

Alan hung his head. He knew me. He knew better than this. Who was the culprit who'd come up with this idea?

I looked around for Blair and Dr. Shaw. They were sleeping with Marquessa and Jenny. I didn't see them. Instead, Sirius caught my gaze. His smile was cunning, and I remembered the feel of those lips against my skin.

"Sirius is sleeping with William," Dimitri said.

I adjusted the bag on my back and nodded. "Great. Let's go to bed." But I was far from tired. We'd all woken up just a few hours ago and would remain awake for hours yet. We'd have portal lag in the morning.

Sirius met me in the hall. "Sleep tight, Daphne."

Lilac gasped and glared between us before Dimitri pushed her up the stone stairway. Sirius ambled down the hall with William at his back.

What was that about? Had he given the pet name to Lilac first? I'd never wanted the name to begin with, but if he had called Lilac that I really didn't want it. I felt dirty and needed a bath.

The bath was starting to relax me when I noticed the water turn black. I jumped to get out, but something clenched my ankle. I opened my mouth to scream, but a head emerged from the water, and then I saw a face I recognized.

Dark hair clung to his stone-like features. Emerald eyes glittered with enough heat to boil the water in the tub. "Miss me?"

I didn't answer with words. Instead, I grabbed a fist full of Ewan's hair and brought his head to my lips.

It had only been days, but he tasted like homemade cookies that had been packed with love and sent in the mail by special delivery.

He moved closer, and I noticed he was naked and smiled. "How did you know I was in the tub?"

"I stalked you from the shadows. I felt you the moment you arrived." He groaned and cupped my jaw before sucking my tongue into his mouth.

I became wet in a whole new way underneath the water.

He cupped one of my breasts and worried my nipple between skillful fingers.

Water splashed over the edge as I arched myself into his hand. A sharp ache sliced its way through my body.

"Whose day is it?" he asked.

"Who cares?" I didn't want him to stop. I knew we had a lot to talk about, but this felt so much more important.

He grabbed my hips and sat me on the edge of the tub. He straightened to his knees and captured my mouth again. He pinched my nipples, and I wanted more. He tugged on my clitoris and I threw my head back and moaned. "More." I wanted him inside me.

"I have a surprise for you."

"What?"

Something pushed against my entrance, and I started to stretch. The object was hard and soft at the same time and far too big to be his finger. I looked down and watched Ewan's baby-making muscle disappear inside me. My body gripped him, and we both groaned in bliss and agony.

"Ewan!" He made me feel wonderful and full, but I had enough sense to try to stop him. "The curse."

He silenced me with a dirty kiss, grabbed my knee, and delivered a hard pounding. Water flew everywhere, hitting the floor and us. His skin spanked mine, and his hips whipped between my spread thighs.

He watched himself take me over. "I've never seen a more beautiful sight."

I watched. It looked as good as it felt. He was slicing me open and forcing himself to the hilt.

His eyes fluttered closed. "So long, I have waited for you."

His thrust submerged me in heat and madness. I planted my feet firmly on the edge and lifted my hips so I could toss myself down on him.

"Lorena!" He grabbed my hips and emptied his seed inside me and continued to wildly thrust. He rubbed the sensitive hood of my slit, causing sweet pain and pleasure until I shattered around him.

He picked me up and arranged us so his back was against the tub and I was on his chest.

His heart was beating so fast it was like a fist hitting my cheek. He drew circles on my back and took deep breaths. "Sorry, I couldn't last long the first time."

I grinned. "That's what the second and third times are for."

He chuckled, and I sat up. "Ewan, I thought we couldn't have sex unless we married."

He took my hand and kissed my knuckles; I forgot how much I missed that. "How are we doing this?"

He wiggled his brows. "I thought you knew how this worked."

I laughed. "I mean it."

He stroked my thighs under the water, his fingers rough against my silky skin. We were still connected, and I had no intention of letting him go any time soon. My body twitched, and I watched his mouth part as ecstasy cascaded over his face. "I defeated Ulgard in a battle. He sleeps in the dungeons under the castle now."

"You defeated the king of the Court of Fire?" I remembered him. He was gigantic, red, and ugly with gray wounds and scars mapped out across his body.

He nodded. "Upon my arrival, I couldn't find my mother. No one would tell me where she was, and Ulgard and Ilgah were acting odd and were once again pushing for a marriage between Ilgah and me that would not happen."

"No surprises there."

He nodded. "We shared a meal, and then later that evening, I found Ulgard with my mother in a way that was clearly nonconsensual. Apparently, she'd told him he could have her after they won the war, but he did not wish to wait. And then, he still wanted revenge for what happened during our wedding procession."

"Oh no." I could already tell this story was about to get really bad. I pushed up, and his deflated shaft slipped out of me. I settled back down on his lap and braced myself.

"It was all a lie. My mother believed she was gaining an ally, but Ulgard turned out to be nothing more than another enemy. Once he was invited to the castle, he'd had her stripped and tied to poles in the courtyard."

I didn't want to hear anymore. This was terrible. I didn't like Titania, but I would never wish this on anyone. "Stop."

"I almost killed him, but I gave him to my mother in exchange for my freedom. My mother is wounded, not so much physically but in every way that truly matters. Her spirit is broken, and even worse, word spread to Oberon. He's calling her all matter of whore, but that's nothing new."

Oberon and Titania were as separated as a married couple could be in the absence of death.

"How long did this go on?"

His hand on my hip tightened. "Twenty days and Oberon did nothing to stop it. He didn't even rescue her in exchange for her kingdom. He left her to her fate."

The water felt cold against my burning skin. Anger built within me. "I have to get to the Court of Water to stop the war."

"Aisling has told me. I spoke to her briefly before I came here." His gaze was elsewhere, lost in some deep, dark place in his mind. He continued to rub my body idly, completely unaware that we were getting pruney.

"Who's Rolo?"

"He was the leader of the firbolgs. He took over after Ulgard's demise."

"And he wants Aisling?"

"So it seems." He rolled his eyes. "Aisling hadn't been a part of the deal, but my sister's beauty has always led people to foolery. It's something I'll have to work out later. You heard about it when I did. My sister has never even met Rolo, not until now."

"Really? Aisling didn't seem surprised by anything that came out of his mouth." But from my angle in the crowd, I hadn't been able to see her face.

"My sister was raised in my mother's court, which is nothing more than a den of thieves. She knows how to play her cards until she can find a way out of the trap. It's just another thing I'll have to worry about. The Court of Fire is a warring group. They take what they want, and he wants Aisling."

"What about Ulgard's daughter, Ilgah?"

"My mother killed her. Apparently, she'd begged Ilgah to free her many times, but the princess denied her request, even though her father would have released her had she asked."

"So, Ilgah could have ended it?"

"And she chose not to. Killing her in front of Ulgard was the first part of my mother's torture. She plans to keep him for twenty years, a year for every day he violated her. She is obsessed with it, so her advisers have placed me in charge."

He swallowed and sighed in frustration. "When she lifted the curse ... I felt it leave me. The curse had been a part of me from birth. I almost feel ... empty without it, like I'm missing a limb." He touched my cheek. "But you've made me whole again." He bent for a kiss, and I gave it to him. He could have anything he wanted from me. He already held a special place in my heart. "I found out something else," he said. "I know where the answers to the soul stone are."

"Where?" I held my breath.

"In the forest. The same place my mother got the soul stones to begin with. My mother's castle is beautiful, but just beyond the trees lies another truth."

"I heard. Aisling told me about the brownies."

"Brownies," he murmured. "A finer way of saying slaves. That's how they all start out. They mine for my mother's precious stones until they are brought by someone looking for a servant. I plan to close those mines as soon as I am given full power and shut down the entire slave market."

"Really?"

"Yes. I've already presented the idea to Mother's advisors. Of course, they hate the idea, which is why I stayed in the shadows when you and the others arrived. I can't let them know how much

I love you or care for my sister. The castle has become a dangerous place."

"It's *become* a dangerous place? Sorry. Hate to break it to you, but this place is the hub for villainy."

His chuckled shined through his eyes. "All right. You're right." He sobered. "And that's the problem. I don't even know who I can trust here."

"You can trust me," I said.

***

After reading over a few spells from Loretta Quinn's book of shadows, I said the magic words and finally crawled into bed. I let Ewan hold me that night and tried to sleep so my body would be on fae time and not Eastern Standard.

I kept thinking about Titania. That his mother had given in without a fight said everything. Titania had been changed by this war. I'd read about wars on Earth. Countries around the globe gloried their soldiers and battles, but there was nothing pretty about the results. Death. Thousands. Sometimes millions. Vengeance played a key role in more than a few wars and always the death that followed tainted the landscape and the people left behind.

While I hated her on behalf of the elves she had enslaved, I felt sorry for the queen of the Unseelie and partially responsible. I shouldn't have waited as long as I had before coming back. I knew a war was brewing, but I'd filled my days warring with Dr. Shaw over a beverage rather than helping the people who'd raised one of the men I loved.

A woman who'd also hurt the man I loved in a land that rejected him for being a vampire.

Maybe that was the reason I hadn't rushed in like Batman and had been chomping at the bit to fight crime. Ewan had been so abused and mistreated in this world that I'd wanted to keep him safe in the mansion and surround him with enough love to fight back the shadows I sometimes glimpsed in his eyes.

I don't think anyone slept except for Ewan. He held me like I was his favorite blanket, draping me halfway over his body. And even though I didn't sleep, I couldn't say the position hadn't been one of the most comfortable I'd ever been in.

Opening my eyes, the first person I saw was Zane. He was sitting on the windowsill. The sun bathed his bronze skin. Chest bare, muscles rippling like water down his body, I fought to squash down the flood of heat.

Nervousness helped me beat back the desire and made it stay down. He was so close to the edge that I couldn't help but worry he'd fall to his death.

Did it matter that he was no longer mine to claim? Not at all. Did I still love him? Definitely. I probably always would. You didn't go on the adventures that we went on, risk our lives for one another, and not have feelings that carried on into eternity.

Would Zane survive a fall like that?

I didn't know if he was like Ewan, who was able to morph into a beast like Dimitri and jump to a nearby tree to save his life. The more I thought about it, I realized that Zane had never shown me was capable of anything more. Did he have a superpower? He was fast, but so were the others.

Maybe it was his ability to look me in the eye and lie.

His head shifted, and he caught me watching.

I didn't turn away. His eyes looked even more gold in the sun. His gaze was almost transparent, and I found myself peeking behind Zane's beautiful barrier of skin and flesh and into his mind.

He was letting me in. I fell into his thoughts and hit a wall of pain. It shattered and stabbed me to the point that I wanted to check myself for blood.

But I wasn't bleeding, he was.

The moment he showed me was our fight in the foyer when I told him I couldn't be with him anymore.

I saw myself as he saw me and had to admit, I looked hotter than when I saw myself in the mirror. I thought myself okay looking, but Zane saw me exactly how he said he did.

As his queen.

I glowed softly in his gaze. My features were softer, my skin ghostly pale and then flushed as he took me to another scene. He was on top of me, thrusting inside me while he held me in his arms. I felt the lust, the memory of my own tightness being spread about his assaulting member.

My head and hands were still on top of Ewan, but my mind was elsewhere.

Heat coiled through my blood, and I broke out into a sweat.

I lowered my gaze and backed out of Zane's thoughts just as a hand landed on my butt underneath the sheets. Ewan squeezed me into his body and forced me down on the abundant wood in his pants.

He groaned as he stretched underneath me.

Zane's libidinous memories were still at the forefront of my mind, filling my own desire and making me ache.

A glance in his direction made me still. He was standing with his fist by his sides. The lines of his body were hard. Was he angered by the sight of Ewan grinding myself against me or turned on?

I reached out and touched him with my necromancy and found that he was still open to me. He was blocking his thoughts but was available to my commands.

I tugged, and he stumbled forward.

Desire flared. I opened my mouth because I could no longer breathe through my nose.

Ewan's heart pounded in my ear.

The sheet was yanked back, and someone grabbed my ankle. The power that linked me to the men in the room told me it was Dimitri.

He slid his large hands up my thighs just as Ewan grabbed the band of my wet underwear and pushed them down. Dimitri helped them off the rest of the way. Then Alan's hands stroked my back and lifted my shirt over my head.

I laid back down on Ewan and found Zane's eyes again.

He watched from up close as the others woke my skin with their rough petting. Lips ran down my spine and up the back of my legs while Ewan continued to rock himself against my clitoris.

Conflicting emotions mingled with my lust. I was still upset about yesterday, but my need was just as strong. I could feel their emotions. Their sorrowful apologies were as present as the hands that spread my thighs.

I mewled when someone dipped their tongue between my slit. The moment those lips took hold of me, my mind was lost to the moment.

Hands on my hips pulled me back while Ewan ran his hands through his hair. He didn't have to send my mind any ideas to tell me what he wanted. I unsnapped his pants. He'd barely shoved them down before I had him in my mouth.

He hissed and pumped himself between my lips as Dimitri fit himself inside my other lips, stretching my soaked slit while I sucked Ewan, running my hand up and down his stiff pole and pulling hard while Dimitri broke me wide open.

The need in our blood was ravenous and filled the room with the scent of passion. I was blinded by the feel of hard muscles and velvet skin.

A tongue danced around my slit, and I knew it was Alan. He sucked my clit between his lips, and I came.

"Alan," Dimitri hissed as he fisted my hips.

I popped Ewan out of my mouth to see what Alan was doing to the beast.

Alan's hand disappeared behind Dimitri's back, and I had a feeling I knew exactly what those deft hands were doing. Dimitri pumped faster, and I took Ewan back into my mouth.

I caught sight of Zane again and stilled as I watched him fist himself. His pants were caught around his ankle. The lust in his eyes was unapologetic and sent wild ideas into my mind as I licked Ewan from base to tip.

I swirled my tongue around the soft, purple mushroom top and turned my gaze back to Ewan. His laden lids and hazy emeralds announced that he was close. He fisted my hair, and I took him into my throat.

"Lorena!" He shot off down my throat at the same time Dimitri roared and emptied himself deep in my gut.

I was rolled and flipped onto my back.

And was presented with the stunning sight of Alan's face. His soft hair felt like feathers against my cheek. He was a pretty combination of soft and hard in all the best ways. His blue eyes were like glass holding back a tide of emotion. "Do you forgive us?"

"This wouldn't be happening if I didn't." I wanted them, but not that much. I could feel their worry pounding through my skin. They were sorry. They'd learned their lesson.

Zane on the other hand … I didn't even want to think about him.

I reached up and threaded my hands through his hair. Then I locked my fingers and tugged his head to an angle that exposed his throat.

He cried out, and I felt his shaft twitch.

"You're lucky you're so pretty."

He smiled.

Without the pulse of a living man, his skin was left luminous and pale, and for some reason, I wanted to bite it.

I realized the idea wasn't mine entirely. Dimitri was beside me, showering my shoulder with kisses.

Giving his throat what it was begging for, I licked him as he nudged my thighs farther apart. I sank my teeth into his skin.

He bottomed out, and I let go to arch myself into his thrust. It felt so good. I wanted to touch him everywhere, experience him and the others in every way possible.

I called them to me and felt their hands against my skin. One pair. Two. Pinching my nipples, rolling my clit in their fingers. Something nudged my mouth, and I inhaled, taking him deep while he pumped into my throat.

Growls and skin slapping were the theme to this coming together.

Wicked tongues flicked across my sensitive places. My senses exploded, heightened. I detonated from the inside out and shuttered as I came.

Alan gave a shout and collapsed on top of me. His simple weight was a comfort.

He righted his head, and I pulled him to me. He kissed me and stuck his tongue into my mouth.

Sharp claps broke the spell. Two palms had never sounded so cynical before. "Well, that was a lovely performance though I've seen more of my brother than I ever wanted to it," Aisling said.

I looked over Alan's shoulder to see who else had seen the show.

A quick glance around had me wondering who hadn't.

Dr. Shaw was flushed. Her chin was in the air. Her gaze was so concentrated that I wondered if she could see through the roof. Thankfully, she had a hand over Blair's eyes, but who knew how much the girl had seen before her mother had acted so quickly?

Jenny and Willow had their mouths parted in equal amounts of shock while Marquessa didn't look surprised in the least.

Want to know what shocked me? My lack of embarrassment. Alan was still lodged inside of me, and I felt nothing but wonder that it had happened. I wrapped my arms around Alan and ran my hand down his back. He was just as buttery soft as me. They couldn't tell us to get a room. We already had one. "Has anyone heard of knocking?"

"It's urgent."

Sirius was struggling to break the hold William and Asher had on him. He was almost foaming at the mouth as he rocked on the floor. William had his knee in the vampire's back.

"What's wrong with him?"

"You called to him." Zane was stretched beside me on the bed, his features softened with sensual sedation. He had a hand on my breast and didn't look inclined to remove it at all. I licked my lips and tasted him on me. He'd been in my mouth. He'd come in my mouth.

Before I could throw him across the room with my fury, he said, "You called to me as well. I tried to hold back, but I'd already let you in so you could read my mind. You sank your hook in all of us. It was impossible to refuse you after that. Even now, I wait for your permission to let go."

I wanted to be furious, but even *I* knew it was right. At the height of my orgasm, I'd called to everyone, and apparently, everyone included the man who was no longer my boyfriend and a guy who wouldn't *ever* be my boyfriend no matter what the Queen of the Trees thought.

I couldn't hate him for this. I'd been wound so tight and so hot I might have let a ghost touch me if he was around.

My necromancy marinated the air in the room, making for any of the men to think. They'd all opened themselves to me and let me dominate their thoughts and body.

They were draped around me, completely nude. Dimitri was underneath my head. Ewan was glued to my other side. Alan was still inside me. At first, I assumed he was keeping his position to keep my modesty, but now I thought otherwise.

I called my necromancy back, and sure enough, they all started dressing. Dimitri and Alan went to take a shower. Zane covered me with a blanket but didn't immediately move away.

"Nothing has changed," I said.

"You're right," he said right back. "Nothing has changed."

Deciphering his meaning meant putting my own anger to the side. Was he assuming sex made him my boyfriend? Well, if that was the case, I was about to pop his little bubble. "Do you have something you want to share with me?"

"I love you."

"And?"

"Everything I do is for your happiness and to make sure you get everything you want."

"And what is it you think I want?"

His eyes glittered like topaz. "Dragons."

I opened my mouth and closed it. My skin burned as I remembered all the nights we'd stayed up together talking about all the things I wanted. Dragons were at the top of the list along with enough magic to make the Earth whole again.

"Zane, tell me the truth."

"Don't," Sirius shouted. He was finally standing, but William hadn't let him go.

"I won't," Zane replied.

"Get out!" I shouted at the people by the door.

Everyone but my lovers filed out. Sirius was dragged.

"Lorena, you will be presented a choice very soon. If I tell you how that choice affects everyone else, you'll never do it." What did that mean? What choice would I be given?

"I don't like this, Zane. I have the right to know."

He narrowed his eyes in pain. "I will never give you this. It is a burden. Fate is a burden. I wish I didn't know. I wish I was like you once again. Trust me. You are free when you don't know."

Zane rolled out of bed.

He felt no shame in his raw state, and he shouldn't. I felt myself getting aroused again as he turned his back to me. I thought about running my tongue down his spine and swirling it in the hollow place at his lower back. His muscles spread like wings.

He looked back and smiled.

I stiffened. Did his ring allow him to read my thoughts?

To test it out, I looked at Dimitri as he emerged from the bathroom. I thought about kicking him.

No reaction.

I turned back to Zane, and he chuckled.

The first order of business? Get my pregnancy hormones in order.

Grabbing my dress, I got up and heard his sharp intake of air. I looked back and smiled. "Take a good look." I wanted to tell him he'd never touch me again, but the way my body was acting left me unsure.

I passed Ewan on the way to the bathroom and noticed his dazed expression.

"What's wrong?" I asked.

He furrowed his brows. "They're up."

"Yeah." Then it hit me. Ewan was surprised when the other vampires got up from their beds in the morning, and I took the opportunity to explain everything that had happened since he had left.

We stopped to shower and then went out to join the others who were waiting in the hall back inside.

Ewan sat next to me in two chairs by the window. "This is unbelievable." He wore one of my rings now. He didn't actually need it, but when I offered, he was honored.

I could no longer read his mind whenever I wanted to, but I didn't really need to anyway. I trusted him completely.

His stone was a diamond.

And so was mine, but my stone was huge. My men had presented me with the ring after I gave Ewan's his. Apparently, they'd been discussing marriage behind my back, and all decided to give me this token of their affection together.

It didn't really solve the question of who I was going to officially marry, but it did solidify our union. We were a very serious thing.

Zane stared at my hand, and I knew what he was thinking. He'd been in the room when Alan had slipped it on my finger. I knew he'd helped pick it out, but that didn't mean he had any claim on me.

The look he gave Ewan's hand was different but just as possessive. He looked like he wanted to cut it off and run with it.

Good, I thought. If he wanted a ring, he had to give me what I wanted, and that was the truth.

Wait. What was I thinking? Zane and I were done. There was no going back.

"All of this happened in three days?" Ewan asked.

Had it only been three days?

"Yup." Dr. Shaw was braiding my hair again. Two days in a row. If she did it a third time, then I'd have no choice but to call it routine. I would become dependent on her patient hands threading through my hair and the soft humming she tried to suppress.

The sound told me that she liked braiding my hair. She enjoyed it just as much as I did. Were we both crazy? She had to be aware that I was using her as a substitute mother.

Thoughts for another day.

Aisling said, "I don't know what I can say to leave the castle. King Rolo won't let me go." She glared at her brother. "Thanks for marrying me off, brother."

"Like I told you last night, I didn't," Ewan said. "He surprised me with his declaration the same as you."

She pouted. "I don't want to marry him, Ewan."

"Then, you won't." Ewan stood. "I've allowed his men to stay because we need his army for the war, but that doesn't mean he can make demands on any person here. Negotiations were closed long before your return."

Ewan could do a lot of things to turn me on. One of those things included breathing, but nothing made me want to throw him onto the floor more than the way he stood up for his sister. He was the prince regent while his mother entertained herself with Ulgard.

Dr. Shaw finished my hair and patted the braid before she stepped away.

"I'll speak to Lord Rolo now," Ewan said. "I'll go downstairs promptly."

"Rolo is not here," his sister said. "He went to fight. He says he finds palace life dull."

Ewan's hand rested on the hilt of his sword. "Well, I'll wait for his return and confront him then." He met his sister's eyes as he made his vow.

Aisling looked away, as if unsure what to do with all the kindness her brother was showing.

I smiled. The words, *I told you so,* danced in my mind, but saying them aloud would be childish.

"I told you so," I whispered. Less childish.

Aisling's face pinked, and when she looked at her brother next, there so much hope and love that it squeezed my heart.

Ewan held out his hand for me. "Are you hungry?"

"Does the queen of England own all the swans in Britain?" I slapped my hand in his.

It was time to get my grub on.

CHAPTER TWENTY

After breakfast, Ewan left for the mines to speak with the leaders. His advisors went with him, as did the troops. Ewan offered to take me, but when I realized going meant riding a horse with Lilac pressed against my back for hours so she could hide my identity, I passed on the offer and instead went to the market.

I wanted to see parts of the kingdom I hadn't the first time. Everyone was out to kill or steal Lorena, but no one was out to kill whomever Lilac had me disguised as.

Our arms were linked as we strolled, but otherwise, we could have been on separate parts of the globe. We said nothing to each other, and I stopped at the stalls or watched wagon caravans of families with children. Their wheels picked up the red dirt road and made a cloud.

Just passed the bridge, the mote was a road that led through the dense forest and then to a small village I hadn't seen the last time I'd left the palace. I'd been flying on Airgead before. Now, we walked.

I saw fae who looked like they'd come from all over. They were moving closer to the castle as the war pressed on, escaping for their lives.

The civilians looked sodden and tired. Their despair was like a cloud that followed them and touched everyone. I wondered if they'd have homes to return to when this was over.

A boy ran past me, and I smiled until I saw the manacle around his throat.

Slaves. I didn't see any of this before. Maybe this was another reason Titania hadn't let me out of her sight. There were no slaves in the palace, at least as far as I'd seen.

Rolo and Ewan's soldiers lined the streets, but their presence didn't subdue the hustle and bustle. In fact, I saw more than a few women bat their eyes with interest at the soldiers, including the scarred ones. I mean, I understood the appeal of the furious bodily damage. The scars told a story that basically ended with the words, "You think this is bad? You should see the other guy." And the other guy was probably dead.

But I had plenty of scars of my own, and while most of the big ones were from battles, I was also clumsy. Who was to say the badly injured soldier wasn't also accident-prone?

Speaking of accidents, Dr. Shaw had insisted on walking with us just in case I needed her. Jenny, Marquessa, and Aisling stayed behind to look over what we'd be taking from the palace for our journey.

I thought of these things so I could avoid thinking about other things, like the fact that we needed to get to the Court of Water and that my arm was linked with a woman I was sure wanted to kill me and that every time I looked in her ex-boyfriend's direction, he was watching me.

I tried to avoid them both, but my eyes were stubborn.

Sirius took the look as an invitation to move closer when, in fact, it was an invitation to jump off a cliff. "Good morning," he purred. He was Scottish today, so the words sounded were more like, "*guid mornin'.*"

While he was around, I decided to ask a question I was dying to know the answer to. "You said Vlad isn't your father."

"He isn't."

"So, who made you?"

He chuckled. "I'll let you in on that little truth when you let me into your body."

I wasn't surprised the conversation had already gone where he wanted it to. "Clue in. That stuff doesn't turn me on."

"Oh, but my tongue will."

Lilac dropped my arm and walked away.

Sirius wrapped an arm around me, protecting me from the view of others while I fumbled with my hood. "Wait here," he whispered. He talked to a merchant and then came back with a beautiful piece of fabric with jewelry adorning the top with dangly pieces. It looked like a belly dancer's veil.

I let him put it on me and took a breath.

"Good?" he asked.

"Great." Now that Lilac was gone, everything was rainbows and sprinkles and puppies in tutus. "Why do you do that to her? Isn't it obvious that she wants you?"

"I can't help her feelings. As I said before, I haven't touched her in decades."

"Then, why live together?"

"Because of last night. The guard at the gate."

"What? You stayed together just for that?"

He chuckled. "You have no idea what secrets the universe holds."

"Does Lilac know?"

"No, and I would suggest you don't tell her. So long as she feels like she's serving a purpose, she's able to hold back the mania. Besides, there are still places in the future where she can be useful." He was like Professor X.

I wondered if there was anything he couldn't see. "Well, that explains a lot. Thanks. Bye."

He caught my hand. "Walk with me. There are things you must know."

I glanced around. William was watching him, but he was strolling with Aisling, still planning the journey to the Court of Water. Dimitri, Alan, and Zane were with them, and I could tell that they'd all come to my aid if I asked for it.

But they also knew to only come if I called. I didn't need them fighting my battles.

I yanked my hand from Sirius. "Touch me again without my permission, and you'll regret it."

"You said the tree at the mansion told you to bring me with you. Did she say why?" His eyes glittered like he knew the answer.

But how?

Did the stars actually instruct him to become my lover? What difference would it make at this point? I was pregnant with Zane's child. "Tell me. Would you want me if the stars hadn't told you to come after me?"

"You could ask the others the same. We've all come to you through fate."

I turned away. I didn't want to believe that, but a portion of me knew it was true. The vampires had first approached me because they wanted to be the father of my child, but that wasn't the reason we were still together.

And it clearly wasn't the reason Sirius wanted me either.

"What do you want from me?" I held up my hand before he could talk. "Let's skip the sexual innuendos and get to the point."

He sighed heavily. "Zane may be the father, but the power of every vampire you take into your body blesses the child's biology through you." He reached for my stomach, but I batted his hand away. The altercation didn't slow his words down. "We are beings made of magic, after all. Think about our vampire bite and what it does to you. There's power in the vampire. I'm sure you've wondered how you got pregnant in the first place."

I had. "How does it work?"

"Magic is a combination of things. Strength, love, shadow, health, foresight, and hope. Your child will need all of these to bring magic back."

I remembered him saying something about the stars holding the answer to those things. "What are you saying? Each of my men has contributed to my child's mystical prowess?"

"Exactly."

I thought about my lovers. Strength was definitely Dimitri. Love, the soft tender emotion that could also be just as powerful, had to be Alan. Shadow was easily Ewan. Health, I didn't know. Sirius had alluded that foresight was his gift.

And hope?

My stomach flipped like an acrobat on a tight string. "Wei."

"Yes."

We made it to a tree, and I ducked into the shade. "Are you confirming that I'll get Wei back?"

He sank to the grass and patted the spot next to him. "Maybe Wei has already given you what you need."

I dropped down beside him and noted how much that pleased him. Clinging to his ocean eyes, I allowed the tide of his beauty to pull me in. "I never slept with Wei."

His eyes dropped to my mouth. "How unfortunate for him," he muttered without an ounce of actual sympathy.

"But Wei has bitten me before."

He lifted his brow and then his eyes. "Yes?"

"Therefore, if his bite was enough, maybe your bite will be enough as well." If I could keep this man out of my vagina, I would count that a victory.

He smiled. "Maybe you're right."

So, I didn't have to sleep with him. Maybe. The man was a riddle and spoke in riddles. I hated it. I was intrigued. I hated that I was intrigued by him.

"How much more about this prophecy are you hiding from me?"

"Plenty."

"Can't you tell me anything? Do we make it to the Court of Water? Will someone I love die during the war?"

He held out his hand for mine, and very slowly, I gave my palm up.

His fingers were rough as they rubbed over the pale lines that mapped out the folds of my hand. "I can tell you that … your skin is soft."

"Is that it?"

He popped my pointer finger into his warm mouth and dragged my fingers to the tip. "And delicious."

I snatched my hand back and glared. All the while, heat flooded between my legs. "You're a pig."

He laughed.

I wanted to walk away, but I also wanted more knowledge. "How come you can tell Zane the future and not me?"

"Because Zane is able to bear the weight of it. He's also willing to make the sacrifice." He was no longer grinning, and I hated that almost as much as I hated his grin.

"What do you mean? What sacrifice?"

He stood. "Go easy on him. He's out of options."

"Because of you."

"I'm sorry." With that, he walked away, leaving me.

"You didn't tell me who your father was," I shouted at his back.

"Don't have one."

He didn't have a father? Then who made him?

I looked around for Zane and saw him with Dr. Shaw and Blair.

I waved, and they came over, breaking off from Zane. He was avoiding me as much as I was avoiding him. Dr. Shaw sat in the grass with me. "How are you feeling?"

"Not too bad."

She ran a warm hand up my arm, and I nearly crawled in her lap. It was official. I was attached to the woman. I wondered how Blair felt about it. When I looked over at her, Blaire had tears in her eyes.

I pulled my arm out of her mother's reach.

Blair shook her head. Her mother had put two French braids in her hair that made her look even younger than she already was. "No. I'm not upset. I'm happy for you."

"Oh. Thanks." This was awkward.

She wiped at her eyes. "I mean, your dad told us more about your mother."

"He did?"

"Blair. You know what? I changed my mind about that meat-stick thing." Dr. Shaw smiled at her. "Would you go get some for me?"

She was barely away before Dr. Shaw turned to me. "Do you mind if I check on the baby?"

I leaned back against the tree to give her better access.

She placed her hand over my womb, and I felt a rush of energy, like a cool wind. Her eyes fluttered closed, and her lips curled into a smile. "Healthy." She pulled back. "I'm sure you'll continue to feed her well after he or she is born?"

"Well, if I don't, I'm sure you'll find a way to slip a few carrots on her plate."

She had the laugh of an angel. Dr. Shaw was perfect. I didn't use that word lightly, but I had never met someone more giving and nurturing than her. And here she was now, attending me while just a few thousand miles from here a war raged that could spill out at any moment.

I was just about to ask her why her husband never came around when Blair returned. There was no meat-stick thing in sight, and her expression was pensive. "Where' the meat stick thing?"

"They ran out." She wrapped her arms around her knees.

I didn't know Blair's lying face, but my Spidey senses were telling me that she was a big fat fibber.

Her mother frowned and then lifted herself from the ground. "Perhaps, they could make more if I ask."

"No." Blair scrambled onto her feet. "They can't. They're busy."

"Did someone threaten you?" Dr. Shaw asked.

"What?" Blair's eyes widened. "Mom, it's fine. I think there's another restaurant in the other direction."

My Spidey senses had been on the right track. I rolled onto my hands and shot up. I knew where the stand was. I'd passed the succulent aroma on my way here.

I started in that direction with Dr. Shaw and Blair at my side. Blair continued to stop us, but I heard the commotion before I even reached the place on the road.

Someone was crouched on the ground. His shirt was ripped open. A manacle was wrapped around his foot. Welts decorated his back, and a large, Unseelie soldier with a flogger was beating him. The man on the ground whimpered.

"Hey!" I shouted as I pushed forward. A small little crowd had appeared.

But the soldier didn't stop. Blood broke from the man on the ground. The soldier lifted the flogger higher.

Dr. Shaw flipped her hand with the palm up but kept it by her side, almost like she was asking for it but didn't want to be obvious. I wondered what she was asking for and then heard something like a drum.

The flogging ceased. Then he tried to whip the man again, but something shimmered over the slave like a shield.

The soldier looked around. "Who prevents me from whipping my slave?"

The crowd shuffled back. Me, Dr. Shaw, and the rest of my people didn't.

Blair tried to pull her mother back and whispered, "Stop this." Her face cracked with worry while Dr. Shaw's was almost tranquil.

I decided to walk over to the slave, but someone grabbed my arm. I swung around and met Sirius's eyes. "Let me go."

"Not yet."

The soldier shouted and kicked the magic barrier between him and the slave.

Dr. Shaw gasped but remained steady.

My mouth fell open. It was her. Dr. Shaw wasn't asking for anything. She was offering something, her protection in the form of magic.

"Mom!" Blair cried.

The soldier kicked and threw his fist against the barrier.

Dr. Shaw shook. The damage to her force field was affecting her. Her nose bled.

I turned to Sirius, ready to give him a piece of my mind, but he let me go. "Now."

I turned to the soldier. I didn't try to call him this time. Now was the time for action.

I pulled my wand from my belt and used a spell I'd read in my grandmother's book of shadows last night.

This one was easy. I drew two parallel lines in the air and then tapped them.

The soldier stiffened and stilled. He was frozen.

Using this spell was better than my other gift because I didn't have to worry about him flying into anyone else. Giving him stiff muscles only affected him.

Five soldiers moved, but my vampires—including Sirius—blocked their way.

"Step aside," the shortest and seemingly more authoritative of them said. "The witch will come with us."

"On what charges?" Alan asked as I moved to the servant and helped him up. The force field was down.

The minute I touched his shoulder, he flinched.

"It's all right," I whispered. "No one is going to hurt you." The servant remained on the ground, shaking.

"She stepped between a master and his slave," the angry soldier replied.

I heard metal moving and looked around.

The soldiers looked ready to fight.

Crap. I didn't want bloodshed. In fact, that's what I'd been trying to stop all along.

I looked up at the solider on pause.

He glared at me. He'd been frozen in rage with his fist over his head. I was sure that if I unpaused him, it'd resume just as he was and come down on me hard.

I touched the servant's cheek and bent to whisper in his ear. "Come, you don't have to be afraid anymore. You're free."

"Only the queen can free me," the man said.

I lowered my voice even more. "Well, the prince is in charge, and he plans to free all the slaves. So, basically, you're free."

The servant uncurled his body and looked up into my eyes. His were a soft brown, the same shade as his spiky hair. "The prince is going to free the slaves?" He'd asked the question aloud.

Too loud.

I looked around. Some of the people in the audience were brownies.

Uh-oh.

The guards by the vampires stopped at hearing the claim. "Who has told you this?"

The servant pointed at me.

The short one pointed his sword at me. "You lie. You shall be punished."

"You'll lose your head before that happens," William said, breaking into the circle. He was bigger than the other people around us.

The soldier looked stunned, and then excitement lit his gray eyes. He was ready to tango, and if I were to go by expression alone, I would say he expected to win. He didn't think the odds were against him but in his favor.

"Mom!"

The shout reached into the atmosphere and grabbed my attention.

Blair was on the ground, holding an unconscious Dr. Shaw against her lap.

More soldiers blocked my men and me before we could reach her.

"Arrest the woman who lies in the prince's name," the soldier said.

"I didn't lie! He told me so himself!" In my panic over Dr. Shaw, nothing else mattered but getting to her and getting her out of here.

"And what are you? His whore?" the soldier asked.

The jig was up. I yanked the hood back and tossed the veil to the ground.

I waited for someone to say my name, for the gasp and shouts of surprise.

Instead, I got silence.

The soldiers stared at me and tilted their heads. Then they began to murmur to one another, and I heard one say, "She looks familiar."

She groaned. "It's me. Lorena." Duh!

Then the gasps came. The bows were a shock to me.

The loudmouth soldier dropped to his knee. "Princess Lorena. We didn't know you were among the travelers."

Princess? I looked down at my ring and decided now wasn't the time to correct his assumption. The title was giving me what I wanted. "How do I make mistreatment illegal?"

"The prince is away, and the advisors have gone with him. As acting queen, you have the right to make such a call."

"Oh, I do?" *Oh, the power.* I looked around. "It's illegal."

"Very well, my land."

Oh, what the heck? I threw my hands in the air. "Also, the slaves are free."

The soldier's heads popped up. "My lady?" He looked troubled.

"You heard me. Let them go." I looked out into the crowd that was gathered. Peter was there. Tears ran down his face, and I knew I'd done the right thing.

The soldiers stood and backed away so I could get to Dr. Shaw.

Dimitri already had her up in his arms but handed her over to Zane, who sped off in the direction of the castle. I'd never seen anyone move as fast as Zane.

I started walking back when two soldiers offered Blair and me rides. We accepted and didn't have to tell the men to ride hard. The horse's hooves beat hard against the ground and jostled me around. I almost missed flying. Almost. Only after I'd dismounted on steady legs did I remember that the soldier I'd frozen was still in the same position back in the village.

Oh well. He'd learn his lesson.

I was all the way to Dr. Shaw's room and found Zane lying next to her on the bed and drinking her blood from her wrist.

A flair of anger twisted my power in the air, but then I thought about it and knew Zane wouldn't do that. He might be a liar, but he wouldn't drink Dr. Shaw while she was weak.

He lifted his mouth from her wrist and said, "I'm trying to heal her."

I didn't know how mouth-to-wrist would heal her, but I didn't know much about healing in general, so I left it alone for now.

Dr. Shaw's eyes were closed. Her skin was ash, and she was sweating. She looked frailer than I'd ever seen her before. She looked frailer than I never wanted to see her.

Blair rushed to the other side and took her mother's free hand.

Dr. Shaw opened her eyes enough to look at Blair and smiled at her. "It's all right. I simply need to rest."

Blair closed her eyes and pressed her mother's hand to her chest. "You shouldn't have done that. You know better than to use anything but aura magic."

Her mother nodded slightly as she fought for air. "I ... had to." She turned to me. "Come, Lorena. Don't be afraid."

Afraid? I wasn't afraid.

Okay, maybe I did have a death grip on the door, and perhaps my heart had decided to enter us both into an Olympic race, and I was bound to medal.

I couldn't breathe. My head was light. "Why can't you use anything but aura magic?"

"My auramancer gifts flow easily from me." She took a deep breath. "Anything else ... takes a great amount of energy."

"Energy you don't have," Blair chastened.

There was a whole lot happening in this room. I felt like someone had suggested I watch their favorite move only to start it in the middle somewhere. I was lost.

Zane lifted his mouth from Dr. Shaw's wrist and then stepped back. "I'll give you all a moment."

He averted his gaze when he passed me and turned his body so he wouldn't brush me. I was glad he didn't. My feet were still unsteady, and I wanted to blame the horse ride for that.

I didn't want to enter the room. It seemed like a trap, and once I crossed the threshold, there'd be no going back.

Dr. Shaw held out her free hand to me, and only then did I step forward. She was weak, and like earlier today, I had a feeling she'd keep her hand out for as long as she deemed necessary.

I took the place Zane had occupied and grabbed her fingers. They were cold. I didn't like that. Her blue eyes were glassy, and I didn't like that either.

She opened her mouth, and I shook my head.

"No. I don't want to hear it." I knew what was coming. I'd crossed the threshold. There was no going back.

"I'm dying."

Air lodged itself in my throat. I looked at Blair, whose eyes were red, but she didn't look shocked at all. Then, with watery eyes, I turned back to Dr. Shaw.

Have you ever played that board game The Game of Life? Well, I felt like I'd been making all the wrong choices until recently, and now that I was finally the final stretch of victory, someone had just come along and tossed the whole board up.

I stiffened, and in the next seconds, a sob broke from my lips, and I was wailing, screaming and not making any sense as my anger, pain, and utter annoyance at life crashed down on me.

Couldn't I have anything?

Was I forever bound to lose everyone I loved?

I didn't remember getting up from the bed, but an hour later, I sat in the corner of the room that I'd destroyed. Wood from chairs and tables I'd smashed into the walls were spread out like waste on the ground. I'd have broken the wall if they weren't made of emerald stone.

The only thing that remained intake was the bed that Dr. Shaw and Blair remained on.

Neither of them was at all surprised by what I'd done. I grabbed my knees and buried my face between my knees.

Hands covered my arms sometime later. I looked up and felt the smile Dr. Shaw gave me. It filled me with warmth, but sadness beat it back. She was dying. What had I ever done to deserve any of this?

My dad had been right to try to keep me from my destiny. I didn't want it. I'd give it up for Dr. Shaw. My baby and I would go on and live a normal life. We didn't have to bring back magic. I'd make that sacrifice if I thought it would save her.

Now all her comments from earlier made sense. She'd been trying to warn me that she wouldn't always be around. I felt stupid, stupid for loving her. I got up and slid across the wall, then walked out.

I didn't know where I was going, but firm hands grabbed me before I could hit my head against a chest.

I looked up and met Sirius' eyes. "Get back in there."

Anger flooded me. "You caused this. I could have stopped her from taking it too far, but you held me back." I gasped as I realized he'd done it on purpose. I pushed his chest and yanked out of his hold. "You did this."

"It had to be done."

"Why?"

He shook his head, his eyes mournful. "I'm sorry, Lorena, but I can't tell you."

"How many more people will die before this is over?"

"Many."

I shook my head. "I quit. I'm going back to Virginia, and I'm taking everyone with me. Do you hear me!" I shouted the last when my declaration of secession gained no reaction. "I'm leaving."

"You can't. Aisling no longer holds the portal key. Rolo had taken them to the frontlines with him. He's making sure she doesn't try to escape."

Sirius knew this. He knew I'd react this way. He knew everything. "Is there anything you don't know?"

He leaned against the wall and crossed his arms. "There is plenty I don't know, and most of the time, I don't know if that makes what I know better or worse."

I understood that. The not knowing what was killing him just as much as the knowing did. I didn't know what I'd do if I had his gift, probably go mad, probably act as repulsive as he sometimes did. "Why? Can you at least tell me why?"

"Go to her," he said. "This time should not be about us."

He was right. I needed to speak to Dr. Shaw. I needed to know what was wrong with her. Maybe I could fix her. Save her.

I wanted to ask Sirius if that was possible, but I also didn't want his answer. The walk back to Dr. Shaw's room seemed longer. Once again, I stepped over the threshold.

The room was dark, thanks to the absence of natural light. Only a candelabra by the bedside was lit.

Blair and Dr. Shaw looked at me when I entered. They were both so pretty. I remembered how perfect I'd assumed their life was. My judgment shamed me.

I moved to the bed before Dr. Shaw would lift her hand and took her fingers once again.

Her color was better, and her eyes as bright as stars.

"What do you have?"

"Lupus. I've been terminally ill for years, but I've been using magic to keep the symptoms back."

"Whenever she takes an ounce of magic for anything else, the symptoms return," Blair whispered.

Her mother nodded. "And they come back uglier and harder than ever."

I frowned and thought about Missy Morton. She'd had lupus.

How strange.

I thought about the photo I'd seen of Missy and my grandfather. Then I stared at Dr. Shaw.

My Spidey senses activated, but I held back the assumption. There was no way. "Why did you come to Colt Valley?"

"Because you needed a doctor.'

"Who told you that? Marquessa and the other witches say it wasn't them."

He smiled. "Your father called me."

"Dad? You know my dad."

She laughed lightly. "We met recently. I was looking for him."

"Why?"

"Because he's my half-brother."

She was Missy's child, which made her my aunt and Blair, my cousin.

"But your last name is Shaw."

"I'm married. My maiden name is Quinn." She looked at Blair. "Blair's last name is Quinn as well. My husband is not her father though he tried to adopt her once or twice."

Blair lowered her gaze. I wondered about the mystery of her father, but I let it go for now.

I had a cousin and an aunt.

But now my aunt was dying.

I asked Blair, "Do you have lupus too?" I couldn't afford any more loss in my life.

Blair shook her head.

"Dr. Shaw …"

"Elizabeth," she corrected. "Or Aunt Beth. I think we've moved beyond the bounds of professionalism." She turned to Blair. "Will you give us a moment?"

Blair hesitated but eventually walked out of the room. The door was quietly closed behind her.

"If I hadn't been so stubborn. If I'd been nicer."

"Shh, no, Lorena. We had our time, and it was wonderful getting to know the real you." She smiled. "I honestly didn't know how to tell you."

"I wish you had told me." I pushed down the anger that pressed at the back of my mind. "Everyone keeps secrets from me."

"Well, this secret was mine, not yours. And don't be mad at your father. I asked him not to say anything because, again, this was my secret. I hadn't planned on telling you, seeing as I don't have long to live. I was going to be your doctor and nothing more." She touched my cheek. "I never meant to get as close as I have, but honestly … you're a very hard girl not to love." She tapped my nose and smiled.

My chin trembled. Why couldn't she have been the villain I tried to make her out to be? That would have made everything so much easier.

She loved me? She thought loving me was easy? I didn't. I'd been so mean to her in the beginning. My mother had really done a number on me where mother figures were concerned. I hadn't wanted Elizabeth's tenderness, but she'd given it to me anyway, and then I'd gotten addicted.

I wanted to be angry, but I knew I didn't have time to be angry because my aunt could die any day now, which only made me angrier.

"I called him to ask him a favor. Then he told me about you, and I knew I had to come and care for you, even if you never knew who I was."

Aunt Beth. I couldn't believe it. I thought it kind of strange that my grandmother had let another woman marry the man she loved. Now my world was being twisted in the other direction as the reality of everything my grandmother had done sunk in.

If she hadn't let Missy marry Jake, there'd have never been an Elizabeth Quinn.

I didn't know how much longer I had with her, but I was thankful for the time I did. "What was the favor you wanted from my father?"

Elizabeth took a deep breath. "I need someone to look after Blair. I don't want to leave her without a foundation."

"What about your husband?"

It was the first time I'd seen Dr. Shaw looked nervous. "He isn't in the picture." There was so much more where those words came from, but she didn't open up, and I had a feeling she wouldn't.

It was her secret, so I let it go. "You want Dad to watch over her?" I asked. "He moves around a lot for work."

"I know, but I didn't realize how much until his visit the other day. Thankfully, Blair is in her final year of high school. Then she'll be off to college. She'll only need someone to spend holidays with."

"She can stay with me and the vampires."

Elizabeth's eyes widened. "Really?"

"Of course." I'd never had a cousin before. "I'll look out for her, I promise."

My beautiful aunt smiled. "Thank you, Lorena. You have no idea how much this means to me. Would you tell her?" She closed her eyes. "I'm feeling rather tired. I think I'll skip dinner."

"Okay." With great gentleness, I put her slender hand down on the bed before I stood.

Blair was down the hall, looking over the balcony railing and down to the next floor. She turned to me as I got close. "What did she say?"

I didn't know how to explain what just happened with her mother. I was still trying to process it all myself. Yesterday, I had the responsibility of motherhood to look forward to. Now, I have a seventeen-year-old cousin as well.

My life was complicated. I hadn't asked for it, but there it was, and until Dr. Who decided to pay a visit and take me on a trip in his time machine, there was no going back.

But what I didn't have to do was take those complications and put them on Blair. I was not going to make her feel like the burden my father had made me feel like for most of my life.

I walked over to the railing and put my arm through hers, linking us together. "She just wanted me to remind you that you're not alone."

Blair smiled sadly. "She asked you to look out for me."

"No, I told her that was what I was going to do because you're a part of the team now."

"The team?" She played with the ends of one of her braids.

"Yeah. Me, the vampires, werewolves, and witches. We're all a team. A family. You're a part of that."

She turned to me and hugged me, squeezing the life out of me. "Thank you."

CHAPTER TWENTY-ONE

I'd have skipped breakfast in favor of sleeping in …

Who was I kidding? I'd have skipped breakfast in favor of yanking every single one of my eyelashes out.

But Titania had summoned me to the grand hall.

The summoned part was the only thing that got me moving. The last thing I wanted to do was start another war.

The great hall was exactly as I remembered. Beautiful. Cold. A combination of pale stones and gleaming silverware. Soft music played from the quartet in the music box high up in the corner of the room. The violin music was a song I recognized and different from her usual playlist.

Who'd introduced her to Bruce Springsteen? She must have picked it up when she crashed the vampires' house back in my world.

I bobbed my head to "Dancing in the Dark" even as I told myself I should tell the band to stop. Titania didn't deserve great music like Bruce.

When I arrived, her staff sat me down next to her in front of the rest of her court.

For a long time, we said nothing.

I know what you're thinking. Me saying nothing was highly unusual for me, but I didn't know what to say, and my thoughts were a thousand miles away from the eggs on my plate. I was thinking about Dr. Shaw and if she'd make the journey to the Court of Water if we'd have to send her back to the human world.

I was thinking about Blair and hoping she didn't turn out anything like me, because it didn't matter what Dr. Shaw had tried to imply, I knew the truth. I was difficult. There hadn't been an easy thing about my life, and thus, I wasn't an easy person.

I wondered where Ewan was and if he was okay. I wondered if Rolo would return from the frontline.

And lastly, I wondered how Titania was doing, but I didn't ask.

For the moment, she was being civil. She ate with gusto as though she'd been putting in hours of work and had hours more ahead of her. She hadn't even said anything about me freeing the slaves.

I noticed the staff numbers seemed lower. How many of the people in the palace had been stuck in indentured servitude to this woman?

I looked out at the court. There were faces I recognized from my imprisonment here, and then there were my friends. Looking at Dr. Shaw, you would never think she'd been ill yesterday. She looked as perfect as she always did, but I couldn't shake the truth out of my vision.

I still hadn't talked to Zane about his "healing" ability, but I would soon.

He and the other vampires had decided to stay away from Titania after Willow strongly suggested it. Not only had Willow been around during Vlad and Aisling's affair, but she'd been the one to introduce them. This relationship might be why Titania allowed Willow to yammer on when she'd come to the table. Titania never sneered or shouted at Willow like she did with everyone else.

Aisling was on her mother's other side, eating quietly. She jumped whenever a door opened, waiting for Rolo's return.

She sipped her drink, and then finally, when she was done, she turned to me. "I ought to kill you."

There she was. That's the Titania I knew. "How are you feeling?"

"Vengeful."

"Great." She didn't want to talk about it. I wasn't going to force it. "Now, can we skip past the threats and get right to the reason you've called me here because I have some things I need to handle?"

There was beauty, and then there was Titania. Her charm was unparalleled by nothing but nature itself. Her hair was the sun, with its beautiful rays of every shade of gold, falling down in curls that danced around her comely face. Her eyes were succulent meadow, a verdant so pure that I almost felt unworthy to meet her gaze. She was a queen through and through, her elegant dominance made more evident by her six-foot stature.

She lifted her glass to a staff member who had been standing by her chair since I'd arrived.

The large man stared down at nothing and only moved and even smiled when Titania paid some attention. He had elf ears though the tips were almost covered up by his wild, black hair. His head and body were boxy.

He smiled at me as he poured Titania another glass of whatever the pink fizzy stuff was. I stared into his black eyes and saw nothing. He turned away and looked forward when he was done.

"You freed my slaves," she said. "All of them. Now, I'm left with creatures like him." He motioned to the big guy by her chair.

I didn't know what a *him* was. What was he?

I thought about pointing out the obvious fact that she didn't need to enslave anyone. She had plenty of wealth. One pearl wall could feed her entire nation for centuries to come. She could afford to pay a fair wage. But what was the point? It was likely she already knew that.

I didn't waste my breath. I had no breath to waste. I barely had the energy to concentrate on her words.

"I'm going to appeal to my advisors to be reinstated as queen. I gave my son the monarchy, believing he'd take care of the kingdom and me, but already he failed at not leaving anyone but you in charge."

I had my limits on how much I was willing to take from this woman. She'd reached him. "Exactly, why do you need slaves?"

"For the mines. You don't stay as powerful as I am and not have slaves. How do you think the Unseelie came to hold the most land in this world? Do you think the others simply gave it to me?" her smile was like poisoned candy.

My stomach boiled. "Your power is made on the backs of others."

"That's all power, dear." She glanced at my stomach. "Your power shall be made on the back of my grandchild. By the way, my grandchild is the reason I won't kill you."

"That's comforting. How's Ulgard?"

Her grace didn't wane at all. Her smile sharpened with true glee. "He's doing very well. You should come down to the dungeons and see all the marvelous ways I've been keeping myself busy."

Barf. "No, thanks."

The great golden doors swung open, and Ewan prowled in like a vision of everything powerful and yummy. My belly flipped, and my happy place squeezed.

He started toward me but then stopped at the sight of his mother. His steps slowed and then picked up before he reached up.

I stood, and he kissed me right there in front of the court.

And I was so ready for him to do so much more to me. I instantly ached for him.

He pulled back, but my fingers were still in his clothes, so he didn't get too far. He grinned and then dipped to my ear. His warm breath put more heat in my blood. "I believe I told you my plans for the slaves was a secret."

"Oops." I gave him my best smile.

His lips twitched, and he sighed. "No matter. It's done." He peeked around me at his mother. "Mother. I'm glad to see you've left the cellars."

Hadn't his mother been coming up for air at all? Surely she couldn't be torturing Ulgard day and night."

Queen Titania threw down her linen napkin. "Well, when my servants didn't return after I sent them off for my evening meal, I had no choice but to come up and discover what you'd done wrong."

Word of freedom seemed to travel fast.

Ewan put a hand on my shoulder. "I'm not going to explain myself to you."

My eyes widened at Ewan's tone. As did Titania's. Her son had never spoken to her that way.

Ewan cut his eyes to Aisling. "Has Rolo returned? Otherwise, I'm off to the front."

"There is no need to hunt me down," Rolo ducked his head underneath the door frame to the right, coming in through the servant's entrance. How long had he been here? He straightened and inhaled, stealing half the air in the room to fill his lungs. "I've saved you the trip."

His men flooded into the room, knocking the tension up by a hundred degrees.

The warriors were dressed in nothing but simple sackcloth around their waste, presenting their abundant scarring to every eye. Aside from the horns that twisted in various directions depending on the man, they wore no weapons.

Ewan looked completely bored of the other fae, who was twice his height, width, and probably five times his weight. "I'm glad you could join us, King Rolo. There is a matter that needs to be discussed."

"And that is?"

"My sister is not for sale."

A quick intake of air had me look over at Aisling. She'd run across the room when she'd heard Rolo's voice. Did she think Ewan had been lying? He couldn't lie and even more charming was the fact that he hadn't beaten around the bush either. He didn't mince his words or explain himself. He just stated the facts.

Titania cleared her throat. "What Ewan means is—"

"I've said exactly what I meant, Mother."

Titania stood up, and the large servant at her back picked up her chair before it could tumble. "You listen to me! I am queen here. I want my slaves back, and Aisling shall … What are you doing? Are you even listening to me?"

Ewan had turned to whisper something to a servant. He didn't speak until the servant was gone. "I sent food down to Ulgard."

Titania's features twisted grotesquely. "No!" She ran from the room. Her need for revenge was more powerful than her need to rule the kingdom.

Our attention returned to Rolo.

The new king of the Court of Fire rubbed his jaw and then twisted his neck until it cracked. The sound echoed against the stone walls. "Has Aisling been promised to another?"

"No, you mistake me. My sister has never been for sale, and so long as I am alive, acting king or not, that shall remain the case. My sister is free to choose her partner."

Oh, Ewan was differently getting some tonight.

Rolo chuckled. "Prince Ewan, forgive me for rushing to the idea. Your sister's beauty caught me off guard. Now, I'm sure you understand that the trade is fair. My men die on the battlefield for your cause—"

"My mother's cause," Ewan countered.

The gray beast flicked up a brow. "Shall I pull my troops back?"

Ewan stiffened. "We had an agreement. You signed a contract. You are being paid handsomely."

"And I agreed to the contract when it was drawn up, but circumstances have changed."

"Circumstances have not changed."

Rolo cut him off. "I don't want your gold or any of the precious stones you people all but worship. The Court of Fire is one made of bones and blood. I want your sister." Rolo turned toward Aisling, and I jumped up, blocked his path, and brought his journey to a quick end.

"I believe the acting monarch has already told you that you can't have her. Shall you hear it from the princess's lips herself?" I looked back at Aisling.

She was trembling a little. She looked nothing like the brave girl who'd been out for vengeance in my world. She didn't look like the tough woman who'd bragged about kicking Corridan last night, either. She looked scared, and I was not about to let what happened to her mother happen to her as well. My personal feelings aside, no one was getting touched without their permission around me.

"Lorena!" Ewan vanished, and then I was taken into a cloud of blackness.

I was wind and darkness. I felt Rolo's hand grazed my face. Caught in the vortex of Ewan's gift, I was shadows. Cold and uncontainable.

The gray king shouted his rage as his fist missed over and over. The shadow shifted around his hands.

He couldn't touch me, but I wondered if I could touch him. It was worth a shot.

I reached out past the shadow and shoved him with my magic.

He hit the ground but jumped right back up and made a beeline for Aisling.

Before his fingers could wrap themselves around her red hair, Rolo was tackled by something large and hairy and slammed to the ground. There was a grunt, and then a crack rang around the room.

Rolo's body shifted but not on its own.

A large gray wolfman was prompting him up. A bone-chilling howl ripped past his snout.

Ewan collected himself and became whole again. He placed me behind him as Rolo's men growled. "Protect her!"

I was immediately surrounded by both the wolves and vampires who seemed to have come out of nowhere. They had their packs on. They were ready to leave.

A fight broke out. Claws, fist, feet, and teeth created a sight of pure carnage.

The people around me started to move me, almost picking me up when I didn't move fast enough. My heart raced as I looked around frantically. "Dr. Shaw! Blair!" They were my responsibilities. I'd dragged them into his world, and I wouldn't go anywhere without them.

I couldn't see them over everyone who was so much taller than me. Sometimes, it sucked being short, especially in those pesky life or death situations.

My shields of flesh began to break off as more soldiers poured in, but Dimitri stayed close and handed me my bag. "Put it on."

I shrugged it on while I continued to look for my friends. There!

Across the room, Jenny and Marquessa were with Blair and Dr. Shaw. The four had their backs to one another. Jenny and Marquessa were blasting attacks back like no one's business while Blair and her mother spun their magic through the air until they'd made a tight shell around them.

"No!" Dr. Shaw couldn't use this kind of magic. "Stop it!"

The determination on their faces was ruthless. They wouldn't listen.

The force field was a blue glass that shimmered whenever someone tried to break through.

The doors were blocked so we couldn't get out that way.

Dimitri spun me around and picked me up. "Hold on."

I didn't think. For once, I listened. My legs and arms went around him just before he thrust himself into the air.

I screamed and looked down just in time to see the last of my friends fall under Rolo's army. Dimitri remained in the air, and I had to look up to see how he was keeping up suspended.

Then I saw. He'd turned his fingers to claws and was climbing across the room.

We were high in the air. I was cradled against his chest.

He climbed out of the window and kept crawling like a monkey. Alan's affectionate term "beast" had never been more accurate until his moment.

Sunlight blinded my vision, but then I looked out and saw the stillness in the courtyard. Everyone could hear the commotion coming from our tower, but no one knew what was going on. William's howl had alerted everyone to action. Some of Ewan's men had their hands on their swords while the giants, trolls, and the goblins (oh my!) had positioned themselves in various states of aggression.

The moment they heard about Rolo's death, the war would spill out.

Dimitri put me down on the flat roof.

I narrowed my gaze. From a distance, the castle had always shined brighter than the sun, but that was nothing compared to seeing it from my position. The light bounced off the white stone and directly into my eyes.

Goodbye twenty-twenty vision. It was nice knowing you. Hopefully, I'd look good with glasses.

I moved to the edge of the roof and grabbed the rails. Finally, I could see but barely.

The courtyard was still at a standstill. Another figure, larger and redder than the others, stepped out of the castle. He was dragging someone with him, a woman.

A violent cry went up as the red demon threw his head back.

Ulgard. Someone had freed him, and I was sure the woman he held by the arm was Titania.

"Dimitri, I have to get down there."

I looked around.

He was gone. He'd left me.

A moment later, I knew why. A pair of winged fae were fighting him, stabbing him with long swords while they flicked around him. Both were beautiful but dressed in rags and heavily scarred.

Dimitri roared as he continued to try to fight them off.

I lifted my hands to shove them back, but they were grabbed before I could send my power out.

Then I was hit, and it was lights out for me.

I might have enjoyed the darkness.

CHAPTER TWENTY-TWO

When I woke up, I wondered about two things. Actually, I wondered about a few things.

One of Dr. Shaw. The second was the queen. Was she dead? I doubted anyone had saved her in time. Ulgard had held her in a death grip, and I couldn't see how anyone could have made it to her in time.

My last thought was more personal.

I was going to have trouble chewing for a week.

My entire jaw radiated with so much pain that I was sure it had its own heartbeat.

My stomach hurt as something swayed underneath me. I opened my eyes and saw a strong jawline and a blue sky.

Dizziness made me close my eyes again. When I opened them again, Zane was staring down at me. I was in his arms, held against his chest while something rocked underneath us. I was almost too queasy to speak and a little fearful I knew what kind of vessel I was in.

"The venom takes a while to work. How are you feeling?" he asked.

There was a tenderness in my throat where I knew he'd bit me. I took a deep breath. "Dr. Shaw."

"She's still with us. She's asleep, though. Blair forced her into stasis."

Good. That settled my mind but not my stomach. "Are we on a boat?"

He grinned. "It's better than flying, right?"

I closed my eyes. It was only a little bit better than flying. I could swim, but drowning seemed like a terrible way to go. "Tell me we're floating down a river, and if I reach out far enough, I can touch the shore."

"I'm sorry, but I can't tell you that. I'm trying not to lie to you anymore." He cupped my cheek, and I turned away before I righted myself. There was only so much of his tenderness I could take.

Pain slash across his features but ignored it.

That pain slipped my mind when I saw where we were.

We were in the middle of the ocean on a small boat. No wonder I could feel the rocking.

A glance around showed me we weren't alone. There was another small boat ahead of me and another behind me. Actually, there was a line of boats. We were all moving at the same speed, but there were no rowers. The boat was very pretty with carvings on the edges. The front of the wood curved and reached up like an arm. A lantern swung with the listless motion.

An orange sun was setting over the pink horizon.

There were no oars, and I couldn't hear a motor.

Zane and I were alone on this little boat. "What's going on?"

"We're heading to the Court of Water. This is the transport Aisling arranged yesterday. At first, we went out in separate boats, but once we were away from land, the boats pulled together in a straight row."

"How is this possible?"

"I don't know."

I knew. The answer was magic.

I couldn't see the shore on either side of me and didn't remember seeing any during my one and only visit.

In fact, I'd arrived at the Court of Water unconscious the first time. Thankfully, I would be awake this time.

Sirius and Titania's odd servant were in the boat ahead of me. For once, the undercover Scotsman wasn't smiling. He tapped the big guy on the shoulder and whispered something.

The giant with the big empty eyes looked at me and smiled. "Princess Lorena."

Sirius nodded. "You will serve Princess Lorena."

"Yes," the giant said.

"And you will never harm her again."

The giant shook his head. "No."

"Very good. Go look at the sunset. You'll paint me a photo of it later."

The thing, because I felt uncomfortable calling him a man, turned away.

I moved to the very edge of the boat, and Sirius did the same in his. We were about a foot away, and I still thought it was too close, but I didn't want to ask my question out loud. I didn't want to offend the other guy in the boat.

"What's wrong with him?"

"He's a shell."

I remembered the term from my grandmother's grimoire. "I'm guessing you don't mean the kind you find on the seashore." Speaking of shores, I wanted to find one and soon.

I kept my eyes on Sirius. His blue was a lot better than looking at the big blue but not by much. Both blues were still dangerous.

"No, a shell is a person without a soul. He was created this way."

I was right. The man on Sirius's boat was the creature spoken about in my book. They couldn't be controlled by necromancer powers. "Who created him?"

"His master."

"I'm going to take a wild guess and say you're talking about Titania."

He nodded his head. "Can you guess how he was made?"

"His soul was ripped from him at birth." And now Aisling's comment about how her mother controlled the slaves made sense. When she said Titania and the elves killed the spirit of the children, she'd actually meant it, not in the figurative context at all.

"Correct." Sirius smirked, and I could tell there was something on his mind, something about me. Maybe pride? "When you freed the slaves, you freed shells like him as well, but he could not be completely freed until Titania died."

Well, there was the answer to that question.

I looked back.

"Ewan isn't here. He had to stay behind."

"I know," but that didn't stop me from looking. I caught Zane's eyes and realized I was surrounded by the two vampires I disliked the most. I swung my head back to Sirius. "Tell me something. How do I know I can trust you? Why did you stop me from helping Dr. Shaw?"

He leaned his arm against the boat and cocked his head. The lanterns were starting to glow as the world darkened around us. "Before I tell you, I have a question of my own. Do you want the blue pill or the red pill?"

"Team red."

He narrowed his eyes. "How is it that you can still surprise me when I already know everything you'll do?"

I lifted a brow. I didn't know how to answer that, so I didn't. Sirius was one of the most intriguing people I'd ever met.

He settled farther against the boat and said, "I'm going to walk you through everything that happened after Dr. Shaw fainted, but this will require your participation. Are you ready?"

"Yeah."

"How did you feel after Dr. Shaw fainted?"

I didn't have to think about it. "Worried. Scared."

"What was your one concern after you saw her injured?"

"Getting her help."

"But there were people in your way, yes?"

Anger burned my skin. "Yes, the soldiers." I slammed my hand on the wood. "Crap! The soldier in the village is still frozen."

"And he makes a wonderful nest for the birds to this day."

I smiled, and then I laughed. "All right. Go on."

"In your haste to get Dr. Shaw to help you did something you weren't supposed to do."

It took a moment for me to remember. "I revealed my identity and then freed the slaves."

He nodded. "The soldiers told Lorena Quinn that you were, in fact, a princess, and Lorena Quinn used your power to help others." He shook his head like he couldn't believe it. "Dr. Shaw was then rushed to the castle where you learned she was your aunt."

"Yes." My heart fluttered with happiness. I loved that lady. I'd eat carrots every day and let them turn me orange if she promised to live forever.

"Now, the domino effect. You spill the secret about the slaves. The news spreads like wildfire. The news reaches Ewan, and he rushes back to the castle, not only in time to confront Rolo before he could hurt Aisling but with an army of slaves who killed their masters and are now willing to fight for the Unseelie Kingdom."

"Wow."

He held up his hand. "I'm not done. The news also spreads to the dungeons. Titania's staff walks out. She decides to confront you and brings her shell with her. The shell, who's was never given a name, hits you over the head at Titania's command." That must be what she whispered to him before she left the great hall. "But when she dies, the shell is free. And what do you know? There lies a necromancer at his feet. He gets you to safety, and here we are."

I looked up at the shell, and he waves. He gives me that empty smile on autopilot and then stares at the last bits of sunset like Sirius asked.

"And all of that because Dr. Shaw fainted?" I asked.

"All of that because your heart is far bigger than your body."

I closed my eyes. I could see it all just like he said.

Suddenly, the rocking of the boat didn't disturb me as much. I'd felt so lost for so long, but now I was feeling more steady than ever. "I'm on the right path, aren't I?"

Sirius laughed. "You are, and I am here to guide you."

"That can't be easy."

He laughed. "It's not. It hurts. Your pain and the pain of others hurts me. Few times in the past, I stepped in to try to save someone, but the results ended up worse than before."

"You stepped in last night. You made me go back and speak to Dr. Shaw. Why?"

He seemed to contemplate whether or not he should spill the beans. Then sighed. "Red pill it is. What happened after you left Dr. Shaw's room?"

"I went to bed."

"No, before that. Who did you see in the hall?"

I thought. "Blaire."

He nodded. "Not only did you tell her that you cared for her, but you told her that you would give her someone else to care for."

"Who?"

"You. When you got hit over the head, she decided she could not stay behind with her mother at the castle. She had to come and make sure you were all right."

"That's sweet, but why is that important?"

The boat rocked, and the lantern light cast shadows over his brow. "Because Blair is needed for the next part."

I looked past him and saw something glow in the distance. It was land, and it was beautiful. The water got rougher. I cling to the side as the waves jerked us. The wood whined underneath my fingers. "What's going on?"

"They're trying to kill us."

"Who?" I asked.

"The Court of Water. You didn't think they'd just take us in, did you? The worlds are at war."

I panicked. "So, why are we going?"

Sirius raised his voice. "I have a gift for you." He held out his hand. "Give me a soul stone."

"Why?"

"Trust me."

I reached back for my sack on the ground and got the stone that was on the left side of my satchel.

Slowly, I moved toward Sirius and held it out.

A wave hit us hard. The cold object slipped from my hands. It made a dunking sound as it hit the water.

My blood froze. It was gone.

I was already in the air, ready to jump out when Zane moved with speed and righted me back in the boat. "My mother!" I cried.

Zane rubbed my back. "I'm sorry."

"You didn't trust me. Give me a soul stone!" Sirius cried.

"No! I already lost one."

"Trust me."

The angry winds wiped my stupid hair, blinding me. "Can't we wait until we get to shore?"

"We will not get to shore unless you trust me, Lorena." He reached his hand out farther.

I closed my eyes and dug into my bag again. Wei's stone bit into my hand. I handed it over. Zane kept me steady.

Sirius turned to the shell and said words that sounded like, "Eat it."

"What!"

The shell swallowed the stone in one gulp. Then he huddled away.

A second later, the shell's skin glowed a fiery red. Cracks formed all over him. He turned to me. His eyes glowed. "Lorena," he said in that empty voice.

Right before he detonated.

I turned away as a brilliant light filled the night.

The waves calmed suddenly.

I looked up and covered my mouth with my hand. Warm, almond-shaped eyes were staring into mine, not in the shade of blue eyes but in priceless onyx.

"Wei." Was it really him?

He reached out for my hand, and I grabbed it in urgency. He yanked me from my boat and into his arms.

It was him. I touched him. I felt his skin, his long, soft hair, the muscles of his arms that circled me, and in the thighs underneath my lap.

He was real. He was here.

He said nothing.

I was a little nervous about that. Was this Wei?

He cupped my face and then buried his head into my neck. Then he inhaled. "I heard you."

I stiffened. "What?"

"On my day, I heard you when you talked to me." He pulled away and cupped my chin. His voice was rich and deep. It was Wei. "I waited for my day to come, just for you to speak to me. I also waited for the day you'd give up."

"I couldn't give up. I love you."

He smiled so rarely that when it came, I burst into tears.

He held me and let me give over to my emotions.

But only for a moment.

Pushing my hair back from my ear, he said, "I heard many things while I was in that stone. Lorena, you can't trust Sirius."

I sniffed. "Why?"
"He's going to kill your son."

To Be Continued ...

***

Dear Reader,

I want to personally thank you for taking your time to read
"House Of Vampires", I hope you enjoyed this latest
installment.

Good news, House Of Vampires Book 7 is available NOW in
paperback and on Kindle.

https://www.amazon.com/gp/product/B08GL2SCLZ

If you want updates on the future releases then please join the
mailing list by going to **SimplyShifters.com**

See you soon :)

Samantha xx

The fun continues in Book 7!
Ending a war is complicated.
Mix in carrying a baby, escaping assassinations, and living through betrayal, and you have chaos, but not for Lorena Quinn.
For a necromancer, it's just another day. Her life is far from normal and with five—or was it six? —lovers to call her own. She'd murdered, buried, and forgotten the need for normalcy long ago.
Now, all she wanted to do was survive.
But when survival means giving up someone she loves, things get kind of tricky.
But Lorena isn't just a witch anymore. Now she's the Queen of the Unseelie, and it's time she started acting like it.

Made in the USA
Monee, IL
27 January 2023

26465727R00134